NEVER TOO OLD FOR LOVE

*A Selection of Recent Titles by Rosie Harris
from Severn House*

CHANCE ENCOUNTERS
GUARDED PASSIONS
HEARTBREAK AND HAPPINESS
THE MIXTURE AS BEFORE
MOVING ON
STOLEN MOMENTS
LOVE OR DUTY
ONLY LOVE CAN HEAL
NEVER TOO OLD FOR LOVE

NEVER TOO OLD FOR LOVE

Rosie Harris

This first world edition published 2018
in Great Britain and the USA by
SEVERN HOUSE PUBLISHERS LTD of
Eardley House, 4 Uxbridge Street, London W8 7SY
Trade paperback edition first published
in Great Britain and the USA 2018 by
SEVERN HOUSE PUBLISHERS LTD

British Library Cataloguing in Publication Data
A CIP catalogue record for this title is available from the British Library.

ISBN-13: 978-0-7278-8777-1 (cased)
ISBN-13: 978-1-84751-893-4 (trade paper)
ISBN-13: 978-1-78010-956-5 (e-book)

All Severn House titles are printed on acid-free paper.

Severn House Publishers support the Forest Stewardship Council™ [FSC™],
the leading international forest certification organisation.
All our titles that are printed on FSC certified paper carry the FSC logo.

Typeset by Palimpsest Book Production Ltd.,
Falkirk, Stirlingshire, Scotland.
Printed and bound in Great Britain by
TJ International, Padstow, Cornwall.

For all my Family and Friends

ONE

Mary Wilson stopped and put down her heavy shopping bags. When she'd left home it had been dull and grey and she'd thought it might rain, so she'd put on her raincoat. Now the sky was blue, the sun was shining and she was far too warm. She would have liked to take her coat off but that not only meant something else to carry, but also she hated to be seen outdoors only half dressed. Women of her generation never went out in simply a dress, or a blouse and skirt. The addition of a jacket, even on a summer day, was imperative.

She really must invest in a shopping trolley, Mary decided. Carrying heavy weights like this not only made her arms ache but also her shoulders. She was getting old, she told herself as she picked up the bags again. At one time carrying home the shopping was no problem at all, now it left her with aching shoulders for the rest of the day.

'Can I help?'

At the sound of a man's voice she looked over her shoulder and saw a tall thin man of about her own age, dressed in grey trousers, an open-necked shirt and a lightweight jacket coming up the road behind her. For a moment she stiffened then, with a sigh, she smiled gratefully and put the two heavy bags down on the pavement by her feet.

'That's very kind of you,' she murmured.

'Not at all. It's quite a walk from the shops,' he said gallantly. 'Have you very far to go?' he asked eyeing the two bags.

'No, it's only the next road, Silver Street, but I seem to have run out of steam! I think it must be a case of getting old.'

'Old! You're not old,' he said with a smile.

'Well, getting older, or something like that. At one time carrying the shopping home didn't bother me, but I was just thinking I must get one of these shopping trolleys, so that I can put everything into it and simply push it along.'

He bent down and picked up the two bags she had placed

on the pavement at her side and started walking. Mary studied
the stranger as they walked along. He was grey-haired, about
her own age and broad-shouldered. Even though he was thin,
he looked very fit.

'We go down here,' she said as they reached the corner.

Halfway down the road she stopped, turned in through a
small iron gate and up a neatly paved path with well-tended
flower borders on either side to a green front door.

'Here we are! I am most grateful for your help Mr . . .' she
hesitated and looked at him enquiringly. Then to cover any
embarrassment said quickly, 'Can I offer you a cup of tea?'

'That would be very nice,' he said with a smile. 'My name
by the way is Bill, Bill Thompson. I live only a couple of roads
away in Coburn Road.'

'Mine is Mary Wilson,' she said as she put her key in the
lock and opened the front door, which led into the hallway of
the semi-detached house.

'Right, Mary, and where would you like me to put these?'
he said nodding towards the two bags of shopping.

'Would you bring them through to the kitchen?' she said
leading the way.

Bill followed her and placed the bags on one of the worktops.
Mary filled the kettle, reached for the teapot and popped in
three teabags from a canister on an opposite worktop.

'I'll put away the perishable stuff while we wait for the tea to
brew,' she murmured as she began unpacking the two bags. Bill
leaned against the kitchen door and watched her. Mary quickly
transferred packages from the shopping bags to the freezer and
fridge while the kettle boiled. She poured the boiling water into
the teapot, then reached down for two pretty pink and green
teacups with matching saucers from a glass fronted cupboard.
She placed them on a tray together with a milk jug, the teapot
and a matching plate on which she arranged some biscuits.

'I'll carry that,' Bill said quickly as she went to pick up the
tray. 'You lead the way,' he told her.

He followed Mary through into the sitting room. It was a
pleasant room, prettily decorated with chintz curtains and shaggy
rugs on a well-polished parquet floor. The three-piece suite was
in dark red, the settee strewn with plump cushions. Bill placed

the tray down on the low table Mary indicated, which stood between the two armchairs.

'Do sit down, Bill, and make yourself comfortable,' Mary murmured gesturing towards one of the armchairs.

Settling back in the armchair Bill looked around the room appreciatively. It was exactly the same size and shape as his own, but so very different in appearance. It was full of feminine touches, from the flowers on the windowsill to the cushions scattered on the settee.

After Lydia had died, he had stuffed all the cushions in his home into a cupboard out of the way, neglected the pot plants until they were past recovery and he could throw them away, and he had put away all the ornaments, because he regarded them as mere dust collectors. For the first time, he regretted having done so. This room, with all its feminine touches, was so much friendlier than his sitting room.

'Milk? Sugar?' Mary asked as she poured out the tea.

'Milk but no sugar please,' he said.

When she passed him his cup of tea he sipped it appreciatively. It tasted good but slightly different from the thick mug he drank from when he was at home. Cautiously, he set the china cup and saucer down on the table, before accepting a chocolate biscuit from the plate she held out to him. They ate in companionable silence for a few minutes. Bill picked up his cup and finished his tea.

'Would you like a refill?' Mary asked as he carefully placed the cup back on the saucer.

'If there is one left in the pot.'

Mary poured him a second cup and one for herself.

'Tell me something about yourself,' she invited.

Bill looked so startled that she almost laughed. She found herself warming towards him. She studied him while she waited for him to gather his thoughts. He was quite broad shouldered but not in any way overweight. He was clean-shaven and his grey hair was well cut. His features were good, his mouth well defined, his chin strong and his blue eyes clear and sharp.

'I imagine you are retired,' she murmured in an effort to put him at his ease and end the awkward silence.

'Oh yes, I've been officially retired for almost twenty years now.'

'What did you do for a living?' Mary asked.

'I was in the army,' Bill told her.

'A professional soldier!' she said admiringly.

'That's right. We moved around a lot, not only in this country but abroad as well. I intended to do so much when I retired. Even thought about carving out a new career for myself, but I never got round to it. Too busy working part time and helping the boys. You think that once you've educated them they would be able to stand on their own two feet, but there's always something happening that takes either your money or your time. I've three sons and they all needed help to get started in life: help with further education, then to set up their own home and then their young families came along and our money seemed to go on helping to buy prams and cots and things like that.

'They're all past that stage now, thank goodness. The eldest grandson will be ten next month and his father has a good job, so he can buy him all the gadgets and sports things he needs.' He rubbed his chin thoughtfully. 'It's amazing what they do need these days. When mine were small all they expected was a pair of football boots or a tennis racket, but today they all have to have the right clothes with the right labels in them. Even their sports shoes, trainers they call them, have to have the right label.'

'Yes, I know what you mean,' smiled Mary.

'You have children?'

'One son, Richard.'

'Is he married?'

'Oh yes!' She stood up and went across to a bookcase and took up a picture of a man and child in a heavily embossed silver frame and held it out to Bill. 'That's Richard and his little boy George.' Bill studied the photograph for a couple of minutes before handing it back to Mary. As she took it from him, she told Bill, 'Richard's a schoolteacher the same as my husband was.'

They sat in silence for a few minutes reflecting about their respective lives.

'When I finally retired we came here to live, that would be about twenty years ago,' Bill told her. 'The boys were all about to start work and we thought there would be plenty of opportunity for them to find good jobs in this area.'

'Your boys didn't want to follow their father into the army?'

'Heavens no! They'd had enough of that way of living. They wanted to put down roots.'

'Do you like it around here?' Mary asked.

'Yes, it suits me fine and Lydia liked it here. She said it was good to feel settled after a lifetime of constantly moving from one place to another. She found there were plenty of interesting places to visit without having to travel away from home and that it was ideal for shopping. What she appreciated most, of course, was having the boys at home. While we were abroad we'd sent all three of them back to England to boarding school. She found that hard. I suppose they did as well, but that was the way of life for most of the other children as well as them.

'When we first moved here we used to get up to London occasionally for family outings or to see a show. Lydia liked that sort of thing and she'd missed being able to go to places like that when I was in the army. We used to have concerts put on at the barracks from time to time but it's not the same, a different atmosphere altogether.'

Mary smiled and nodded understandingly.

'Do you get up to London?'

Mary made a face. 'Not very often,' she murmured. 'I find it is so crowded and so noisy. I grew up in a very quiet part of Dorset and I sometimes long to be back there. We lived in a little stone cottage surrounded by fields and there was a stream at the bottom of the garden.'

'Sounds idyllic!'

'Yes,' she sighed. 'It was.'

'So why not go back there?'

'My son and grandson live here, it's as simple as that.'

'Yes,' he nodded understandingly. 'We like to be near them don't we? Even though we don't see a lot of them, they all have such busy lives.'

'Yes, very true,' Mary agreed, 'but then so do we,' she added.

'And I'm keeping you from getting on with yours,' Bill said quickly. 'Thank you for the tea,' he added as he stood up and straightened his jacket. He moved towards the door, then suddenly stopped and walked over to look at an oil painting hanging on the adjacent wall.

'Lovely isn't it?' Mary said with a sigh. 'Whenever I feel homesick I imagine myself back there.'

He stood staring at it intently studying every detail, even the signature in the bottom right hand corner. Then he turned towards Mary, 'Is this where you used to live?'

'No, not really. But it is so similar to the countryside where I lived that I absolutely love it. It brings back so many memories.' They stood together looking at the picture of gently rolling green hills, with a cart track running between them, meandering through the trees to where a five-bar gate led up to a stone cottage.

'I must be on my way,' Bill reflected, buttoning his jacket. As they reached the front door, he paused and looked back at Mary. 'I've really enjoyed this morning I . . . I.' He hesitated, unsure of himself, then said quickly, 'I was wondering if you'd like to come to the pictures with me. Sometime next week perhaps?'

Mary looked surprised then with a quick smile said, 'Yes that would be very nice.'

'Tuesday? I'll pick you up.'

'What are we going to see?'

He looked slightly taken aback, 'I don't really know what's on. I'll find out and let you know.' Without another word, he strode down the path and through the little gate, shutting it carefully behind him.

Mary watched him walk off up the road, noting the squared shoulders and brisk stride that reflected his years in the army. Then she closed the front door and went back into the living room to gather up their cups and saucers, and took them through to the kitchen to wash them up.

TWO

As he walked home, there was a spring in Bill Thompson's step as he went over the events of the day. Lydia had died four years ago and, since then, he had practically had no social life at all outside his family. The boys either came to see him or phoned once a week to check he was OK, but he rarely saw their families. One of his daughter-in-laws popped in occasionally to make sure he was keeping the house in order and that he hadn't starved to death. Now and again she brought a homemade cake, or a pot of jam, or even some cooked ham or chicken left over from their own meal the night before.

Lydia had not had many friends and he hadn't really got on with any of them. Whenever they came to visit, he usually made himself scarce by either going outside and pottering in the garden or going for a walk. In fact, even when Lydia was alive, they hadn't socialised very much at all. They were both content with each other's company, especially since he had retired.

He wished Lydia could have known Mary Wilson. She was so charming, so refreshing to talk to that he was sure they would have been good friends. Still, it was no good thinking like that. Now Lydia was gone, he'd been on his own for the past four years, and although he had never considered himself to be lonely, he suddenly realised that to some extent he was.

He had cut himself off from the rest of the world apart from his boys and, as long as he was self-sufficient and made no demands on them, they didn't offer any help. In some ways, he was glad that things were like that. He didn't want them to be bothering about him all the time. They had their own lives to live and, from what he could see of things, they all had very full lives and he was glad about that.

Yet, he had thoroughly enjoyed Mary Wilson's company and he hoped they could go on seeing each other. It would be nice to occasionally go to the pictures or even to go out for a meal together. Not too often of course; he didn't want her

taking over his life, but somehow he didn't think that would
happen. She seemed to be a very independent lady with intelligent forthcoming views on most subjects. Of course, there
was her family to be considered. He didn't know just how
involved she was with bringing up her grandchild, or how
much her son depended on her. He was quite sure she didn't
depend on him. She was self-sufficient. That was proven by
the fact she was struggling to carry home two heavy bags of
shopping instead of asking him or her daughter-in-law to do
it for her.

Yes, she was a plucky little woman he thought admiringly.
She was quite attractive as well. He imagined that at one time
she had been something of a beauty. She still had good features
and a thick head of hair even though it was grey. He judged
that she must be in her mid-seventies which was about his own
age. Yes, he'd enjoyed meeting her and he hoped taking her to
the pictures would be the start of a long-term friendship. He'd
wait and see how their next meeting turned out before making
any further plans.

Suddenly he remembered they hadn't fixed the time or place.
He automatically decided on the Odeon in Maidenhead. That
was where he usually went on the few occasions that he had
been to the pictures since Lydia died. Well, he'd have to ring
her up and tell her. Then with a shock he realised he didn't
know her telephone number. He hoped she was in the phone-
book; if not then he wondered if she was on the Internet. He
hadn't seen a computer, but then he'd only been in her sitting
room and she didn't seem to be the type of woman who would
keep her desktop sitting in the middle of her lounge.

There were so many things he didn't know about her it was
like a voyage of discovery. He was pretty sure she would have
a computer and that she would be able to use it efficiently,
therefore they would be able to email each other. It was a much
better way of making contact. When you phoned someone or
they phoned you then you had to think on the spot; with an
email you could consider what you wanted to say before you
committed yourself. However, since he didn't know for certain
if she was in the phone book or had a computer, he would
have to walk round to her house again to let her know the

details of where they were going once he had made the necessary arrangements.

He wondered if a matinee would be a better idea than an evening show. Somehow she didn't look like the sort of woman who went out at night. She would probably be nervous about doing so in the dark, especially with someone who was more or less a complete stranger. No, since this was their first time it would be far better to take her to a matinee, and then afterwards they could have a cup of tea perhaps at a nearby café before they returned home.

He toyed with the alternatives for the rest of the day. First thing next morning he went into Maidenhead to check what was on at the Odeon and on what days there would be a matinee. Armed with this knowledge, he went back home and wrote a short note telling her that he would pick her up at two o'clock the following Tuesday. He put his own phone number on the sheet of paper with his address, and then he waited until it was dark, walked round and slipped it through her letterbox. Now, he told himself, it was up to her to acknowledge it and to confirm that they would be meeting.

As she put away the used cups and saucers Mary Wilson thought about her visitor. It was the first time she had entertained a man on his own since Sam died. In fact, she had entertained very few people in the three years since he'd died. Now, for the first time, she realised how much she missed adult company – not that they had ever been in the habit of entertaining very often.

In the early days of their marriage, it had been his profession as a schoolmaster that had made this difficult. They had avoided socialising with the parents of any of the children Sam taught, because usually the entire conversation centred on the achievements or otherwise of their children.

Sometimes this was quite embarrassing because the parent concerned, usually the mother, either thought that her child was brilliant and not being recognised as a little genius, or – if the child was not doing too well – that the teaching was not of the right kind to bring out the best in her child. Either way Mary had found that it was embarrassing to listen to Sam being criticised and equally embarrassing for him, as he tried to explain the situation to the parent.

As she went back into the sitting room and picked up the photograph of Richard and George, she looked at it with a smile on her face. Richard was very considerate. He made a point of visiting her at least once a week, as well as phoning from time to time in between to make sure she was all right.

She wasn't too sure how she felt about his wife, Megan.

Megan was tall, beautiful and always looked elegant. She was a very clever career woman. She had gone on working after she and Richard married and continued to do so even after George was born. She had put him into a nursery when he was two months old. Her job at a leading London fashion house sometimes kept her away from home for days at a time, so she had installed an au pair and expected her to look after George. This had not been successful. Mary had deplored what was happening because this meant that, whenever Megan was away from home, George was neglected and so she had tentatively offered to look after him.

'At your age!' Megan had said, raising a pencilled eyebrow and giving her a supercilious smile. 'I don't think so. He's far too much of a handful for you to be able to cope with.'

Mary hadn't offered again. She had felt humiliated.

Megan had solved the problem by installing a housekeeper. Lucia was an Italian woman in her mid-thirties. She had not long been widowed and Megan had met her on one of her business trips abroad. Lucia was eager to get away from her home and sad memories, and she had settled in well. She had taken to little George, mothering him as if he was her own. George thrived on her attention and they soon became inseparable. Mary liked her and trusted her, and was happy that George was being so well looked after. She was also delighted that Lucia secretly brought George to see her at least once a week. After the first time, Megan had told Lucia that it wasn't necessary.

'Surely it's a duty to do so, you are his grandmother,' Lucia had declared to Mary and continued the visits without Megan knowing.

Mary sighed. She was sure that Megan not only disliked her but also resented the attention she received from Richard. Megan was possessive and wanted both Richard and George all to herself. She rarely let Richard bring George with him when he came to see her and often, while Richard was visiting, Megan would phone to ask when he was coming home. There was always some pretence or another but Mary saw through it every time.

Even so, Mary reflected, she still had a good relationship with him and with her grandson. She was a very lucky woman. She might be seventy-five but she was still fit and well enough to look after herself, to do her own shopping and to live the way she wanted.

For the first time, she realised that her world was extremely restricted. True, she read the papers each day, listened to the news on the television or radio and so she was well acquainted with what was going on in the world, even though she was playing no part in it.

Mary sighed. When Sam had been alive he had enjoyed a wide-ranging group of friends, but most of them had been people Sam had known from the gliding club, where after his retirement he spent a good deal of his leisure time. They were very nice people and very interesting, but they had really been his friends, not hers. She had never cultivated women friends. Again, this had been partly because of Sam being a schoolteacher and all those mothers wanted to talk about was their children's education.

Since he had retired she and Sam had spent more and more time in each other's company. When he became too old to fly solo, he had joined the local golf club but it had not been a serious commitment. He had never become overly friendly with any of the other members, nor accepted any invitations to their homes or to meet their families. As a consequence, she hadn't got to know their wives and, as she never attended golf club functions, she only knew the men he had played with by name. After Richard left home she and Sam had been quite self-sufficient and neither of them felt that they needed outside stimulus.

Now, having spent an hour in the company of a complete stranger, she wondered if she had been remiss in not making friends. She had found it extremely interesting talking to Bill

Thompson and hearing his views on life and things in general.
It was a funny thing, she mused, that men looked at most things
in a different way to women. To get a balanced perspective it
was necessary to have both points of view, she reflected.

The idea of going to the pictures with him intrigued her. She
hadn't been to the pictures for years. Sam hadn't been very
interested in doing so. He preferred to sit at home at night and
watch television, and she had never dreamed of going on her
own. Somehow it didn't seem right to do so.

As she finished tidying up, she suddenly thought that they
hadn't fixed a time or a place where they would meet. Perhaps
she should meet him at the cinema? That might be the best
choice, then she was under no commitment. But which cinema?
He hadn't said and she hadn't asked. Well that meant phoning
him, but she didn't know his phone number. It was all so
ridiculous she thought with a wry smile. I really am out of
practice in making friends and being with other people. That's
got to end and going to the pictures with Bill Thompson will
be a start.

Or would it?

Suddenly she was filled with doubt. Had it all been a lot of
talk on his part? Had he deliberately not said a time or place?

THREE

As she carefully applied her lipstick, Mary Wilson studied
her reflection critically in the dressing-table mirror. For
her age she supposed she didn't look too bad, but even
so, it was the face of an elderly woman.

Still, Bill Thompson was no chicken himself, she thought
with an inward smile. They probably suited each other. No one
would give them a second look, although they might have done
if one of them had been twenty years younger than the other.
Especially if it had been him; people would have laughed behind
her back and said she had a toy boy.

Ever since Bill's letter had arrived saying he would come

and pick her up at two o'clock on Tuesday the sixth, she had been planning what she would wear and how she would look.

She'd immediately booked a morning appointment at the hairdressers, so that her hair at least would be at its best. Now, as she patted it into place and used a tail comb to slightly lift it at one side – to give more fullness to it – she decided that her eyebrows needed touching up. Nervously she used a black eyebrow pencil to define them. With a sigh, she put down the pencil, studied her mouth and then picked up a tissue and blotted it. She didn't want too much lipstick on; she didn't want to look overly made-up.

There was nothing she could do about the wrinkles, she reflected uneasily, turning her head to study her profile. There seem to be more and more of them every day and she couldn't understand why because she wasn't worried about anything. Well, that wasn't quite true. Ever since Bill's letter had arrived she had been worrying about what to wear and how to look her best.

Standing up, she smoothed down the red and black patterned dress, and slipped on the loose white jacket that she intended to wear over it. She turned to study her herself in the mirror, adjusting the shoulders of the jacket so that it fitted more smoothly. She looked as good as she was able to look. Anyway, she didn't know what she was worrying about since they would be in the dark most of the time. Now it was just a case of waiting for Bill to arrive.

She had barely finished tidying up her dressing table when the doorbell rang. As she hurried downstairs to open it she could feel her heart pounding. What on earth was the matter with her? Anyone would think she was a schoolgirl on a first date, she told herself crossly.

When she opened the door, she found Bill there waiting patiently and looking over his shoulder she could see a rather ancient Ford Capri parked outside the gate.

'Is that your car?' she asked in surprise.

'Yes, it's my car. Rather an old banger but not quite as old as I am.'

'I didn't mean to sound so surprised,' Mary said contritely, 'but I never thought you still had a car because you never mentioned it.'

'There are lots of things we didn't mention. I can see we need to have another long chat but not at the moment.' He looked at his watch. 'We don't want to be late. The matinee starts at three o'clock promptly and we want to be in our seats before then.'

'Well I'm ready.'

'Yes, I can see that and very nice you look too. I'm beginning to wonder if I should have put on a suit.'

He was wearing very light grey slacks, a pale blue shirt with a dark blue tie and a smooth, worsted, well-tailored, navy blue jacket.

'You look very smart just as you are,' she told him.

'Thank you and we will be sitting in the dark anyway for most of the time.'

She nodded thinking how she had had the same thought only a few minutes earlier. She locked the front door and they walked down the garden path together. He closed the gate behind them and then quickly moved forward to open the passenger door of the Capri for her. Bill waited until she was comfortably seated, made sure the skirt of her dress was clear of the door and then pulled out the seatbelt and handed it to her to fix around herself. When she'd done this he slammed the car door shut, walked round to the other side and got in behind the steering wheel.

It was only a short journey, less than five miles, to the Odeon cinema in Maidenhead but they encountered holdups with heavy traffic along the A4. She saw him once or twice look anxiously at his watch. He was a man who didn't like to be late for things, she thought with an inward smile. She assumed that it was because of his time in the army. She had once been told that you were never late for anything in the army, because if you were then you received a punishment; excuses were never accepted.

Sam hadn't liked being late either. She thought fondly of him as they drove the short distance in fits and starts. Sam had been a really good driver, although in the later years he had done very little.

She had never taken the wheel since he'd retired. In fact, she reflected, it was almost twenty years since she had driven a car.

She was so out of practice that when Sam had died she had sold their Mercedes. The general traffic had increased so much that, after one attempt to drive it, she'd been so nervous and unsure of herself that she felt she would be a danger on the road.

There was a short queue at the pay desk and, although she fully intended that they would go Dutch, she made no protest when Bill went up to the pay desk and bought the tickets. They could settle things afterwards she decided. Why spoil the occasion with an argument over money? Anyway, she thought, he wanted the pleasure of her company or he wouldn't have invited her.

They found their seats and had just settled comfortably when the lights went down. For the next two hours, she kept her eyes focused on the big screen. The picture was set in some unknown European city and was basically a thriller of a very mild nature, with a great deal of love interest woven in.

Mary enjoyed it. Once or twice she cast a surreptitious glance at Bill to see how he was taking it, because she was not at all sure if it was his type of picture or not. He seemed to be as utterly absorbed in what was happening on the big screen as she was. When the picture ended and they left the cinema and came out into the late afternoon sunshine, she screwed up her eyes in protest and grabbed his arm.

'Bright isn't it,' he commented, tightening his arm to give her better support.

He noticed that she was still clutching the box of chocolates, which he had bought for her.

'Here, let me throw that empty box away,' he said reaching out to take it from her hand.

'No, I've only eaten two of them and I'm taking the rest home.'

'Only two! I had four!'

Mary gave a little sigh. 'I know, they were delicious but I have to be careful.'

'Careful!' He laughed derisively. 'You ladies and your dieting! You don't need to worry, you look very trim,' he told her gallantly.

'I'm afraid it is far more serious than my weight or shape.

I'm diabetic,' Mary explained. 'I have to be very careful about eating chocolate, cakes and pastries or anything very sweet,' she said.

'So I should have bought you a bacon butty then, should I?' he joked.

'No, that would have been equally bad for me, too much starch in the bread and starch turns to sugar after you've consumed it.'

'Really?' He looked surprised. 'I didn't know that!'

'Not many people do or if they do they don't think it's very important. In my case it is. Too much starch or sugar and my blood sugar goes dangerously high.'

'Isn't there anything you can do to stop that happening? Pills you can take?' he asked, his brow furrowing anxiously.

'I do take pills; special ones of course. I take them regularly twice a day.'

'I see.'

There was silence between them for a minute or so and then he gave a resigned sigh.

'I'm sorry about the chocolates, I must try and remember to bring you flowers next time,' he said as they reached the car. He opened the passenger door and waited for her to get settled before walking round and taking the driver's seat.

'It doesn't mean I didn't appreciate what you bought me,' Mary told him as he started the engine. 'They were lovely and I shall eat all the others in due course.'

'One a day for the next two weeks?'

'Something like that.'

'And what about drink?' he frowned as they drove out of the car park.

'I have to be careful. I usually have a small glass of red wine or a small dry sherry, but I never drink sweet wines like port or sweet sherry.'

'Do you drink spirits?'

'A small whiskey with lots of soda or a small vodka with lots of sugar-free tonic.'

'Is that better than orange squash or something like that?'

'It is certainly safer when you're drinking out. You can never be sure in a pub or restaurant if they are giving you the diabetic version which is supposed to be sugar free. If they say it is you still have to be careful because it may use artificial sweeteners which can affect you in other ways,' she said with a laugh.

'I must try and remember all that. You never said anything the first time we met and we had tea and biscuits at your house.'

'Yes, but I had to watch my diet very carefully the next day to bring my blood sugar back down to what it should be,' she said quietly. They sat in contemplative silence for the rest of their journey. When he pulled up outside her house she asked 'Are you coming in for a cup of tea?'

Bill hesitated. 'Yes, I'd like that,' he said.

He had been on the point of suggesting that they went for a meal but then he thought that it might be too much for one day, especially with her dietary problems. He didn't want to rush things. He enjoyed her company but he had no way of knowing if she felt the same about being with him. Take it slowly, he told himself. You've got the rest of your life to get to know each other better.

As they went into the house, Mary remembered she hadn't paid for her ticket. She had fully intended to do so, but somehow it seemed churlish to do so now. Some men were very sensitive about that sort of thing. She remembered Sam had always been so careful to stand his ground when they met up with friends. He most certainly would never let a woman pay for her own drink.

She decided that, even if she let it go this time, if they went out together again then she would insist that they went Dutch. Or else that the outing was one she chose, so that she could book their tickets in advance and she could be the one to pay. This time she'd simply thank him very much for taking her and assume that it was something he had wanted to do. He had been so concerned about his mistake in giving her chocolates that it wouldn't be very gracious for her to make a fuss about the ticket. What she would do she decided, as she went through to the kitchen and switched the kettle on, was to make him a really substantial tea. A plate of ham and cheese sandwiches as well as some biscuits.

Next time she would make sure that she had some cake to offer him. She must try and find out what kind of cake he preferred, whether it was fruit, walnut or chocolate.

FOUR

It took Mary and Bill several weeks to come to some agreement over paying when they went to the pictures. Bill was adamant that it was a privilege to pay for her and he wouldn't dream of not doing so.

'Let you pay for your own ticket!' he said aghast. 'Whatever kind of man do you think I am?'

'A very nice one,' she said with a smile.

'That settles it then,' he said firmly. 'No more talk about you paying.'

It didn't settle it though, not as far as Mary was concerned. She didn't know his circumstances but he was a pensioner the same as she was and, like her, he no doubt had to budget his income fairly carefully. So she was determined to repay him in some way. They say that food was a way to a man's heart, so perhaps she could offer to cook him a main meal once a week. She sorted out her old cookery books and went through them, trying to remember which dishes she had liked cooking. She hadn't cooked for anyone except herself since Sam died and they'd had very conventional meals. Sam had enjoyed his food but he too had preferred what he termed 'plain English cooking'.

She thought about it for several days before she mentioned the idea to Bill that they should have a meal together once a week and that she would prepare it. When she did suggest the idea to him he looked dubious.

'I'm not into fancy foods,' he said bluntly. 'I like meat, two veg and a pudding of some sort afterwards. In fact, I would go as far as to say that it's the puddings I like best. None of these fancy ones, mind you. Apple tart, Rhubarb crumble, steamed pudding or bread and butter pudding, that sort of thing.'

'That sounds ideal,' Mary murmured. Her cooking was of the standard family kind. Meat and two veg followed by a tasty pudding. Nothing fancy.

He looked at her with raised eyebrows. 'From what you told me about your diet puddings aren't the sort of food you indulge in.'

'Well, the meat and two veg is OK. As for the puddings, I would enjoy a very small portion of all of the ones you've mentioned.'

'Really!' He looked surprised yet relieved.

She nodded. 'I don't make any of them at the moment because it's not worth all the fuss to make one serving, and a small one at that.'

'Right, then, let's give it a try,' he said enthusiastically.

'Good,' Mary said and they smiled at each other understandingly.

'Now does that make you feel any better,' he asked with a broad smile. 'I know what you're trying to do you know.'

Mary sighed. 'I know; appease my conscience by giving you something in return for taking me out.'

'As I told you before, it's a great pleasure to do so but I would certainly like to give this new arrangement a trial. We'll go to the pictures on Tuesday afternoons and I will come here for lunch every Thursday. How does that sound?'

'It sounds fine,' Mary told him. 'I must keep the weekends free in case Richard calls round and brings little George with him. Saturday and Sunday are the only times he does so because he's working during the week.'

'Doesn't his wife bring the little one round to see you?'

'Good heavens no! Megan's far too busy working. She travels abroad quite a lot. Once a week, Lucia, who looks after little George, brings him to see me, but she has to be careful because Megan doesn't approve of her doing that.'

The new arrangement worked quite well. Mary thoroughly enjoyed her weekly visits to the Odeon in Maidenhead. Bill always phoned a quarter of an hour before he was due to pick her up. Whether this was to make sure she was ready and he wouldn't be kept waiting or to reassure her that he was taking her, she wasn't sure. It didn't matter. In some ways it was good because, if she happened to be running late, she knew exactly how long she had before the doorbell would ring.

Sometimes the picture was very much to her liking, but then she felt anxious at the thought that Bill might only be pretending to enjoy it, simply to please her or be polite. At other times, when it was not to her taste, she did her best not to let him know this. Afterwards, they invariably laughed about the slight difference in their opinions about what they had seen but agreed that it was well worth the experience. Both of them were seeing pictures they would never have dreamed of going to see and it broadened their outlook in so many ways.

The Thursday lunches were a great success. Bill enjoyed the home cooking and was lavish with his praise. Sometimes, when they'd been to a picture that he knew she hadn't been too keen on, then he would bring her a bunch of flowers as a way of compensation. So far he had not found any of her meals not to his taste. He simply revelled in the puddings she produced and sitting back replete, a satisfied smile on his face, declared that they were simply scrumptious.

'My word you are a good cook, Mrs Wilson,' he would say approvingly. There was always some left over which Mary put into a container for him to take home for his own lunch the next day.

'I believe you make too much on purpose,' he would grin as he took the container from her.

'No, it's difficult to make a pudding any smaller,' she said with a smile, 'and I don't want to have it lying around here because I will eat it and upset my own diet.'

'Yes, I should imagine your diet is going to the wall with all the meals you're cooking when I come for lunch.'

'Not at all, I am very careful.'

'I can see that! The portion you dish out for yourself is only about a quarter of what you put in my dish, then I often have a second helping and you still have some left for me to take home!'

They smiled at each other understandingly and Mary felt a warm glow encompass her. She was so glad she had met Bill and that they had become such good friends. His companionship gave reason to her life and, for the first time since Sam had died, she felt wanted.

Having her hair done and getting dressed up on a Tuesday had become a very important routine. She noticed that Bill also took care about how he looked and always wore a suit when they went to Maidenhead.

On Thursday they were more relaxed. Bill usually came in slacks, a sports jacket and an open-necked shirt. She dressed more casually as well, but was careful to choose one of her cotton dresses or a skirt and pretty blouse. If it was cold she kept a cardigan handy for when she had finished in the hot kitchen. At first she tried to have her apron off before Bill arrived, but having spilled gravy down one of her favourite skirts while dishing up she no longer did this. However, she always took it off before she sat down at the table with him to enjoy their meal.

After their meal she would take the coffee into the sitting room and they would both relax and talk of anything and every-thing. Bit by bit they began to know more about each other. Bill told her tales about army life and some of the outlandish overseas postings he had during his long service.

'You make my life as a schoolmaster's wife seem very tame and uninteresting,' she said, after he had told her about one of his postings in Germany.

They said very little about their respective families. Bill mentioned where each of his sons lived and how many chil-dren they had, but told her resignedly that they were all so caught up in their own lives that he rarely saw anything of them.

'Brian, the eldest, is talking about going to live in Canada. Len emigrated to Australia when he was twenty and he hasn't been back since. And Gary lives in Cardiff, he changes his job so often that I don't even know what he is doing at the moment. Before he moved there he lived near Reading and that was when his wife, Jane, used to call on me occasionally. Since they moved to Cardiff she hasn't even written me a letter or made a phone call.'

'You haven't been to visit any of them?'

Bill shook his head. 'When Lydia was alive we occasionally went to see Gary and Jane. Jane got on well with Lydia.'

'You make me feel extremely lucky that I see Richard fairly often and little George. I'd like to see more of them but they have so many other calls on their time. Richard is a keen glider pilot and spends a lot of his time at Booker when the weather if fine.'

'He doesn't take little George up there does he?' Bill frowned.

'Oh no! Lucia looks after him when Richard goes flying. She is very accommodating and willing to take her time off to suit what he is doing. He's very lucky in that way.'

'And your daughter-in-law?'

'Megan,' Mary sighed. 'She's rarely at home. She lives a very erratic life. She is always buzzing off to Paris or Milan, or working up in London. Sometimes I don't see her for months at a time.'

Two Thursdays later, when they were enjoying a coffee together after their dinner, Megan herself arrived unexpectedly.

Mary felt quite startled when she answered the door and saw who it was. Megan looked so bandbox fresh and glamorous in a sleeveless, green silk dress that clung to her perfect figure like a second skin, that Mary felt old and dowdy. She knew her hair was untidy and that she was wearing a rather outdated cotton dress, because she didn't want to spoil any of her better clothes when she was working in the kitchen. Hesitantly she invited Megan in.

'This is a surprise,' she murmured as she led the way to the sitting room.

Megan paused in the doorway of the sitting room staring hostilely at the man sitting in Sam's armchair. 'You've got a visitor?' she said in an accusing tone.

'Yes, come and meet my friend, Bill Thompson. We're just having a coffee, will you have one with us?'

'No, I am in a hurry,' Megan said ignoring Bill who had stood up and was holding out his hand in greeting. 'I wanted to let you know that I'm off to New York at the weekend and since it is half term I am taking Richard with me. He doesn't know yet and I don't want you trying to dissuade him from going if he mentions it to you after I tell him.'

'What about George?' Mary asked.

'What about George? He is far too young for that sort of holiday! He will stay home with Lucia. I have given her your telephone number in case he is taken ill or anything.'

'I see.' Mary tried to assess what she was being told. 'Perhaps . . . perhaps you should also tell Lucia to bring him round to see me every day,' she stuttered.

'Every day! Whatever for?'

'Well, he might be feeling lonely with both of you away,' Mary said lamely.

'He might miss Richard but I'm sure he won't miss me,' Megan retorted. She looked at her watch. 'I must go. Remember what I've told you,' she added as she opened the door into the hall.

'Yes, I will, and you remember what I told you about Lucia,' Mary said as she accompanied her to the front door.

At the door Megan paused. 'You must be careful about inviting strangers into your home,' she warned.

'Strangers?' Mary looked puzzled.

'That old man. You gave him dinner didn't you?'

'Yes, but he's a friend,' Mary defended Bill.

'*Friend!*' Megan repeated scathingly. 'He's seen you for a soft touch,' she added as she started to walk down the path to where her gleaming white sports car was parked outside the gate.

'Rubbish!' Mary retorted crossly, her eyes flashing and her colour rising. 'He's a very good friend who helps me carry my shopping home and who takes me to the pictures once a week.'

'*What?*' Megan's voice was shrill with disapproval.

Refusing to explain her actions Mary hurriedly shut the door. She hoped Bill hadn't been able to hear their exchanges, but as she went back into the sitting room she realised that he had.

'She's a bit of a tartar that one, isn't she?' he chuckled.

Mary gave him a watery smile. She felt too close to tears to speak.

'Very lovely to look at but not so nice inside,' Bill murmured.

Mary looked at him in surprise. He was very observant she thought gratefully. That summed Megan up perfectly.

FIVE

Megan lost no time in telling Richard about the old man who had been at his mother's when she had called to see her.

'Sitting there in your father's armchair as if he owned the place,' she said in a highly annoyed voice.

'Really? Mum has never mentioned him and I've never bumped into him when I've called to see her.'

'They probably make sure you don't,' Megan said acidly.

'Well good for Mum. I'm glad she's found a friend.'

'Really!' Megan interrupted cuttingly. 'You are naive Richard. He's taking her for a soft touch. She'd even cooked lunch for him!'

Richard laughed. 'Well that's no bad thing because it means she's getting a proper meal herself. I know she finds cooking for one something of a bore and I suspect that half the time she lives off a bowl of soup or one of those ready meals from the supermarket.'

'Maybe she is, but it's not costing her as much as preparing a full-scale meal for some unknown old man. What happens when she runs out of money?'

'She'll have to ask him to pay,' Richard said with a laugh.

'By the sound of that he's already doing so in kind by taking her to the pictures once a week.'

Richard let out a low whistle. 'The old dog,' he said admiringly.

'Old *fraud*! He's probably making her pay for the tickets,' she added cryptically, her green eyes narrowing.

'Well that's what friends are for,' Richard commented philosophically. 'Share and share alike. When you have the money you treat your friends, when you haven't then they treat you, or else you both go without.'

'You do talk a lot of nonsense,' Megan said scathingly. 'I hope you feel that way when she runs out of money and comes begging you to help her.'

'I don't think that's very likely. My moocher is very prudent. She works out her budget to the last penny and always makes sure there's some left over for emergencies.'

'That's what you think, or hope,' Megan retorted.

'Apart from that she's not exactly living hand to mouth. She has a healthy nest egg she can always fall back on if necessary.'

'That's not hers!' Megan exclaimed in an annoyed voice. 'That's our inheritance.'

'It's hers,' Richard stated firmly, his handsome face hardening.

'No it's not! It's what your father left her when he died.'

'Yes, money he had accrued because she was thrifty and always made sure that they had a healthy bank balance. As I've just said, she worked very much to a budget. She wasn't stingy but she never wasted a penny piece.'

'Well she's wasting it now feeding an old man that you've never met and don't want to know.'

'Oh I'm not so sure about that. He's probably quite an interesting character, Mum wouldn't bother entertaining him or going out with him if he wasn't.'

'Rubbish!'

Angrily Megan stood up and began pacing the room. Why was Richard always so obtuse? Like his mother, he seemed to see the good in everyone and ignore their faults. For a grown man he was far too naïve and ready to take things at their face value. Couldn't he see that this old chap was taking his mother for a soft touch? Buttering up to her, being her friend, carrying her shopping home and taking her to the pictures; it was all so obvious.

And what came next, Megan thought bitterly. He would start staying the night and, in no time at all, he would have moved in and persuaded her to marry him. She was of the generation who would think that was necessary if they were living together. Once he was legally her husband then he had control of her possessions including her bank account. And Mary Wilson was trusting enough to let him do so.

Sam Wilson had been a mild man but still quite astute. Even so, Megan had never forgiven him for leaving everything he had to his wife. Not a penny had come their way.

When the will had been read, Richard had said pleadingly to Megan, 'Dad probably thought that I was earning enough to stand on my own two feet and that Mum needed it more than I did. He also knew that I had a wealthy wife,' he added teasingly, trying to calm her down. That remark had infuriated her and she had resolved that she would make sure he could never touch a penny piece of what she earned. Every penny she had would go to George; that was if there was anything left in her bank balance apart from an overdraft.

She worked hard, she spent hard. She liked the good life and she was a career woman, not a dull shadow of her husband, no matter what his career might be. She had worked and schemed to achieve the professional standard she now enjoyed. It took money to hold onto her glamorous reputation, but she was determined to do so. That was one of the reasons why she had gone on working after she had married Richard, even though at that time she had been nowhere as high on the ladder as she was now. It was why she had refused to give up working when George was born.

She knew she had pleased Richard by giving him a son, but George wasn't the be-all of her life. She had a career that was taking her to dizzy heights and she had no intention of giving up before she absolutely had to do so. She intended to live life to the full. If Richard couldn't find the time to join in then she'd do it on her own. Within months of being married, she had decided that the dull uneventful life of a schoolmaster's wife was not to her liking.

'You've met him,' Richard went on, cutting into her thoughts but ignoring her acid comment, 'what did you say his name was?'

'Thompson, Bill Thompson.'

'Did he look respectable?'

'He was reasonably well dressed but that doesn't mean a thing. Con men are usually careful to give the impressions of being well dressed and polite.'

'Any idea what he did for a living?'

'Your mother said something about him being in the army.'

'A professional soldier eh! Well, that's a very admirable occupation.'

'Not one where you end up well off though.'

'No, but he must have been retired for a good many years if he is about Mum's age, so he may have had some sort of career or profession after he left the army. If he was a professional soldier then he will also have quite a good pension.'

'All the same, he appears to be looking for a comfortable billet. If he gets too friendly with your mother he may even scheme to marry her and take over her house and persuade her to change her will in his favour.'

Richard laughed. 'You must think that everyone is as materialistic and scheming as you are!'

Colour stained Megan's face at his jibe but she made no attempt to withdraw what she had said.

'Richard, I know you don't think that this Bill Thompson is a threat, but I do. We may not need your inheritance from your mother, but we have little George to think about. That child is going to cost us a fortune. Think about it, there will be school fees, university, a car and an allowance after university until he gets established. I don't see why we have to spend our money providing these, when it's all there waiting for him when your mother dies.'

'My mother is only in her seventies. She's healthy and fit and may live for another twenty years, by then George should be able to look after himself.'

'Maybe, but we will have spent a great deal of our money getting him to that point and your inheritance would recover our loss.'

Richard looked at Megan with disdain written all over his face. 'I hope by then she will have spent whatever money she has enjoying her life or at least making it comfortable,' he said acidly. 'Anyway,' he added without stopping for breath, 'she may leave her money to a cats' home.'

'Not if that old dog who has latched onto her has his way,' Megan said tartly.

'You don't know that and neither do I. If she is happy in his company, having him for a friend, then as far as I'm concerned good luck to her. I know she won't do anything foolish.'

Megan knew when she had been beaten, but inwardly she

was furious. Richard might accept the situation but she didn't. She'd keep a watchful eye on what was going on, she resolved.

Although Richard had been dismissive about Megan's suspicions and accusations, he was worried. He was well aware that his mother was lonely and to some extent he knew that he and Megan were to blame. Megan rarely went to see her and, although he endeavoured to do so once a week, there were times when his visits were so fleeting that he barely had time to say more than hello.

He encouraged Lucia to take George to see her, even though he knew that this annoyed Megan. He ignored her complaints because he knew his mother derived so much pleasure from seeing George that he thought it was essential that she should do so and George liked visiting her. He knew she always had time to listen to his prattle, to ask him questions and that she rarely reprimanded him, told him what he ought to be doing or criticized him in any way. George also loved going to see her because she kept a stack of the biscuits he liked and other little treats that Megan frowned on.

Lucia too seemed to enjoy his mother's company. She and Lucia appeared to have long discussions about Lucia's family and her childhood, comparing the differences in their two countries. For Lucia, his mother in some ways compensated for the family she had left behind in Italy. Her house was where Lucia could relax and be herself, not the nanny who had to insist on making sure that George was always doing and saying the correct things.

Richard sensed that it was anger more than concern that was making Megan so annoyed with his mother. Although he professed to be in favour of what she was doing, deep down he was equally worried. He must try and find a way of meeting this man and making sure, in his own mind, that it was simply a matter of two old people befriending each other because they were lonely and not anything sinister going on.

SIX

With the coming of autumn and the darker evenings after the clocks went back an hour, Mary didn't feel at all confident about Bill driving them home from the cinema. True, the Bath Road was well lit, but it was also very busy with cars and lorries in both directions. She found that many of the headlights dazzled her and she was pretty sure that they affected Bill because his driving was slightly erratic at times.

'I don't think it is just the headlights . . .' he said when she tactfully broached the subject. '. . . It's my eyes. I'm not seeing as well as I did. I find it is getting more and more difficult to read the newspaper. The words seem to dance around on the page.'

'Have you been to the optician?' Mary asked.

'No, I suppose I should. It may be that I need new glasses.'

'Can you see what's on the screen when we go to the pictures?'

'Well the screen is exceptionally large and once you are into the story then I think the brain takes over and I seem to be able to see all right. I've never really thought about it.'

'When you're driving it bothers you though?'

'Yes, it does.'

'Then the sooner you make an appointment to have your eyes tested the better. It certainly sounds as though you need to have your glasses changed,' she added as she refilled his cup and held out the plate of ginger biscuits that she knew were his favourite. Mentally, she made a note that she would check up with Bill, when he came for lunch the following week, to make sure that he had taken the trouble to go and see the optician.

The rest of the week she spent preparing for winter. Now that the clocks had gone back the sun seemed to have less warmth in it. She busied herself putting away her summer clothes and getting out her winter ones, making sure that they were crease-free before she hung them up in her wardrobe.

Mary didn't like the winter. She felt the cold more and more each year and, although she kept her home warm and cosy, going out troubled her. When it became frosty and the roads were covered with ice, she was always scared of slipping. A broken leg or hip meant a stay in hospital, most likely followed by several weeks in a nursing home, and she knew that the cost of that would bite sharply into her savings.

At the moment, that weather was far away, she hoped. Although it was several degrees colder there was no sign of frost or snow. The trees were glorious as the leaves changed from green to gold or red, especially when the sunshine transformed them into glowing beacons. This year the hedgerows seemed to be bright with berries and she hoped this didn't mean that there was going to be a hard winter ahead.

No, the only disadvantage so far, she consoled herself, was that it was dark by four o'clock and that meant long evenings. It also meant less time to get the garden tidied up. At the moment, there was pruning to be done and fallen leaves to be swept up so she had better get on and do it, she told herself. Bill had offered to give her a hand but she didn't want to be one of those women who had to lean on a man to do the jobs she didn't want to do. Anyway, the exercise would be good for her and much better than sitting here contemplating the drawbacks of the coming winter. If she didn't want Bill doing it then the best thing was for her to get it done before he came for lunch the following week.

When Bill did come for lunch the following Thursday the state of the garden was of little concern to either of them. He arrived white-faced and agitated.

'Whatever is the matter, Bill? Are you ill?' Mary asked worriedly.

He was shaking like a leaf when the wind catches a branch. He shook his head as if unable to speak.

'Come and sit down, you look as if you need a drink.'

He nodded and clutched at her arm for support.

Frowning, she went to the cupboard and found the small bottle of brandy she kept there for emergencies. She poured some into a glass and handed it to Bill. His hand was trembling so much that he could hardly take it. He took a deep gulp, shook himself and then drained the glass and sat back in the armchair closing his eyes. She left him for a moment then she touched him on the arm.

'Are you going to tell me what's wrong?'

He opened his eyes and stared at her. His eyes, normally a light blue, were dark with fear.

'I . . . I had an accident. I . . . I hit a dog on the way here. I didn't see it!'

He buried his face in his hands and his shoulders shook.

'Is the dog all right?' Mary asked squeezing his arm in a comforting gesture.

Bill shook his head. 'I don't know. It squealed a terrible cry so I know it was hurt, but it had disappeared before I could get out of the car.'

'It probably ran home,' Mary said in a reassuring voice. 'It shouldn't have been out on the road running free. It wasn't your fault.'

'It was,' Bill argued. 'I should have seen it and braked or swerved. I think I am supposed to report it to the police.'

Mary frowned. 'I think that is only if you kill it,' she told him.

'I may have killed it,' he pointed out in a shaky voice. 'It ran off somewhere . . . perhaps to die.'

'I hope not and, even so, there's nothing you can do about it,' Mary told him in a practical tone.

'Supposing it had been a child!'

'It wasn't; it was a dog!'

'Even so, the police might follow it up if the owners report it and then trace it back to me.'

'Yes, so you had better report it. Explain that it ran out in front of you, you tried to break but it was too late and that, because it ran away, you think it is probably all right.'

Bill stared at her. 'What if they make me have an eyesight test? They'll know I can't see properly.'

'Have you been to the opticians?' Mary asked sharply.

Bill shook his head. 'I haven't got round to doing so yet.'

Mary's lips tightened. She went over to where she kept the phone, checked through the telephone numbers and made a call.

'Come on, your meal is all ready,' she said when she came back to where Bill was still sitting in the armchair. 'As soon as we've eaten you're going to see the optician and have your eyes checked.'

'Today? Just like that!'

'Yes, just like that and I'm coming with you.'

'I thought I would have to wait weeks to get an appointment,' Bill protested.

'Normally you would, but I know them quite well and said it was important that they should see you right away.'

Bill started to argue but Mary was having none of it. She served up their meal, sat down and began eating hers. After a minute Bill followed suit. The moment their meal was finished Mary stacked the dishes in the sink.

'I'll do those when we get back. Come on.' She handed him his overcoat. 'We don't want to be late.'

While Bill was in the optometrist's consulting room, Mary sat in the waiting room flicking through the latest edition of *Homes and Gardens* magazine. Though she couldn't concentrate, she was too anxious about what was happening.

When Bill finally emerged she could tell from the shocked look on his face that it hadn't been good news, but she waited patiently until they were outside and back on the village High Street before asking what the result was.

'I've got to go the eye hospital in Windsor,' he said in a shaky voice.

'When? Today?'

He shook his head. 'No I will be getting an appointment letter from them in a few days' time. The optician I've just seen was very thorough. She sat me in front of some sort of machine and said she was taking pictures of the back of my eye and that was why I had to go to the hospital. She said I needed treatment for Macular Degeneration, whatever that is.'

'It's bleeding behind the eye,' Mary said quietly. 'That's why your sight is not as good as it once was.'

'Really!' Bill looked at her in surprise. 'How do you know that?'

'They will give you an injection to stop it bleeding,' she told him ignoring his question.

'An injection in my eye!' Bill said in a dubious voice. 'I don't like the sound of that.'

'A mere pin prick and it will be over in minutes.'

'You sure about that?'

'Yes, but you can confirm it after you've had the injection.' They walked in silence for a few minutes and then Mary asked, 'Would you like me to come with you?'

'Would you?' His response was so quick that she suspected he was somewhat apprehensive about going.

'Of course I will. We'll have to go by taxi.'

'So you don't trust me to drive?' he said in a slightly bitter tone.

'It's not that, but you won't be able to see to drive afterwards. They put drops in your eyes and it will be several hours before you can see properly. It's like a haze or seeing through a fog for about four hours afterwards.'

'You seem to know an awful lot about this Macular Degeneration,' he commented frowning at her.

'I should do, Sam had it. He didn't get treatment early enough and he went almost blind in one eye. He was stopped from driving.'

Bill let out a low whistle. 'I can see from what you are saying that the sooner I get it put right the better,' he muttered.

'Too true!' Mary agreed. The memory of the shock it had been to them both, when Sam had been diagnosed, came back vividly to her mind. He had scoffed at the idea of going to the hospital for treatment and felt resentful when he was told that he had left it too late.

'Nobody tells you these things,' he had grumbled. 'When you find it more and more difficult to read or see things clearly, you think it is because you are getting older. I thought it might be a cataract,' he admitted, 'but I knew you had to wait until they were what they called "ripe" before they would do anything about it. I was quite sure that it hadn't reached that stage, because my mother had had hers attended to. She was almost blind before they operated, but afterwards she claimed it was marvellous. She could see birds in the sky, leaves on the trees and everything was bright and new. I wonder how long they will take to let me know about an appointment,' Bill said worriedly. 'I hope they don't keep me hanging about for weeks and weeks.'

'You are a new patient so I'm sure they will see you as soon as possible,' she consoled.

'Well, you've been right about everything else so let's hope you are right about that,' he said with a forced laugh. 'I am grateful to you, Mary, that you made that appointment and made me go along to the optician,' he added, reaching out and taking her hand and squeezing it.

'That's what friends are for,' she told him with a smile.

'Can I take you out for a coffee or a pot of tea?' he asked.

'I think that might be what we both need,' she agreed. 'I've been as concerned as you have about what the optician was going to say. I rather suspected that it was going to be more than merely new glasses.'

SEVEN

Four days later, Mary received a phone call from Bill to say that he had heard from Windsor and he had an appointment at the Prince Charles Eye Unit at King Edward VII Hospital.

'That's wonderful,' Mary exclaimed. 'When is it?'

'That's the problem. It's the day I normally take you to the pictures.'

'Well, this is far more important than going to the pictures,' Mary said briskly. 'What time do we have to be there?'

'Eleven thirty in the morning.'

'Right, then I'll order a taxi for a quarter to eleven. Can you walk round here or shall I ask the taxi to collect you?'

'I'll come to your house,' Bill said quickly. 'I'll order the taxi though.'

'No you won't, I'll do it,' Mary said firmly. 'Be here for half ten. OK?'

'Very well.' He hung up without another word and Mary immediately checked her phone list and arranged for the taxi for the next morning.

Throughout the rest of the day she wondered if she ought to phone him and try and reassure him, but decided against it. Less said the better, she thought sagely, time enough to commiserate when he had had his injection.

Bill arrived promptly the next morning. It was a bright sunny day but extremely cold. He looked very nervous and seemed to be shaking. He took a deep breath as he came into the warmth of the house, rubbing his hands together and exclaiming how cold it was outside.

After a mild autumn, winter had suddenly arrived and, instead of going into the colder weather gradually, it was a case of sudden biting cold that set old bones and joints aching.

Mary offered him a cup of coffee but he declined.

Their taxi arrived promptly and, after assuring the driver that it was the King Edward's Hospital in Windsor that they wanted, silence reigned more or less throughout the journey. As they sped along the relief road and Windsor Castle came into view, Mary commented on how lovely it looked with the Round Tower sparkling in the sunlight. Bill merely grunted his agreement. Mary looked at him sharply but he avoided her eyes. She felt at a loss of what to say. A few minutes later they were in Windsor, turning down Gosling Way and heading for the hospital.

'Have you brought your appointment letter?' she asked as they approached the reception desk.

Bill fumbled in an inside pocket of his jacket and pulled it out. Mary took the letter from him and passed it across to the girl. She checked it against an entry on her computer, asked him to confirm his date of birth, address and telephone number, and then handed it back telling them to take a seat. There were about thirty other people sitting waiting and Bill pursed his lips in concern.

'We'll be here all day,' he muttered.

'Not all the people waiting here are for the same clinic,' Mary whispered back.

Ten minutes later, Bill's name was called and he was taken into a curtained off cubicle. When he came out he looked slightly dazed.

'They checked what I could read of the letters on a chart and I didn't do too well,' he frowned. 'The first couple of lines were all right, but after that, although I could see that there were letters written there, I couldn't make out what they were. Not even using the pinhole device which they said would help to make them clearer. I guessed at a couple of them but I'm not sure if I was right or not. The nurse then measured the pressure in my eyes and said that was all right. Then she put in drops, which stung like a bee. They said to go along to the next room and sit on one of the yellow chairs.'

'Well, come on then, that's what we have to do,' Mary told him. She stood up gathered up their belongings and accompanied him to the AMD section of the next waiting room. Almost immediately Bill's name was called and he was taken into a small room and seated in front of a machine to have the back of his eye photographed.

'The optician did all this,' he told the girl who was operating the camera device.

'We like to have our own record,' she told him. 'Now put your chin on that little ledge and watch the screen. You see the green cross, well focus on that and ignore the red line. Now have a blink and then keep your eye open and keep still. There will be a bright flash.'

'That almost blinded me,' Bill gasped.

'Now we do the other eye,' the operator told him. 'Same again, chin on the ledge, watch the green cross and ignore the red line and don't blink.'

Again there was a bright flash and Bill shook his head after it.

'Is that me done?' he asked hopefully.

'Yes, now you can go back outside to the yellow chairs and the consultant will see you as soon as she has studied these pictures,' she told him with a smile.

Again there was a wait and this time it seemed to be longer and Bill began fidgeting uneasily.

'Not long now,' Mary told him.

Five minutes later his name was called again and this time he went into a consulting room. Mary expected him to be back out in a few minutes but there seemed to be a considerable delay. Mary sat there thinking back to the numerous times she had accompanied Sam to this hospital for treatment. He had been diagnosed with Age-related Macular Degeneration, or AMD as they called it, almost five years before he died.

At first his visits had been monthly, sometimes for injections of Lucentis, at others as a check-up to make sure that there was no further bleeding behind the eye. It had become so routine that in the end they took it as a matter of course.

Bill felt nervous as he went into the consulting room. The consultant, a youngish woman with dark hair and horn-rimmed glasses looked serious as she studied something on her computer.

She indicated a special chair adjacent to a movable worktop holding some sort of magnifying equipment and indicated that he was to sit in it. Then she slid the device so that it was in line with his face and told him to rest his chin on the special ledge and look straight into the screen. She studied both his eyes, then peered at them through a very bright light that she held in her hand and finally marked a cross on his forehead over his right eye.

'You have slight bleeding in both eyes,' she told him, 'but the right one is more advanced so we will treat that one today.' As she moved the equipment to one side a nurse appeared and put drops into his right eye. They stung so much that it brought tears to his eyes and she handed him a tissue to wipe the moisture from his face.

A couple of minutes later, he was taken through from the consulting room to a small but well equipped surgery where he was asked to lie on a narrow bed. The nurse advanced towards him and put more drops into his right eye. This was to anaesthetise it, she told him.

He knew he was trembling as he lay there, feeling vulnerable and wondering what was going to happen next.

He only had to wait a few minutes before the consultant who had seen him came bustling in and was helped into an enveloping green robe and a cap to cover her hair. A net cap also covered her head and a large piece of sterile green cloth had been placed over her face. The consultant took her place behind his head and placed a green cloth over his face. Bill began to shiver as he felt her cut a slit into the green cloth immediately over his right eye. It was so close that he was afraid she would dig the scissors into his eye.

'Relax,' she said in a low firm voice. 'You will feel a slight pressure, that is all, nothing to worry about.'

He waited holding his breath, afraid to move. As she had said, he felt the pressure on his eyeball followed by a tiny prick. Then his eye was swamped with swirling red and green, like oil on a puddle when the sun shines on it. The next moment the green cloth was whipped off and he lay there blinking for a couple of seconds before he was helped to his feet. The consultant had already gone. A nurse helped him off the bed and onto his feet.

'Do you have someone with you?' she asked.

'Yes, a friend,' he told her. Bill was still white-faced and shaking with the nurse still holding his arm as she helped him back into the waiting area.

'Before you leave, sit here for ten minutes until you are feeling better,' she said as she guided him into a chair. 'Are you together?' the nurse asked as Mary immediately moved to the chair next to him.

'Yes, I'll take care of him.'

'Ten minutes then, until he feels steady,' the nurse repeated.

'As soon as you feel ready to leave we'll go along to the canteen and have a coffee or a cup of tea,' Mary told him as she pressed his arm reassuringly.

'What about getting home?' he asked.

'I'll ring for a taxi while we're having a drink,' Mary told him. 'It will take ten minutes or so for them to get here.'

'It's a good job you insisted that we take a taxi. I certainly wouldn't be able to drive home; everything is misty and distorted. One good thing though is that it doesn't hurt.'

'Well it may do once the anaesthetic wears off,' Mary warned him. 'The best thing to do is go home and go to bed for an hour or two. Then, when you wake up, apart from perhaps some cloudiness for another few hours, you will feel all right.'

'Bed?'

'Well, if you don't want to go to bed then have a snooze in your armchair. It is the best thing to do believe me. It's what Sam always did.'

'Mmm . . . well let's see how I feel when I reach home. Shall we go and have that cup of tea now?'

'I feel better for that,' Bill smiled as he drained his cup. 'My mouth was so dry I could hardly speak.'

'You don't feel shaky anymore?'

'No, I'm as right as rain.'

'Right then, I'll ring for a taxi and we'll make our way back to the waiting area by the entrance, so that we can see when it pulls up.'

'You mean you can see,' Bill smiled. 'Everything is still very cloudy to me. I don't know how I would have managed if you hadn't come with me,' he said squeezing her hand gratefully.

As they emerged from the hospital to the taxi, Mary heard Bill's sharp intake of breath and his hand went involuntarily to his face to shield his eyes from the bright winter sunshine. Mary waited until they were both strapped in and the taxi was moving before she extracted a pair of dark glasses from her handbag and handed them to Bill.

'Here, put these on, then the sun won't hurt your eyes.'

He took them from her and began fumbling to take off his normal glasses.

'It might stop them hurting but I won't be able to see a thing, not even with my good eye, without my glasses.'

'Keep your glasses on. These are supposed to go over them. Try.'

Bill did as she instructed. 'That's better!' he exclaimed when he had fixed them into place. 'You've no idea how that sun hurt my eyes.'

'No, but I know how it used to affect Sam. That's why I brought those dark glasses along with me.'

Mary saw Bill home and, for the very first time, went into his house with him.

'You go and sit in your most comfortable chair and I'll make you a drink,' she offered.

He didn't argue. She went into his kitchen, surprised at how Spartan it was and how tidy it was. Everything seemed to be in its allotted place. She filled the kettle and switched it on and while it was boiling she reached down for three cups: one each for them for their tea and one to make soup in before she left. She had brought a packet of soup with her and she felt that would sustain him and even help him to sleep for an hour or so, after she went home.

Then, by the time he woke up the uncomfortable feeling as the anaesthetic wore off would have passed. He had also been given a creamy ointment to put into his eye to soothe it. By the next day he would not only be feeling fine but also he would be able to see fairly clearly.

EIGHT

The phone was ringing when Mary returned home. Leaving her keys still in the door, she rushed to answer it.

'Mother? Are you all right?'

'Hello Richard. Yes, of course I'm all right. Why are you sounding so worried?'

'Someone told Lucia that they had seen you at King Edward's Hospital in Windsor today.'

'Yes, I was there but not for me. I went there with my friend, Bill Thompson. He has developed AMD, you know, the sight problem like your father had and he was there for treatment.'

'Well, I'm glad that was all it was. We were quite worried about you.'

'There's no need to be. I'm as fit as a fiddle. How is little George?'

'He's all right,' Richard said dismissively. 'Getting back to what you said, about what you had been doing and why you were at the hospital, don't you think you are a bit old to be playing nursemaid to an old man? Hasn't he got a daughter or daughter-in-law or someone who could go with him?'

'No, he hasn't.' Mary's tone was cold and clipped.

It surprised Richard; it was almost as if she had squared her shoulders defiantly, warning him that she wasn't prepared to argue or even discuss the matter. He hadn't intended to upset her, merely to warn her not to take too much onto her shoulders. He knew from her reaction, though, that she considered he had overstepped the mark and so he decided the best thing was to retreat.

'I'd better ring off now or I'll be marked as absent when they call the school register,' he said with a dry laugh. 'Bye for now.'

'Why oh why can't people mind their own business?' she muttered as she slammed down her own receiver. As she went back to take her keys out of the front door, Mary wondered who had seen her. As far she could recollect she hadn't seen anybody that she knew. Why did people have to gossip and spread tittle-tattle? she thought crossly. Still, she had made it quite clear to Richard that she wasn't prepared to talk about it, apart from telling him that Bill had AMD.

She understood his concern about her looking after Bill and comparing it with when Sam had AMD, but that was altogether different. Then she had been responsible not only for escorting him to hospital but putting drops in his eye. He had hated it and had made quite a fuss. Once or twice when she had had to go out, she had asked Richard to do it and from what she remembered he and his father had nearly come to blows. Sam had complained that Richard was clumsy and heavy handed, and Richard had turned round and told him to do it himself then.

'Other people have to do it for themselves,' he had argued. 'Mum spoils you and panders to you.'

Sam knew he was right but he resented Richard being the one to tell him so. Their quarrel had been heated and full of accusations and anger. Afterwards, neither of them would apologise to the other. Sam had accused Richard of being arrogant and immature. Richard had accused his father of being a selfish old bore. After that she had tried her best to always be on hand to put the drops in Sam's eyes and no more was said about the matter.

She was quite sure that Bill would be able to put the drops in himself. He was so much more self-sufficient than Sam had ever been. She supposed it was because of his army training; there was no one they could fall back on, whatever needed doing they had to get on and do it. She thought that Richard's call would be the end of the matter but she quickly found that it wasn't.

Megan was on the case the moment Richard reached home that evening and told her about what had transpired when he'd phoned his mother as she had ordered him to do.

'I hope you discouraged her and warned her not to start dancing attendance on him, like she did on your father,' she said sharply.

'I tried to do so but she didn't want to talk about it.'

'Really!' Megan's tone was caustic. 'I knew right from the beginning that this Bill Thompson was going to be trouble,' she went on in an angry voice. 'He's a clever old devil! He's latched on to your mother and wormed his way in, making sure she trusts him and feels sorry for him. Taking her to the pictures indeed! All he is doing that for is so that he gets a good cooked meal at least once a week. In next to no time it will be a cooked meal every day.'

'I don't think she would want to go to the pictures every day,' Richard joked.

Megan gave him a withering look. Her green eyes were like daggers and there wasn't even the ghost of a smile on her face.

'You don't have to be so obtuse, Richard. You know quite well what I'm trying to imply and now look where it's leading. She spent years nursing your father because of his eye trouble. In the end, he was practically blind and he couldn't read or see to even sign his name. Is she going to go through all that again?'

'I don't know,' Richard said mildly. 'As I said, she doesn't appear to want to talk about it.'

'Well we are going to talk about it whether she likes doing so or not. I'm going round to see her. She must be warned about the danger of doing things like that. The next thing is he'll be taking to his bed and expecting your mother to look after him full time.'

'That's nonsense,' Richard argued. 'He's having treatment because he is losing his sight. He's not ill; you don't take to your bed with AMD.'

'If I remember rightly your father spent a great deal of his time in bed,' Megan said acidly.

'Yes, that's true, but he had other things wrong with him as well.'

'Or so he claimed,' Megan said in a disparaging voice. 'Anyway, this Bill might have all sorts of other health problems that we know nothing about and he might start to play up about them in order to ensure your mother helps him.'

'Well I did point out to mother that she was rather too old to be acting as a nurse,' Richard responded lamely.

'Yes, and I bet she laughed at you.'

'No, she didn't do that but as I've already told you she did make it quite clear that it was none of my business and refused to discuss it.'

Megan said no more but there was a strained atmosphere between her and Richard for the rest of the evening.

Next morning, Megan wasted no time in confronting Mary. Although she had an appointment in London, she made it her business to go and call on Mary first.

'I've heard that you've been taking this Bill chap to the hospital. Do you think that's wise?' she demanded in an aggressive voice the moment Mary opened the door to her. 'You look absolutely worn out!' she added as she studied her mother-in-law's appearance.

Mary felt at a disadvantage as she saw how perfectly made up Megan was, her hair immaculate as if newly set and her sharply fashionable outfit. Megan was elegant from the tip of her high-heeled shoes, to the glittering earrings that matched perfectly; and with the silver and diamante necklet at the neck of her emerald green dress, she looked bandbox glamorous. Mary mentally compared them with the shabby skirt and blouse that she was wearing. Normally she kept these for doing her chores in. She had simply combed her hair so that it was tidy but not styled in any way and she wasn't even wearing any lipstick.

'Wise? I don't know about being wise, it's simply something one does for friends,' she defended.

'For family, perhaps, but not for complete strangers, not unless you are hired as a carer or as a nurse and expected to take him to hospital as part of your duties.'

'Wouldn't you do it for your friends?' Mary asked mildly.

'No, of course not! None of them would expect it,' Megan said dismissively.

'So they wouldn't do it for you either,' Mary commented dryly.

'I wouldn't dream of asking them to do so,' Megan retorted. 'If I was well enough to take a taxi then I'd go on my own, otherwise I would expect Richard to take me,' Megan told her huffily.

'I see,' Mary said with a sigh. She knew that it was pointless trying to explain the situation to Megan. Whether she was telling the truth or not she didn't know, nor did it matter. Megan had taken a dislike to Bill from the moment she had first met him and there seemed to be nothing that would change that, Mary decided with a mental shrug. She pulled herself together and gave Megan weak smile.

'Will you have a cup of tea or coffee while you are here?'

Megan pulled back the cuff on her elegant coat, looked at her slim gold watch and frowned.

'Heavens no! It's far later than I thought. I have an appointment in London. I must go. Just bear in mind what I've said. Richard thinks the same,' she added ominously. 'At your age it is enough for you to look after yourself and not worry about strangers.'

Mary opened her mouth to point out that Bill wasn't a stranger but then thought better of it. She would never change Megan's opinion on that point so why antagonize her further? She thought resignedly. There was nothing to be gained from doing that and Megan would only take it out on Richard when she got home.

She wasn't sure if Richard understood anyway or whether he sided with Megan. It didn't really matter, she told herself. She wasn't going to be bullied into breaking off her friendship with Bill Thompson simply to please them. She'd had such a long lonely time since Sam had died and she was quite sure that he would approve of the fact that she had found a friend. It wasn't as though it made any difference to Richard and

Megan, she told herself. She wasn't expecting them to entertain him, she wouldn't dream of taking him round to their house.

As she got on with her cleaning – catching up on the jobs she had neglected the day before because of going to the hospital – she resolved that, far from listening to either Richard or Megan, she would go round and see Bill later in the day to make sure that he was all right and that he was managing to put the drops in his eye.

She looked at the clock. There was still time to make a cake to take with her, a Victoria sponge perhaps with jam and cream in it. He'd love that. They could have a cup of tea together and a chat. It would relieve the boredom for him and it would set her mind at rest that he was all right.

NINE

Mary Wilson felt like a naughty schoolgirl as she put her coat on over her smart navy dress in readiness for when the taxi arrived. She was taking Bill back to the hospital for a check-up after his injection. It was purely routine but she knew that if either Richard or Megan found out what she had been doing, then she would receive a lecture from them reminding her that it wasn't up to her to do that.

They had a right to their opinion, of course, but as far as she was concerned she was doing the right thing. Bill was her friend and he had no one else to go with him. He could go on his own, of course, but she was afraid he mightn't do so. He hated the whole procedure, the same as Sam had done, and she knew Sam would never have kept his appointments if she hadn't gone with him.

The taxi arrived promptly and Bill was ready and waiting when they arrived at his house. He was looking very smart in his best navy blue suit, pale blue shirt and blue and black tie. Mary was glad that she too had taken the trouble to put on her smart navy dress and coat, and that she had a navy and white scarf tucked into the neck of her coat.

It was a bright, crisp November morning as they drove to Windsor. Mary enjoyed the scenery, especially when Windsor castle came into view and she noticed that the Royal Standard was flying which meant that the Queen was in residence. Bill didn't seem interested when she pointed this out to him. She suspected that he was worried about what lay ahead and she tried to reassure him that he wouldn't be having an injection, only a check-up, and that would only take about an hour.

'They'll go through the same procedure of getting you to read the chart, putting drops in your eye, testing for pressure and then you'll have to have the back of the eyes photographed, of course,' she reminded him.

'What, both of my eyes?'

She almost laughed at the look of dismay on Bill's face. His heavy eyebrows were drawn together in a frown that made him look quite fierce.

'Yes, both of your eyes,' she repeated. 'Then you will be seen by the consultant and he will study the X-ray of your eyes and examine them himself with a very bright light. If there is no sign of any further bleeding then he will probably tell you that he will want to see you again in about a month's time.'

'Seems a lot of fuss,' Bill grumbled. 'Why can't they just look at the eye where I had the injection in and leave it at that?'

Mary gave an imperceptible shrug. 'That's the procedure,' she said. 'I understand that it is to make quite sure that the problem hasn't spread to the other eye. If it has then they can do something about it right away and that means the treatment has a greater chance of success.'

Bill sighed and looked more worried than ever but he didn't ask any more questions and Mary knew when it was better to say nothing.

When they arrived at the hospital Mary paid the taxi driver and said she would phone his office when they were ready to come home. She then accompanied Bill inside the hospital to the eye clinic reception desk. They were very busy; the waiting room was packed. After he had registered they managed to find adjacent chairs. Mary noticed he was looking very gloomy but he brightened up slightly when his name was called ten minutes later.

Everything went according to plan and less than an hour later they were leaving the hospital.

'The specialist said he would see me again in a month's time,' Bill told her.

'I take it that will be before Christmas,' Mary commented.

'They'll write and let me know the date and time.'

'Good. So we can forget about it until then,' Mary smiled.

'Yes, and I hope that next time will be the last time and that it will be the end of the problem. I don't fancy having another injection in my eye. It wasn't all that painful but all the fuss beforehand and that green mask over your face was claustrophobic.'

'Think yourself lucky that you only had to put a cream in your eye afterwards for the rest of the day. When Sam was attending that clinic there was far more fuss, he had to put drops in his eye three times a day for two weeks.'

'Did it do any good?'

'Well, the Lucentis injections stopped the bleeding but it didn't really make his eyesight any better, only stopped it from getting any worse. He had already lost the central vision but still had peripheral vision and saving that was the most they could do.'

'You mean that no matter how many injections I have,' Bill said gloomily, 'I'm not going to be able to focus enough to read a book or the newspaper ever again?'

'I'm afraid not. You still have peripheral vision though. You can see people and objects still.'

'Yes, but until I am right up close to them, I can't be certain who they are because I can't focus on their face.'

'Well, you still have one good eye and you can still drive,' Mary said consolingly. 'You've got to stay positive and enjoy life as much as you can.'

'Enjoy life! How can I enjoy life when I can't see properly?' Bill's voice was bitter.

'Yes, enjoy life,' Mary repeated a little sharply. 'Take care of yourself, eat a sensible diet and make sure you go for a walk or do some gardening every day or some other exercise. It all helps with your blood sugar and if that is under control then it helps to keep your eyes healthy.'

Bill sighed. 'All I want to do is read the newspaper or a book,' he grumbled. 'Is that asking a lot?'

'No, but for the moment it is difficult. You'll adjust. Sam did and he wasn't the most patient of men. A good magnifying glass helps so ask at the hospital next time you go there if they can help you.'

'Ask them for a magnifying glass!' Bill sounded cross and contemptuous but Mary knew it was frustration. He hated to think that he was losing his sight and it was making him grumpy. She had been through it all before with Sam so she took no notice, but answered in as calm a voice as possible.

'Yes, that's right. Ask the Eye Clinic Liaison Officer. She will make an appointment for you to go to the right department for a magnifying glass and anything else they think might help you. At the moment, I don't think you are bad enough to be registered as having impaired vision but when it comes to that then she will help you.'

'I don't want a white stick so that the whole world knows I'm half blind,' he said aggressively. 'I suppose you will expect me to have one of those, or else a guide dog next.'

'If you need it then it is advisable to have a white stick. It helps other road users know you may not be able to see them and so they can take your progress into consideration.'

'I don't need a walking stick!' Bill exclaimed angrily.

'It doesn't have to be a walking stick. They issue a white wand to people who don't need a walking stick. As for registering with the authorities that you have sight problems, well, that can give you some advantages. It helps with your income tax and also you get a reduction on your rates.'

'Really?' Bill looked interested. 'Well, I didn't know that,' he muttered.

'There's probably a great many things you don't know but are worth looking into,' Mary told him. 'It's not all bad news,' she added with a smile.

'I suppose you are right,' Bill admitted. 'I don't know how I would manage without you. I don't think I would have come back again, not after that injection, if you hadn't made me.'

'Enough of that for the moment,' Mary said taking his arm firmly. 'Let's go along to the hospital canteen and have a cup of tea. I will phone for the taxi to take us home and by the time we've drunk our tea it should be here.'

TEN

Megan was far more concerned about Mary's friendship with Bill Thompson than Richard was. She really couldn't understand him, he seemed to accept it quite placidly and not be able to see any underlying danger. It became a subject that she broached whenever they were alone together. Something she even found herself brooding on when they were apart. Why oh why couldn't Richard see the risk his mother was taking in opening up her home to this man? Or why this man was becoming so friendly with his mother?

Normally Richard was no fool, she told herself. He might only be a schoolmaster but he was as sharp as a needle, especially when it came to financial matters. Richard vetted all her business contracts and investments and his advice was always sound. He even booked hotels and travel for her when she was working in Paris or New York, and he was always meticulous about the service she would be getting and the cost of it. In many ways he was her manager, although she would never admit that. She regarded it as his duty to vet her contracts and take care of her finances since she earned a great deal more than he did. It was obviously his duty to take care of the family finances generally. She left it to him to make sure that Lucia shopped wisely for their household needs and, when it came to buying clothes for George, that she wasn't unduly extravagant or cheated over the value of them or short changed in any way.

Yet, for all that, Richard didn't seem to see the danger in this Bill Thompson becoming so friendly with his mother. He looked either annoyed or puzzled whenever she raised the matter. What if Bill Thompson managed to persuade Mary to move in with him, or she decided to let him move in with her?

She had no idea, of course, whether Bill Thompson had enough money of his own to live comfortably or whether he was looking for some rich old widow to keep him in comfort for the rest of his days. She rather suspected it might be the latter and that Richard's mother was too naïve to realise this.

True this Bill dressed smartly and kept himself looking spruce. In fact, she had to admit that he was quite a present-able figure. But what was Mary thinking about to be going out with a man at her age? Sam had been a devoted husband and he had lived into his late seventies, so what on earth did she need a replacement for now? She must be in her late seventies and there was something objectionable about her taking up with another man at her age. She was making a laughing stock of herself.

Richard's argument that the two of them were merely friends and that his mother was probably lonely certainly didn't cut any ice with her, Megan decided. Sometimes she did wonder if he was giving her the hint that they didn't visit his mother as often as they should. That was nonsense, of course. She and his mother had nothing in common, except Richard, and since his mother thought he was perfect she could hardly sit and point out all his faults and shortcomings, without causing a bad atmosphere between them.

Richard hated gossip so there wasn't much his mother could talk to him about except little George. That certainly was a subject that Richard and his mother had in common. They both idolized the child. Megan only hoped that they weren't spoiling him behind her back. She was constantly reminding Lucia that she must make him behave and teach him good manners because she suspected that perhaps Lucia was also spoiling him. She made a mental note to discuss this with Richard and decide what was the best thing to do about George over Christmas.

She had persuaded Richard to go with her to Monaco at the invitation of one of her most important business contacts and, of course, taking George with them was out of the question. He would be staying at home with Lucia. He wasn't yet five so it wouldn't really make all that much difference to him whether they were at home over the Christmas holiday or not, as he was far too young to know what it was all about. They would have a party for him when she and Richard returned early in the New Year and bring him back a present of some sort.

Lucia had wanted to go home to her family in Italy for Christmas and she had even offered to take George with her, but Megan had decided that was out of the question. On reflection though, she wondered if that mightn't be better than leaving him at home. Unless she forbids Lucia to take him to see his grandmother over the Christmas holiday and she didn't think she dared to do that. Richard was bound to hear about it and object; it might even end up with him deciding to stay at home with the child and not go with her to Monaco.

Richard couldn't understand why Megan was so averse to his mother being friendly with Bill Thompson. He had briefly met the man himself whilst visiting his mother and Bill seemed to be a nice enough old man. He was clean-shaven, always neatly dressed, well spoken, his eyes were bright and his conversations intelligent. It was obvious that his mother enjoyed Bill's company. He was still driving and apparently, from time to time, took her to one of the big supermarkets to stock up on groceries and commodities not available in the local village stores.

Their outings seemed to be innocuous enough. A visit to the cinema in Maidenhead once a week and a meal at her place once a week. What was wrong with that? Old people like the reassurance of a routine so it probably suited them both. This Bill was obviously of the old school and wouldn't let her pay for her seat at the pictures, so her idea of giving him a meal was a way of recompensing him without taking his pride away from him. This business about him having eye problems was a shame, because it could eventually result in him not being able to drive, but they could worry about that when it happened. There are always taxis.

He quite understood why his mother felt she should accompany Bill to the eye hospital when he went for treatment. She had been through the scenario with his father and, even though his dad had never admitted to being nervous about going for treatment, Richard knew that he hadn't liked doing it and that his mother going along with him each time had boosted his confidence. This was what she was now doing with her friend Bill; there was nothing more to it than that.

Megan worrying about Bill moving in with his mother was utter rubbish. Since his father had died she had established a routine that suited her and she loathed to deviate from it. She didn't want to go on holiday because she said she couldn't be bothered with all the hassle of packing and travelling. She didn't even want to stay at their place overnight, not that he'd asked her to do so for the last couple of years.

No, he told himself confidently, his mother was happy with her life as it was but, naturally, she enjoyed the friendship of someone her own age and going to the pictures once a week didn't really ruffle her serenity. He felt a twinge of guilt because he knew he should visit his mother far more often than he did. She so enjoyed his visits, especially when he took little George with him. George loved going to see his grandmother. She always had time to chat to him and to listen to what he had to say. He was always eager to tell her about what he had been doing since he last saw her. George also enjoyed the biscuits she kept in a special tin for him, a tin that had his name printed on the outside.

Richard sighed. He tried to make his visits once a week, but so often there were things going on at school at the end of the day that seemed to take priority. At the weekends, if Megan was at home then there were social occasions either with friends or her business contacts that took up all his time. They would even be away over Christmas, he thought guiltily. He wondered what his mother would think about that! She would accept it, of course, and she never criticised what they did but he knew that deep down she would be very concerned, especially when she found out that they weren't taking George.

His mind spun back to the Christmases he had known as a child. They'd been magical affairs, with parties and high jinks from a couple of weeks before Christmas right through to the New Year. He remembered sitting at the kitchen table with his mother making decorations; looping strips of colour paper into a chain to hang across the ceiling of the sitting room. There had been the excitement of Christmas cards arriving and they had strung these all up so that they hung from the top of the doors right down to the ground. They'd decorated the hall with holly and ivy, the red berries glowing like rubies when the light was turned on. His father had helped to decorate the Christmas tree and was always in charge of the Christmas lights on the tree and the ones they put out around the window frame.

By the time Christmas Eve came Richard remembered he had been so excited that he was sure he would never sleep. All throughout the evening he had fancied that he'd heard the bells of Santa's sleigh jingling. It was only his mother's warning that if he wasn't asleep when Santa arrived then he wouldn't leave him any presents, which had finally persuaded him to go to bed. He had been determined to stay awake and see Santa when he came but the minute his head touched the pillow he was asleep.

When he woke the next morning there it was! His stocking bulging with surprises and, when he eventually came down-stairs, there were mysterious presents for one and all spread out underneath the Christmas tree. Their tradition had been not to open these until after they had eaten the roast chicken or turkey, which his mother spent all morning basting and turning so that it would be cooked to perfection. Friends and neighbours popped in for a glass of Christmas cheer, to wish them well and usually brought him a present. By the end of the day he was surrounded by new books, toys, games and new clothes. There were so many wonderful things that he found himself moving from one to the other, too excited to settle down and enjoy any of them.

The days between Christmas and New Year were spent enjoying all his new possessions. If there was any snow, then he would abandon them temporarily to go out and make a snowman or throw snowballs, or simply trundle through the magical white stuff, kicking it away from under his feet as he walked and wishing that Christmas could last forever.

George had never known that sort of Christmas, Richard thought sadly. Megan thought it was all old-fashioned nonsense; she didn't even exchange Christmas cards. She certainly wouldn't tolerate having streamers and lights all over their very modern home. He knew his mother still put up decorations but, much as he would have liked to do so, he never found the time to go along and help her. Megan discouraged Lucia from taking George and found countless other things that she wanted her to do, so George didn't visit his grandmother at Christmas, although Mary always bought him a present.

This year though, if they were away, Lucia would have a chance to take George along and he wondered what the little boy would make of it all. Richard wished he could be there to see his little face. He felt guilty that he was putting his wife's wishes before his duty to his son. He should be stronger, he told himself, and stand up to Megan.

Next year, George would be at school so he would find out for himself what Christmas was all about. He ought to discover it before then, Richard thought worriedly, otherwise the other children would tease him. Megan didn't seem to understand that when he tried to point it out to her. In fact, she laughed derisively and told him he wasn't playing at teacher at school and she had no time for such nonsense.

ELEVEN

Bill had one more appointment at the eye hospital before Christmas and, to his great relief, he was told that his eyes were stable at the moment. He didn't need another injection, so they would see him again in the New Year. Mary was also relieved at some good news. The evening before, she had had a brief phone call from Megan to say that she and Richard were going to be away over Christmas. She had rung off abruptly, not giving Mary a chance to ask her where they were going or whether they were taking little George with them.

If they were not taking him, then what were they going to do with George? What would Christmas be like for the little chap without them there? She'd had a sleepless night worrying about it and now that she knew Bill was all right, she brought the subject up with him.

'Of course they'll be taking him with them. Probably the reason she didn't tell you was because she knew how upset you would be because you wouldn't be seeing him over Christmas, or seeing them come to that. It means you'll be on your own over the holiday,' he said, his voice registering shock.

'Yes, that's true,' Mary agreed. 'Still, I don't mind that so much as long as I know little George is having a good time. I wonder if they're planning to take him to Lapland to see Father Christmas and they are keeping it secret and she was afraid he might overhear if she told me?'

'It might well have been that,' Bill agreed.

'I just hope he has a good time,' Mary repeated.

'He will. I'm sure of that. It's the kids that make Christmas and seeing their little faces light up when they unwrap their presents.' He sighed. 'Seems like another world when you look back. Our boys loved Christmas and all the preparations leading up to it. I can see them now, stirring the Christmas pudding and screwing up their little eyes as they made their wish. Or sitting at the kitchen table, laboriously writing their list to Santa telling him about all the things they wanted. Whenever we were in England in December we used to take them out before Christmas to see Santa in his Grotto. While they were on his knee, he'd listen to what they wanted and then give them a little present before he sent them on their way.

'Yes, those were magical times. Not that we were in England as often as we would have liked, but Lydia took Christmas with us and we celebrated in style no matter whether we were in the Far East, Africa or no-man's land. She had this huge tin box and it had a big black "X" marked on it. We all knew what was inside and made sure it always came with us when we had a fresh a new posting.

'A couple of weeks before Christmas, we'd have a family gathering and open the box. The "ooh's" and "ah's" as the boys rediscovered their favourite decorations for the tree echoed round the room. We had an artificial Christmas tree and this was given a place of honour in the living room. When we'd decided where it was to go, the boys took part in finding their own special trinkets to hang on it.

'Once Christmas was over the tree was dismantled and put back in the huge tin box and securely strapped up ready for the next Christmas.' Bill sighed. 'Then, of course, they grew up and considered themselves to be too old for such childish celebrations. They preferred to spend Christmas partying with their peers. It was always a festive season, of course, and whenever my duties allowed it, we always all sat down to Christmas dinner together and pulled crackers and so on, even when they were grown up. That is until they left home and moved so far away that they couldn't come home for Christmas anymore.'

Mary patted his arm. She could hear his voice shaking but she didn't know what to say. In some ways, she thought wryly, he was better off than her. Bill didn't live in the hope Mary had each year, that she might be invited to join Richard and Megan for the day. No, she had to think herself lucky if she caught a glimpse of little George for half an hour. This year she wasn't even sure about that.

It was such a pity that it had been Megan and not Richard who had phoned, Mary mulled again the next morning. Richard wouldn't have rung off so abruptly as that and she would have been able to ask for more details, to find out where they were going and if it was suitable for George. Not that there was very much she could do or say if she had doubts about their holiday. It had obviously been arranged by Megan and was cut and dried before Megan had phoned.

Ah well, Mary told herself, she must make the best of it she supposed. She'd invite Bill to come to her place for Christmas dinner. It would make it a bit festive for both of them. She'd go out shopping tomorrow and buy a small turkey and a small piece of ham to boil. She'd buy a jar of mincemeat because she still had time to make her own mince pies. She'd have to buy the Christmas pudding because it was less than a week to Christmas and far too late now to make one.

If she was going to keep all this secret from Bill for the moment, then she'd have to do the shopping on her own. She looked through her list again; it was going to be pretty heavy to carry home. Perhaps she ought to ask him to drive her.

No, she resolved, she wouldn't do that as it would spoil the surprise. What she would do was get a taxi home.

The moment she'd had her porridge and washed up her breakfast dishes, she set off for the shops. Better to do it early before they became busy, she thought. It was a crisp bright morning but very cold. She shivered as she set out and she suspected that there had been a frost overnight. Still, if she walked briskly she'd soon warm up.

She was so busy thinking about the purchases she planned to make that she didn't notice the patch of ice caused by a leaking gutter or drainpipe. The next minute she was sliding, lost her balance and crashed to the ground. She felt very foolish and hoped no one had seen what happened. She took a moment to get her breath back and hoped she hadn't torn her winter coat.

Then she tried to get up.

The searing pain in her leg brought the tears to her eyes and made her yell out as she fell back onto the ground again.

'You all right missus?' called out a workman passing by on his bike. He stopped, dismounted and came over to where she was lying. He laid his bike down on the ground and held out a hand to her. 'Here, let me help you up.'

Mary shook her head. 'Thank you, but I don't think that I can stand,' she said with a ghost of a smile. 'I think I've broken my leg,' she added in a rather tremulous voice. 'I didn't see the ice.'

'Nasty!' His lips pursed in a whistle. Then he turned and waved to a car that was coming along the road to stop.

'Lady here thinks she's broken her leg,' he told the driver. 'Can you help?'

The middle-aged man hesitated and then shook his head. 'I'd better not. Might do more harm than good,' he said in a clipped voice. 'I'll phone for an ambulance.'

By now, a small crowd had gathered and they were all murmuring words of sympathy or offering advice. Mary felt both annoyed by her own foolish mess and distressed by the situation she found herself in. She knew they meant well but she wished the ambulance would come and that they would all go on their way and leave her in peace.

It felt like ages before she heard the ambulance approaching. The pain in her leg was becoming more unbearable by the minute and she was shaking partly with cold and partly with shock. Once the ambulance did arrive, the paramedics quickly had her on a stretcher and transferred into the ambulance. She

tried not to cry out, but the pain was so intense that she had a
hard job not to do so. Before they pulled away, they made her
as comfortable as possible, covered her with several blankets
and gave her an injection to make the pain more bearable.

Even so, the journey to the hospital was uncomfortable and
transferring her from the ambulance onto a stretcher and then
into a bed. In the A&E ward it was excruciatingly painful.
Before they took her for an X-ray they took down all her details
and asked so many questions that she felt dizzy. She managed
to retain enough of her senses not to tell them Richard's name
or address and let them believe that not only was she living on
her own but that she had no relations.

'Is there anyone at all you would like us to notify?' she was
asked.

For a wild moment, Mary thought of asking them to phone
Bill. Then common sense prevailed and she shook her head.
Time enough to let him know when she felt better. He would
assume that, after taking him to hospital, she hadn't been in
touch because it was so near to Christmas that she wanted to
catch up with things in her own life. She hoped he wouldn't
worry if she didn't contact him for a couple of days, but knew
he would understand when she eventually told him what had
happened. It was Mary's last thought after she had been taken
into the theatre and before she went under the anaesthetic.

She had no idea how much time elapsed between that
moment and when she woke up dazed and bewildered in the
hospital recovery room. Her mouth was dry and her throat so
sore that she was sure she had been sleeping with her mouth
open and she felt both uneasy and guilty. She hoped she hadn't
been snoring. If only she knew where she was, she thought
uneasily. She certainly wasn't at home because the bed she was
lying in was nowhere near as comfortable as her own bed at
home. She wanted to get up and find out, but she felt so tired
and so lethargic that she couldn't make the effort. She closed
her eyes and drifted off into a hazy state of dreamlessness that
seemed to last for hours.

When she woke again her throat was even drier and she tried
to call out for a drink. She felt helpless. When she moved she felt
uncomfortable. She slid her hands down to see if she was lying

on something hard, then stopped in shock as she encountered something encasing one of her legs.

Panic swept through her. What was wrong with her?

Before she could answer her unspoken question a nurse was bending over her, murmuring comforting words and holding a glass of water to her lips. Mary gulped thirstily, it made her cough but it cleared her throat sufficiently for her to ask, 'Where am I? What's happened to me?'

'You had an accident and broke your leg. You've been in theatre for surgery to repair the damage. We will move you to a bed in one of the wards soon.'

With that the nurse bustled off, leaving Mary to recall the events of the day in flashback spasms, as once again she drifted in and out of consciousness.

TWELVE

The next morning Mary awoke at the time she normally did. She lay for a few moments staring round, wondering where she was. Then with a sudden burst of recall she remembered the accident, the pain, being brought into hospital. After that it was all a misty dream. Had it really happened or had it been a nightmare?

She made to sit up but the pain in her lower back and leg brought a whimper to her lips and she fell back against the pillows. Gingerly she ran her hands down her body. The left one contacted something encasing the upper part of her left leg. So she really had broken her leg. What on earth was she going to do now? How long would they keep her in hospital, she wondered, and even more importantly, what was she going to do if they sent her home? Would she be able to look after herself, get up and down stairs, shop for food? She wondered what the date was. How near it was to Christmas. She had intended on asking Bill to come to her place for his Christmas dinner. Had she asked him already? If so she must let him know that it wasn't going to be possible.

But that meant telling him about what had happened to her and she was determined not to tell anybody. She wasn't even going to tell Richard.

Then she remembered that Richard, Megan and little George were all going to be away at Christmas. She wouldn't even be able to see little George's face when he opened his present. Well, she corrected her thoughts, she would because she wouldn't be giving it to him until after Christmas. Had they already left? She wished she could remember but then she didn't even know what day it was, or the date.

She closed her eyes to try and concentrate, then opened them, startled when she heard someone speaking to her. A nurse was standing at her bedside waiting to check her blood pressure and take her temperature. After she had done this and given her an injection in her arm she asked, 'Are you ready for your breakfast, Mrs Wilson?'

Without waiting for a reply, the nurse propped her up with the aid of several pillows into a partial sitting position. Mary found that the bowl of porridge, piece of toast and cup of tea revived her. They made her feel almost normal again. She felt impatient to know what was going to happen next, but when she asked the nurse gave a shrug and told her she must wait and see what the doctor said when he did his rounds later that morning.

The doctor was a middle-aged man with grey hair and a brusque manner.

'Do you live on your own?'

'Yes, but I am quite fit and capable,' Mary said defensively.

'Is there anyone at home to look after you?' he questioned.

'No, but if I am able to walk then I can look after myself,' Mary told him.

'I'll see how you are tomorrow and then try and get a package put in place.'

'A package?'

'Someone to help you dress and prepare breakfast for you,' he told her.

'I don't want that. I can't stand anyone interfering in my kitchen,' she told him.

He stared at her as if he thought she was deranged then turned away and spoke to the nurse who was accompanying him. His voice was so quiet that Mary couldn't hear what he was saying, but she knew from the way they were both looking at her that they were talking about her and she didn't like it. She felt tears of frustration rising to her eyes and she swallowed quickly. If she gave way like that they certainly would think she was incapable of managing, she thought angrily.

'Are you sure you haven't a neighbour who could help you for a couple of weeks?' the nurse asked after the doctor had gone.

Mary shook her head. Her neighbours were all much younger than her and went out to work so apart from 'good morning' she hadn't chatted to any of them. She had never felt the need to do so.

'You've no children who could help?' the nurse persisted.

'I have a son but he and his family are away on holiday and I have no idea when they will be back,' Mary told her. 'Anyway, my daughter-in-law has a very demanding job.'

'And no other friends who could help or you could go and stay with for a couple of weeks?' the nurse persisted.

'I keep telling you, I can look after myself,' Mary stated firmly.

'A very independent lady, I can see that,' the nurse said with a frosty smile.

Mary said nothing. She closed her eyes and lay back against the pillows. The argument with the doctor and now with the nurse had left her exhausted and she wasn't at all convinced that they believed her.

Later in the morning, a youngish woman in a tailored black coat and carrying a notebook and pen came to her bedside and introduced herself as Pat. She said she wanted to take down details of Mary's circumstances and see what they could do to help her. She asked if she had her house keys with her and, if so, to let her have them and she would go and check if there were any aids she might need when she got home.

Mary looked aghast. 'Hand my keys over to you so that you can go in my house, even though I'm not there?' she exclaimed in disbelief.

'I won't do any damage I assure you,' Pat smiled.

'Maybe not, but I don't know you from Adam,' Mary told her sharply. 'No one but me has the keys to my home,' she declared.

'I only want to make sure that your chair is the right height for you and that your kitchen is safe for use. You may not be perfectly mobile for weeks, you know.'

'I don't need any aids,' Mary reiterated. 'Thank you for your concern but I know I can manage. I don't want any of your packages either.'

Pat snapped shut her notebook. 'We're only trying to help you,' she admonished.

'I know and it's very kind of you, but I couldn't stand someone fussing in my kitchen or interfering with my belongings, thank you very much.'

It was late in the afternoon when Mary had a surprise visitor. For a moment she couldn't believe her eyes.

'Bill? Is it really you?' she exclaimed.

He laughed as he sat down in the chair beside her bed. 'It is but I'm the one who should be saying that to you. What on earth are you doing here? And, even more important, why didn't you let me know!'

'I didn't want anyone to know, that's why,' she retorted. 'I didn't want to spoil Christmas for anybody.'

'Well, you're not likely to do that now are you? Your Richard and his family are away for the Christmas holiday.'

'Yes, but have they left yet?' Mary asked. 'I'm a bit fuzzy about the dates. I didn't want Richard to hear it before he left because he would only worry.'

'Tomorrow is the twenty-third of December. Only two days before Christmas. Richard left three days ago. Do you have an address for him?'

'I wouldn't tell you in case you got in touch with him and told him what had happened.'

'Now, would I do a thing like that?' Bill chortled. 'So, you'll be staying in here for Christmas will you?' he asked.

'I certainly hope not. I want to get home as soon as possible.'

'Will you be able to manage?' he frowned.

'Oh don't you start. The doctor, nurse and some sort of social worker have interrogated me and trying to convince them that I can manage has worn me out. They even wanted me to have a package; some young girl to come in and dress me in the morning and get my breakfast. Ridiculous! I hate people interfering in my affairs as you well know.'

'I am well aware of that,' Bill told her. 'It's one of the reasons why I have had such a hard time tracking you down. I went to your house several times, asked around and so on but no one knew where you were or when they had last seen you. Then I tried the police and they suggested ringing round the local hospitals. No,' he sighed, 'it hasn't been easy.'

Mary stretched out a hand and caught at his arm.

'I'm sorry,' she said contritely. 'I should have asked them to let you know. I . . . I wasn't thinking clearly. I didn't mean you when I said I wanted no one to know where I was. I was thinking of Richard. I didn't want to worry him or spoil his holiday.'

He took her hand and squeezed it. 'I understand,' he told her and his voice was a mere whisper and there were tears in his eyes as he stared down at her. 'Well,' he gathered himself together. 'Now that I am here what are we going to do? Do you know when they are sending you home?'

'No but from all the questions they've been asking they are anxious to do so as soon as possible. I suppose they need the bed. Lots of silly old dears like me falling all over the place and breaking their bones at this time of the year. There must have been ice on the road and I didn't see it.'

'Perhaps I had better ask them so that we can make some plans,' Bill said.

'Plans, what do you mean?' Mary asked sharply.

'What we are going to do when they send you home of course. You don't think I'm going to shut my eyes to the pickle you are in do you!'

'What can you do?' Mary asked. 'I'm not having you play nursemaid and I am not coming to stay at your place, so don't think I am,' she added forcefully.

'I haven't invited you to do so,' Bill retorted brusquely but the twinkle in his eye took away the harshness of his statement.

Mary lay back against her pillows and sighed deeply. 'I hate

people fussing over me and I hate being dependent on anyone,'
she muttered softly.

'I know, I know.' Bill patted her arm. 'If me telling them
that I'll look after you, means that they let you come home,
then will you let me pop in each day to make sure you are all
right and do any bits of shopping you need?'

'I suppose so. If it's the only way I can get them to agree to
my going home, then I have no choice,' Mary muttered with a
wry smile.

'Well, Christmas is only a few days away so you could ask
them to let you stay on here. You'd be warm and well looked
after, you know.'

'No!' Mary pursed her lips angrily. 'I want to go home. I'll
manage, don't worry.'

'So you want me to go and tell that nurse that if they let you
out I'll be looking after you?'

'Yes, as long as picking up any shopping I may need is all
the looking after you are going to do.'

Bill didn't answer. He stood up and walked down to where
the nurse was sitting in front of a computer entering records.
Mary watched as they spent the next five minutes talking about
her and her future. She wished she could hear what they were
saying but, although they kept looking towards her, they made
no attempt to come over and include her in their discussion.

'They're going to keep you in for another day because your
temperature is still high,' Bill told her when he came back to
her bedside. 'Then, if they think you are fit enough they will
send you home by ambulance. They are going to phone me and
tell me what time of day that will be so that I can be at your
place when they arrive.'

'They haven't said anything about packages have they?' Mary
asked apprehensively.

'Of course not! You won't need any carers if I am there to
look after you.' He held a finger to his lips as he spoke, warning
Mary not to start making a fuss. 'I'm off now,' he told her. 'Do
you want me to take your front door key so that I can make
sure the place is warm when you get home?'

'There's no need. The storage heaters will see to that. I leave
them on all the time in this weather.'

'Right. Well I'll get you some bread and some milk. See you tomorrow or whenever they send you home.'

He was gone before she could thank him. She should have let him have her key, she thought guiltily. It made it look as though she didn't trust him and it meant that he'd have to hang around outside waiting for the ambulance when he could have been indoors in the warm.

THIRTEEN

For the next few hours Mary felt light-hearted. She was going home. She would be in her own surroundings for Christmas Day, and even though Richard and his family were away, it didn't matter. She would sooner be quiet and on her own in her own home than here; where the comings and goings night and day kept her from sleeping or even thinking, because she couldn't concentrate.

Now, relieved and content she tried to plan ahead, working out how she was going to manage. A woman coming to her bedside with two crutches disturbed her thoughts.

'These are for you, Mrs Wilson. I understand you are hoping to go home but, before you can do that, you have to be able to use these,' she said pushing the crutches towards Mary.

'Crutches! I'd rather not try them; I'd probably fall over and break my neck, thank you all the same,' Mary said, shaking her head.

'You won't fall over once you've mastered how to use them and it's the only way you will be able to move around, because you mustn't put any weight on your broken leg for at least three weeks, maybe longer.'

The woman consulted the notes she was holding. 'I see it's the left leg,' she murmured half to herself. 'Left leg and you now have a steel rod and screw in it.'

'I've got what?' Mary stared at the woman aghast. She knew her leg hurt and she had wondered why it wasn't in plaster but a steel rod in it! Whatever was going on?

The woman ignored her question.

'Come along, put on your dressing gown and I will show you how to use the crutches.'

The next half hour was a form of torture for Mary. She had never used crutches in her life before and she found it so uncomfortable. They seemed to be pushing her armpits up into her shoulder. She wasn't very heavy so she was surprised at the effort it took to support herself on them. She wondered how big heavy people managed.

At the end of half an hour, she was told that she had done enough for the moment and to rest. The woman said she would be returning again later in the day, however, for a further session. Mary lay back on her bed exhausted. She closed her eyes and wondered if perhaps it would be better if she gave in and stayed at the hospital instead of struggling to get home. She would never be able to move around on those things, she told herself. The pain under her arms for one thing was excruciating.

Leaving her dressing gown on, she pulled up the covers and turned her face into the pillow so that no one could see the tears of frustration sliding down her cheeks. When she finally sat up again, it was because someone was tapping her on the arm and telling her that her meal was ready. They moved the bed table over to her, uncovering a plate of savoury smelling food. Still in a daze she ate it almost automatically, slowly aware that the hot food was making her feel better. Then she saw the crutches propped against the foot of her bed and all her fears came back. This is ridiculous, she told herself, I've never given in ever in my life and I'm not going to do so now.

Purposefully, she pushed away the bedside table and put her feet, which were still in her slippers, onto the floor. The searing pain in her left leg as she tried to stand up took her breath away. Shuddering she pulled her foot clear of the ground. She'd have to learn to use those awful crutches or she would be bedbound forever, she told herself.

When the physiotherapist returned for a second session Mary was as cooperative as she could possibly be. By the time the woman left, she was not only balancing on the crutches but managing to take a tentative step or two, only using her right foot and the crutches for leverage and balance. A sense of achievement filled her as the woman congratulated her on what she had managed to achieve.

'Now have a good night's sleep, I'll be back in the morning and then we'll try a little walk.'

The next morning, Mary not only managed the promised little walk, but also manoeuvred her way up three steps and down again. She felt really proud of herself. There was nothing she couldn't do if she put her mind to it, she told herself. She rested for half an hour after the physio had left, and then she began slowly to walk up and down the ward.

'You'll wear the floor out if you go on like that,' one of the nurses told her laughingly. 'We'll have to send you home if you are that capable.'

'That's exactly what I am hoping will happen,' Mary said smiling back. 'You've all been very kind to me and I am truly grateful, but I'm sure you will agree; there's nowhere quite like your own home.'

'Yes, well we'll have to wait and see what the doctor says,' the nurse countered. 'Now pop back on your bed and rest like a good girl,' she told her.

Mary nodded and gritted her teeth. Why oh why did they have to be so condescending. 'Like a good girl' indeed, who the hell did the nurse think she was talking to? She may be old enough to be her mother, or perhaps even her grandmother, but there was no need for the nurse to speak to her as if she was out of her mind or a young child, Mary thought resentfully.

So Mary propped the crutches against a chair and awkwardly clambered back onto the bed, well aware that the nurse was watching her every movement. She lay back against the pillows and closed her eyes, so that the nurse wouldn't see the tears of frustration that came welling up into them. The doctor looked at her with raised eyebrows when, later that day, she asked him if she could go home.

'Is there someone there to look after you?' he questioned.

'Not exactly,' Mary admitted after a slight hesitation. 'Not living there that is, but I have a very good friend who will come in each day and do my shopping and things like that.'

The doctor bit down on his lower lip and looked

questioningly at the Sister who was accompanying him on his round. 'Has the patient's house been checked and has a package been put in place for this lady?'

The Sister shook her head.

'Why not?'

'Mrs Wilson wasn't prepared to hand over her keys so we couldn't carry out an inspection, and,' her mouth tightened perceptibly, 'she says she doesn't want a package; she doesn't like strangers in her home.'

'Hmm!' the doctor tightened his lips, whether in disapproval or to stop himself laughing Mary wasn't too sure, but from the twinkle in his brown eyes as they met hers she suspected it was the latter.

'So you are very independent are you, Mrs Wilson?' he said at last.

'I try to be,' Mary told him spiritedly.

'You really think you can manage?'

'Yes, I do,' Mary said quietly

'Very well, we'll let you go home tomorrow, providing we are confident you can manage. One more night in hospital and then it's up to you to take care of yourself.'

'We will want to see you back here again for an X-ray and check-up in about six weeks' time to make sure that your leg has healed and to check that you are walking properly. Until then, use your crutches.'

'Shouldn't I be able to walk without them by then?' Mary questioned.

'Later you will be able to manage with a stick, but not at the moment. On no account put weight on your damaged leg. Is that quite clear?'

'Yes, I understand what you are saying,' Mary said quietly.

'Good! One other thing,' he went on, 'if you have any trouble such as serious discomfort and pain, or another fall, or anything like that, then come back so that we can check you haven't done any further damage to your leg. Is that understood?'

'Yes, I understand,' Mary repeated.

Mary could hardly sleep that night for excitement. Later in the afternoon, she'd had another session of moving around on her crutches under the eagle eye of the physio and she was sure she would be all right, providing she went slowly and was careful. She promised that she wouldn't attempt going out, not until she felt really confident.

The only thing that worried her, and she was thankful that no one had questioned her too closely, was that her bathroom at home was upstairs and she wasn't at all sure that she would be able to go up and down stairs on her crutches. There was a toilet downstairs and for the moment she would have to have a wash at the kitchen sink, she resolved. She could have a strip wash there, although it would not be as good as showering or a bath of course. Still, she wouldn't be able to get into the bath with her leg, not on her own, and she certainly wasn't going to ask Bill to help her. Anyway, they'd told her not to get her leg wet so she didn't really need a bathroom, she reminded herself.

She had a single bed that would be easy enough to bring downstairs and, by moving things around in the sitting room, it could be put in there as a temporary measure. Or, if Bill wasn't able to do that on his own, then she would sleep on the settee. It would only be for a short time, she told herself. Only until Richard came back from his Christmas holiday and could put the bed down in the living room, or she had more confidence about manoeuvring on steps with her crutches and could face going upstairs.

Being at home, in her own surroundings, doing things at her own pace was what she wanted most in the world. She would ask Bill to get her some ready cooked meals from the supermarket so that she could put them in the freezer and then she could heat one up each day. A pint of milk would last her at least two days and a loaf of bread almost a week, she told herself. She'd have porridge for breakfast, it would be a simple enough matter to make that, and she could make a cup of tea or coffee whenever she wanted them.

Yes, she told herself, looking after herself would be simple enough. Then she remembered that she had intended cooking a full Christmas dinner for Bill on Christmas Day. She sighed. That was out of the question but she was sure he would understand. He'd already had three Christmases on his own so another one wouldn't matter. Next year she'd really go to town and cook him a splendid meal. By then, she would have thrown away the crutches, all her problems would be over and she would be walking normally.

FOURTEEN

Mary was awake and began struggling to get dressed before it was even light the next morning. She had slept very fitfully, drifting in her mind from hospital to home, imagining all the obstacles she was likely to encounter and then trying to solve them. She felt tired but that didn't matter, she told herself, as soon as she was at home she could have a nap.

She wondered what time the ambulance would be ready to take her. Did they take the people who were being sent home first, or did they have to be slotted in between emergency and routine calls? She didn't care when she went as long as she did eventually get home.

Bill had said he would be there when the ambulance arrived, so she must make sure that she telephoned him and let him know what time she was leaving the hospital. She mustn't be impatient nor must she keep asking, she told herself, just let it happened when they were ready. There was some business about being signed out and waiting for the pharmacy to send up the medicines that had been ordered for her to take home. The morning dragged by.

With the help of a nurse, Mary had packed all her belongings, except her coat, into a large hospital bag ready to leave. Every time a nurse came into the ward Mary brightened, thinking she was coming to tell her that they were ready to take her home. It was mid-afternoon before the summons came. She had picked her way through her midday meal, making herself eat it because she wasn't sure when or where she would get her next meal.

The two paramedics were suddenly at her side. One was middle aged and tired-looking, with grey hair and watery blue eyes. The other was very young, freckled and with a wide grin as if he found the whole world one big joke. The younger one picked up her bag, the elder one handed her the crutches.

'Do you need these?' he asked.

Before she could answer, a nurse came bustling over and handed him another bag which she explained contained Mary's medication.

'Haven't you brought a stretcher or a wheel chair?' she demanded of the eldest paramedic. 'Mrs Wilson can't walk all the way to the ambulance from here and she will need to be conveyed from your ambulance into her house at the other end.'

'I'll go. Which is it to be?' the younger one asked.

The elder of the two looked at the nurse. 'Think she can manage with a chair?'

She pursed her lips. 'Possibly, but you will have to be careful. No weight bearing on the left leg remember.'

'Fetch a chair,' the older man ordered. 'We'll be careful,' he told the nurse.

Ten minutes later, after a shift into the wheelchair which Mary considered to be quite traumatic, she was taken from the ward down a long corridor and then into a lift, only to emerge in another long corridor; along which the younger paramedic pushed her at what she thought was terrific speed.

She looked around with interest as she found herself in the main reception area and then outside, to where the ambulance was parked. He wheeled the chair up a ramp at the rear of the ambulance and then carefully anchored it to a seat, using a series of straps so that the chair was immovable. The bags containing her belongings and her crutches were also safely stowed away. Then the ambulance doors were slammed shut and she was finally on her way home. Mary found it overwhelming to look out and see familiar roads and shops, and waited eagerly for her first glimpse of her own house as they drew nearer.

They lowered the ramp at the back of the ambulance and wheeled her out onto the driveway. Then they assisted her to stand up with the aid of her crutches. With their assistance, she was able to walk from the ambulance up to her own front door. Bill was waiting there as he had promised to be and Mary felt

tears of gratitude brimming up in her eyes. Slowly she manoeuvred her way into the sitting room and within minutes was
sitting in her favourite armchair, comfortable and happy to be
there.

'Now is there anything else we can do for you, Mrs Wilson?'
the oldest paramedic, she now knew as Jim, asked.

'No, you have been very kind,' she told him.

'Where you going to sleep tonight?' the younger one, Tommy,
asked whilst looking around the room. 'You're not going to try
and get upstairs are you?'

Mary bit her lip. 'There's a single bed upstairs in the back
bedroom and . . . I'm planning on having that brought down.
Until I can manage to do that I can curl up on that settee.'

'I'm going to see if I can find someone to help me get it down,'
Bill said quickly.

The two men looked at each other.

'Lead the way, show us where it is and while we get it down
you make us a brew,' they told him.

Ten minutes later they had dismantled the single bed, brought
it downstairs, moved the furniture around so that there was
room for it and reassembled it.

'That is simply wonderful and so very kind of you,' Mary
told them as Bill handed them both a mug of coffee and then
offered them some biscuits. They wasted very little time in
drinking their coffee and after wishing Mary a speedy recovery,
they were on their way.

Left on their own, Bill and Mary breathed sighs of relief.

'That was good of them,' Bill commented.

'Two very helpful men,' Mary agreed. 'It seems I am all set
up now with no worries other than managing those wretched
crutches. I am so afraid that one of them will slip.'

'Don't attempt to walk without them,' Bill warned. 'Take
your time, be careful and make sure they are firm before you
put your weight on them. Give it a couple of days and you will
have mastered them and not give it a second thought.'

'I hope you are right,' Mary said dubiously.

'I do think you should get rid of some of the rugs though,'
Bill advised. 'It would make it much easier for you to get
around. Shall I roll them up for you?'

'Yes, very well, if you think it is necessary.'

She watched Bill remove the rug from the middle of the room, the one in the kitchen and the one in the hall. Without them the room looked bare but much larger. She could see what he meant; the space was now clutter free and there was nothing to catch the crutches in.

'I've brought you some milk and bread, and also some tins of soup, cheese and one or two frozen meals. Enough to keep you going for a day or so and I'll be round in the morning to make you some breakfast and see if there's anything else you need.'

'You'd better take my key,' Mary said.

'I'll call out when I come in so that you won't be startled or wonder who it is.'

'I'll know it must be you because no one else has a key, except Richard and he's away,' Mary reminded him with a smile.

'True, true!' Bill agreed. 'Now is there anything else you need before I go?'

'Nothing at all and thank you for all you've done,' Mary told him warmly.

As she heard the front door close behind him, she took in a deep breath. She was home on her own at last. The silence was overwhelming but it was an atmosphere she loved. Quiet, peaceful and orderly. She sat back in her chair and closed her eyes. She suddenly felt so tired that she was almost tempted to get into the bed that had been left ready for her.

The only disturbing thought that nagged away in her mind was that there was only one day left before Christmas Day. She knew there was no chance she would be able to provide the Christmas dinner for herself and Bill that she had intended to do. She didn't know whether to tell him now how sorry she was about this or to simply say nothing and hope that perhaps he would forget that it was Christmas Day.

That, of course, was nonsense she told herself. He would know it was Christmas Day the same as she did. She finally went to sleep hoping that a solution would come to her in the next twenty-four hours.

As it turned out, Bill solved the problem. When he arrived next morning, he wished her a Merry Christmas and handed her a Christmas card before he went about the usual chore of making tea and a bowl of porridge for her breakfast. All the time he was whistling happily, as if he hadn't a care in the world. Breakfast over, he didn't go off to attend to his own home. He sat there talking to her and enjoying a TV programme with her.

'See you tomorrow,' he said as he left.

It was the same on Christmas morning. Bill arrived bright and cheerful, made her breakfast and cleared up afterwards, and then sat there with her.

At midday, he looked at his watch once or twice, his brows drawn together in a frown, and Mary thought he was anxious to get home. When she asked him he shook his head and then his face brightened as the doorbell sounded. Mary looked puzzled. Who on earth could be calling? Surely Richard hadn't come back already, not on Christmas Day.

Bill went to answer the door and returned to the living room accompanied by a smart young man wearing a high-necked white jacket and black pinstripe trousers. He was carrying a heavy tray covered over by a snowy white cloth, which he took through into the kitchen.

'Whatever is going on?' Mary gasped.

Bill held a finger to his lips, accompanied the young man back to the door and in a couple of minutes they returned; the young man carrying another covered tray and Bill an ice bucket with a bottle in it.

The young man, whom Bill introduced to Mary as François, whipped out a crisp red tablecloth, spread it on the dining table and started to lay it up for four people.

'What on earth is going on?' Mary asked again.

'Christmas dinner,' Bill announced proudly.

'There are only two of us so why is he laying for four?'

Before Bill could answer there was a ring at the doorbell and with a beaming smile of triumph Bill hurried to answer it. Mary felt tense. Surely he hadn't been in touch with Richard and asked him back? He couldn't have done so because he didn't have a contact number for him, she reminded herself. As Bill came back into the room Mary thought she was dreaming. He was shepherding Lucia and little George. They were both laughing at her surprise and George flung himself into her arms, almost knocking her out of her chair.

'Is your daddy . . .?' Mary began but Bill quickly silenced her by shaking his head and frowning.

'We'll explain everything after we have eaten our Christmas dinner,' Bill promised. 'Come on, coats off and let's sit down and enjoy our feast. We have everything from champagne to turkey and Christmas pudding. The food is all piping hot so sit up to the table and enjoy.'

It was a meal Mary would remember forever. François opened the champagne with a flourish and a loud pop and poured a glass for the three of them, and a glass of apple juice for George. While they were drinking their drinks, François finished laying the dining table. The napkin rings had holly and mistletoe on them, the placemats had a festive snowman and the larger mats for hot dishes depicted a bright Christmas scene. George was entranced; he kept looking from one to the other of them, pointing out things he recognised.

François then served them with a traditional Christmas dinner of the highest order. He made sure that the portion he placed in front of George was the right size for the small boy, and that the turkey was diced so that George was able to eat unaided. The meal over, they sat drinking their coffee and eating a mince pie, while George, his eyes wide with wonder, unwrapped the big box of Lego that Bill had bought for him.

Silently and efficiently François whisked away all the dirty dishes, cleared the table, and after wishing theme all a Happy Christmas, departed.

'Did that really happen or have I dreamed it all?' Mary gasped as the door slammed shut behind him.

'Bit of all right, wasn't it?' grinned Bill proudly.

'Absolutely perfect! I'll certainly never forget it,' Mary beamed, her eyes misting with tears of happiness. 'Thank you Bill, it really was wonderful,' she added, stretching out a hand to take his.

FIFTEEN

Mary's wonderful Christmas had filled her with a purpose for the coming year. She was going to regain her mobility, she told herself, even if it meant using a stick for the rest of her life. She was intent on discarding her crutches as soon as she possibly could and followed the physiotherapist's instructions assiduously, about what she must or must not do. On her next visit to the hospital, they praised her progress but said they wanted to see her again in three weeks' time. Even so, Mary was delighted. She was winning, she told herself. She was now weight bearing on her broken leg and, provided she took care, she would be back to normal in next to no time.

Bill was equally enthusiastic about her progress. Although he had not minded looking after her, he had found the additional shopping and other duties very tiring. It had made him very much aware that he was not as young as he used to be. His joints ached at the end of the day and he often felt stiff when he woke up in the morning. His eye was troubling him and, because of his concern about Mary, he had skipped his last appointment at the eye hospital. He told them that he had a heavy cold so he was now behind with his treatment. He hadn't told Mary because he knew it would worry her and he hoped she wouldn't find out. She had enough problems of her own without adding his to them. He had the date of his next appointment and he vowed he would keep that no matter what happened.

It was five days into the New Year when Richard and Megan returned home. George was very excited to see them again and ran straight into Richard's arms shrieking, 'Daddy, Daddy, I love you and I've lots and lots to tell you.'

'Have you now?' Richard exclaimed swinging the boy up in his arms and hugging and kissing him. 'Well, go and kiss

Mummy first and then you can tell me all your news.' George's news was a gabbled account of the fun he and Lucia had had over Christmas at Silver Street with his grandmother and Bill. His eyes were shining as he told his father about the wonderful box of Lego that Bill had given him and how Bill had helped him to build things.

Megan's frown increased with every word George uttered. Richard put a finger to his lips, signalling her to be quiet until George had finished and then visibly squared his shoulders for the onslaught he knew would follow.

Megan was incandescent with anger. 'I gave strict instructions to Lucia that she was not to take George to visit your mother,' she fumed. 'She will have to go; I will not stand for such disobedience.'

'Don't be silly; it sounds as though it all turned out for the best. George had an exciting Christmas and I am pleased to hear it. I've had quite a conscience about leaving him without us over the festive season.'

'Lucia was with him,' Megan retorted. 'He probably wasn't even aware that it was Christmas.'

'No, he probably wasn't and that was our fault. We didn't even fill a stocking for him before we left, or leave him and Lucia any presents.'

'George doesn't need any more toys. He has plenty and he will be off to school soon and won't need babyish things like that.'

'Toys aren't babyish, Megan,' Richard said reprovingly. 'Look how excited he is over the Lego that Bill bought for him.'

'Yes, and that's one of the things I object to. It can go straight into the bin.'

'Megan! You can't do a thing like that. It was a present and very kind of Bill to buy it for him.'

'Kind! Don't be so gullible, Richard. As I've told you before, that old man is trying to inveigle his way into your mother's life.'

'By the sound of it he has been very good to her. Where would she have been without his help after her accident?'

'She should have stayed in hospital or told them to send her to a nursing home. It's a disgrace sending her home with no

one there to look after her. It certainly gave that old man a
wonderful opportunity to worm his way still further into
her home. I also want to know the truth from Lucia about
what happened. Why did she succumb to his scheming ways?
How did he get in touch with her? Did he come round here
looking for her?'

'Wait until we have heard my mother's side of the story,'
Richard said placating. 'I'll go round to see her later on to let
her know we are home and hear what she has to say about this
wonderful Christmas George tells us he had.'

Mary's version was more lucid. She explained that Bill
had bumped into Lucia and George while out shopping and had
naturally invited them to come on Christmas Day, because he
thought it would be a lovely surprise for her. Richard accepted
her story that it had all happened in good faith and said he
understood. He said nothing about Megan's orders to Lucia
because he thought his mother would be very hurt. When he
returned home and tried to explain all this to Megan, however,
she was far from mollified.

'Lucia should have refused his invitation, she had my orders
not to go there,' she said stubbornly.

'Very difficult for Lucia to do that when she knew it was
being done to please my mother,' Richard pointed out. 'Anyway,
George was there at the time and he knew what Bill was saying
and of course he wanted to go and see his grandmother.'

'I gave Lucia strict instructions not to visit her and from
what George says they have been back there several times
since Christmas,' Megan pointed out angrily.

'Well, I suppose Lucia felt she had to do so if my mother
invited her.'

'Not when I had expressly told her not to visit,' Megan
repeated angrily.

Richard sighed. 'Well, what's done is done and there's nothing
we can do about it now, so I think the best thing to do is forget
it happened.'

'I shall certainly be having strong words with Lucia. She must
be made to understand that she has to do what I tell her and not
ignore the instructions I give her.'

SIXTEEN

Mary Wilson felt worried. Although she was making good progress with her walking, even though she was much slower in her movements than she would have liked, she was concerned about Bill.

Bill Thompson didn't seem to be anywhere as alert as he had once been. He had become clumsy, bumping into chairs and tables, knocking over a glass and not bothering to read the newspaper when she offered it to him. His excuse that he hadn't the time to sit down and read it now was so unconvincing that she wondered if he was making excuses because his sight was deteriorating.

When she found him pouring boiling water down the side of the teapot instead of inside it, she felt the time had come to question him about what was happening. She waited until he had brought their tea into the sitting room and they were both in their armchairs before asking, 'What did they tell you about your eyes the last time you went to Windsor hospital?'

'They said they would see me again in a month.'

'Have you had an appointment?'

Bill didn't answer. Instead he picked up her cup and saucer and asked, 'Would you like another?'

'Yes in a minute, after you've told me when you have to go to the hospital again.'

Bill concentrated on drinking his tea and didn't answer.

'Bill, you haven't missed an appointment have you?' Mary asked, her voice full of dismay.

'I think I have,' he admitted. 'I forgot the date.'

'So when should it have been?'

'I told you, I can't remember.'

'Then we'd better ring up the hospital and find out,' Mary said, picking up the phone that stood on the small table beside her chair.

'I don't know the number or any of the details they always ask for when you phone them,' Bill prevaricated.

'Don't worry, I do,' she said calmly.

She saw Bill scowl but dialled the number anyway and, when the girl answered, asked to be put through to the eye appointments office.

'I'm checking the date for Bill Thompson's next appointment,' she told the receptionist in the appointments office.

'Can you give me his hospital number, please?'

'So sorry, I am afraid I haven't got it handy but I can give you his date of birth.'

'That will do,' the girl said, and within a couple of minutes she came back on the line to say that it should have been on 10th January but he hadn't turned up.

'No, sorry about that but he wasn't well,' Mary said quietly.

'Then he should have let us know and we could have offered the appointment to someone else,' the girl said reprovingly.

'Yes, very sorry about that. When can you fit him in?'

'Well, he should have let us know,' the girl repeated.

'I know, and he's very sorry about that. He's here, would you like to speak to him?'

'No, it doesn't matter,' the girl said curtly.

'So when can you see him,' Mary persisted.

'There's been a cancellation so I can give you an appointment on 24th February,' the girl said hesitantly.

'Oh dear, not until then! What time?'

'It's at 9.30 a.m.'

'Right. He'll be there and thank you for being so helpful,' Mary said sweetly.

'You heard all that?' she asked Bill as she replaced the receiver. 'I'll order a taxi so be ready.'

'You're not thinking of coming with me, are you?' Bill said in an astonished voice.

'I most certainly am. I can't trust you to keep it otherwise, now can I?'

'Sorry about missing the other one,' he said rather shame-faced. 'I didn't forget; I couldn't face it.'

'I understand,' Mary said quietly.

She cast her mind back to the days when Sam had to attend

the eye hospital for AMD and how reluctant he had always been, even when he knew that it was only for a check-up.

'I don't think you should come with me, Mary,' he said, his brow furrowing.

'Of course I'm coming with you!'

'You are in no fit state to do that. It will upset Richard if he finds out.'

'Then we'd better make sure he doesn't,' Mary said. 'No arguing, I'm coming with you.'

'You are still on crutches,' he protested.

'I know that, but I have a hospital appointment in the middle of February, before your appointment, so with any luck they will say I can use a walking stick and not have to use the crutches any longer. My leg is so much better and I'm able to put my weight on it now.'

Bill shook his head. 'I wouldn't count on it. These things take time.'

'Then I'll simply have to use my crutches,' Mary snapped. 'Let's forget the whole thing. My tea is almost cold,' she said changing the subject. 'What about making a fresh pot?'

Bill was right, of course, Mary knew. She still wasn't walking well enough to give up the crutches. When they had agreed to see her again in February she had hoped that it was because they thought that, by then, she could discard the crutches in favour of a stick and she was determined this would happen, because she disliked the crutches so much.

Now there was an added incentive.

She was very disappointed when she kept her appointment and, after her leg had been X-rayed, was told that – although it was healing well – she still needed the support of crutches.

'Your age has a lot to do with the healing process, Mrs Wilson, and we don't want to take any risks now, do we?' the surgeon told her when she protested.

Bill's visit to the eye clinic was equally disappointing. The trauma of getting there and back was something that imprinted it on Mary's memory. The taxi arrived promptly and fortunately the driver had been the one who had taken them to the hospital before. He gave a low whistle when he saw Mary was on crutches.

'What you been up to? Been skiing?'

'No, nothing so exotic,' Mary told him. 'I slipped on some ice when I was out shopping and broke my leg.'

'Sorry to hear that!' He opened the front passenger door. 'Climb in here, you'll find it easier than getting in the back.' He waited patiently as she manoeuvred into the seat, then he took her crutches and stowed them in the back of the car. 'Same routine?' He asked as he fastened her seat belt for her. 'Pick up your friend and then the eye hospital in Windsor?'

'Yes, that's right.'

Bill was surprised to see she was sitting in the front passenger seat but nodded understandingly when she told him why she was doing so. Mary left Bill to sign in at the reception desk. Walking down the long corridor from the entrance had made her very nervous and she wanted to sit down. The initial procedures for Bill's eyes seemed to take longer than usual but the outcome was devastating for both of them.

The AMD was now in both eyes.

The doctors had decided he must have an injection in the newly affected eye right away. There was a fairly long wait but, as Mary pointed out to him, the fact that they were doing something immediately increased the chances of lessening the damage it might do.

'At least you know the procedure,' she said consolingly.

'That's the problem,' Bill said. 'I know the procedure and I don't like it.'

'Never mind, it will all be over soon and we'll go and have a cup of tea or coffee before we go home.' She looked at her watch. 'In fact, we could have lunch here. They do an excellent jacket potato.'

Bill didn't answer. At the moment food was far from his mind. All he wanted was to have the injection and get it over with. He was also secretly wondering if, by missing his last appointment, he had made matters worse. If he had come back then, a month ago, would he be here today with these results? It was almost midday before Bill was called in for his injection. Half an hour later, he came out of the surgery smiling with relief that it was all over.

'Sit quietly for ten minutes and if you feel all right then you can go,' the nurse told him.

'Shall we have lunch here?' Mary reiterated ten minutes later, when Bill said he was ready to leave. She picked up her crutches and started walking in the direction of the restaurant. She knew that at the moment, coupled with his sensation of relief that it was over with, he would not be feeling any discomfort. In another hour or so, when the anaesthetic had worn off, then his eye would feel painful as if it was full of gravel and most uncomfortable.

The moment they had finished their meal and drunk their coffee, Mary phoned for the taxi. She wished she had asked the driver who brought them here his name, so that she could ask for him, but the chances were that he would be out on another job anyway.

The driver who arrived was a complete stranger and he raised his eyebrows in surprise when she said she wanted to ride in the front passenger seat. Bill held the door for her and then took her crutches into the back of the car. She gave Bill's address and when they arrived in Coburn Road, she could tell from the look on his face that his eye was beginning to become uncomfortable.

'Bed as soon as you get in,' she said. 'I'll phone you some-time this evening to see how you are.'

He nodded but said nothing.

She then gave the driver her address in Silver Street. When he stopped on the opposite side of the road she looked slightly dismayed but said nothing. It wasn't a busy road so she shouldn't have any trouble getting across. She paid him before she got out of the car and was slightly annoyed when he made no attempt to help her retrieve her crutches from the back of the car.

As she stood holding onto the door and struggling to balance she asked, 'Could you pass over my crutches, please?'

He didn't seem to understand what she was saying but, when she waved a hand towards the back of the car, he looked over his shoulder into the rear and then leaned back and pressed down the door handle. However, he made no attempt to get out

of his seat or to reach them out for her. Balancing awkwardly
she moved her hold from the passenger door to the rear door
of the car and painfully hobbled round, so that she could bend
down and extricate the crutches.

It took her another minute or so to move her hold from the
door to the crutches, and she was very aware that the driver
merely sat there watching her struggle and made no attempt to
help her. Angrily, she hobbled away, leaving the car door open
and hoping he'd have as much difficulty in closing that as she'd
had in getting out of his car.

SEVENTEEN

M ary was very surprised when the following week
Megan came to see her. It was so unusual that, for
one brief moment when she opened the door, she
thought there must be something wrong with either Richard
of George. Then she realised that Megan was looking extremely
elegant in a very smart suit with a crisp white blouse underneath it. She certainly wasn't looking like a harassed wife or
concerned mother.

'You're still hobbling around on those things then,' Megan
commented as Mary awkwardly backed away from the door so
that Megan could enter.

'Yes and I will be for another few weeks I'm afraid,' Mary
said with a small sigh.

'I thought you were going back to the hospital about a week
ago for a check-up,' Megan frowned.

'I did and the surgeon advised using the crutches for a little
bit longer,' Mary told her.

Megan raised her carefully pencilled eyebrows but said
nothing.

'Can I make you a cup of tea?' Mary asked in an attempt to
overcome the chilly atmosphere that seemed to have arisen
between them.

Megan hesitated for a moment and then nodded. 'Very

well, it might be easier to say what I have to say if we have some tea.'

'So what is it you have to say?' Mary asked as she switched on the kettle and popped some teabags into the teapot.

Megan didn't answer for a moment, then she said, 'There's no hurry; we'll wait until we are sitting down.'

She stood in the kitchen watching Mary take two blue and white cups down from the cupboard over the worktop. Mary put these together with a jug of milk and biscuits onto a tray. As soon as the kettle boiled, she filled the teapot and put that also on the tray.

'Right, it's all ready but I'm afraid you will have to carry the tray,' Mary said with a smile.

'I can see that,' Megan said. 'Why did you put everything on the tray when you knew you wouldn't be able to carry it?'

'I thought you could do it,' Mary said briefly. 'So, what do you normally do when you make a cup of tea, stand here in the kitchen and drink it?'

'No, I can manage to carry one cup, if I'm careful. Anything more than that and I have a trolley on wheels that I put everything on, and then use one crutch and with my other hand push the trolley to where I want it,' Mary told her.

'I imagine there is every chance doing that that you will fall over and break your other leg,' Megan said critically.

'Well I haven't done so yet,' Mary contended. 'Anyway come on and sit down and I'll pour the tea before it gets cold and you can tell me what it is you have come to tell me.' When they were in the sitting room Mary sat in her armchair and Megan sat on the adjacent settee. 'I know you take milk but do you take sugar?' Mary questioned as she began to pour milk into the cups.

'I don't take sugar,' Megan told her. 'Stop a moment and take a closer look at those cups,' Megan said, her voice laced with disapproval.

'Why? What's wrong with them?'

'Can't you see that they are not clean!'

'Clean, of course they're clean. They were washed up this morning after breakfast.'

'Really!'

'Bill Thompson comes in every morning and clears away my breakfast dishes. We have a cup of coffee and then he washes the whole lot up.'

'Well he doesn't do a very good job. I would have thought you could see that for yourself,' Megan said sharply. 'They're dirty! There's stains inside them.'

Mary picked up one of the cups and peered closely. It was quite true there was a slight brown mark inside but it was so small that only someone with eagle-sharp eyes would have noticed it.

'I'll fetch another cup, a clean one this time,' Mary said.

She struggled to her feet and hobbled away on her crutches. She went to the cupboard and took out a cup that she knew had not been used for weeks and, dangling it from one finger, hobbled her way back into the sitting room

'This one is perfectly clean because it hasn't been used since I've been laid up,' she said holding it out so that Megan could inspect the interior.

'Thank you that does look better,' Megan said.

They sat for a few minutes in silence after Mary poured the tea and waited for it to cool down enough to drink. The tension in the room was palpable. Megan sat looking around critically and Mary felt so uncomfortable that she wished Megan would speak out or leave.

'So what is it you have to say to me?' Mary asked bluntly, unable to tolerate the silence any longer.

Megan put her cup and saucer back on the tray.

'I would have thought it was obvious you are not looking after yourself as you should be.' She held up a hand as Mary went to speak. 'Those cups for example; they're not clean and I wonder how many other things there are in this house that are not clean.'

Mary felt the colour rising in her cheeks, but she was so incensed that she couldn't find the right words to refute Megan's accusation.

'Looking round this room I can see dust on most of the surfaces. I was shocked when I heard that you had refused to have a carer come in to help you.'

'I don't need a carer,' Mary said. 'I manage quite well on

my own and, as I've told you, Bill does my shopping and he clears away my breakfast things, and if there's anything else I need doing I have only to ask him.'

'Yes, ask and look at the way it's done! The next thing you will have wrong with you is food poisoning.'

'What, from the stain on a cup?' said Mary derisively.

Megan shook her head. 'It won't do; you know it won't do. You should either go into a nursing home until you are fully mobile or else have some help around the house. Since you refused to have the help that was offered to you by the hospital, then you will have to pay for someone to come in and clean and make sure your place is hygienic.'

'Fiddlesticks!' Mary said dismissively.

Her temper was mounting and it was taking her all her strength not to retaliate in full voice. She didn't want to fall out with Megan but neither was she going to sit there and let Megan tell her how she was to run her life.

Sensing the atmosphere had become hostile Megan stood up. 'Well that is all I have to say. I have to go, I have an appointment.'

'You usually have,' Mary muttered.

'Yes, I'm a busy working woman and I am not too proud to have help in the home. For Richard, it is very good as there are lots of things he doesn't do and which I wouldn't expect him to do. By the way, have you got a dishwasher apart from Bill? He's obviously useless. If he has AMD then he probably can't see what he's doing.'

Mary didn't trust herself to answer. Nevertheless, Megan's criticism upset her and she brooded over it for the rest of the day. In her dreams she found herself tackling an enormous sinful pile of dirty dishes, while Megan stood there watching her. She woke up so angry that she didn't enjoy her breakfast and found herself looking at every cup and dish she used with critical eyes.

The next day she was not at all surprised to see Richard. Nor was she surprised when she found him prowling round the sitting room, picking up ornaments and inspecting the surface underneath them. She came in from the kitchen to tell him that she'd made the coffee and ask if he would bring it in for her.

'Well, come on, have your say,' she invited. 'I suppose Megan has told you that I live in squalor. Perhaps I should have let you check your cup before I made the coffee so that you could see it was clean.'

'Mum, don't take it so much to heart. Megan meant it for the best.'

'Did she? It sounded more like a way of putting me down.'

'Look, we both know you have had a hard time of it recently and we are also aware that we haven't been very helpful.'

'Yes, that's true,' Mary agreed stiffly.

'Well,' Richard went on, 'Megan says that you haven't got a dishwasher so we thought we would get you one as a late Christmas present.'

'That's very kind of you but I don't want one.'

'Why not?'

'A dishwasher for one person, who only cooks about once a week,' she said scathingly. 'It would take me a week to fill it.'

'Would that matter?'

'Having dirty dishes around for all that time? No thank you. I prefer to wash up as I go, clear up after each meal in the proper way.'

'At the moment you would find it a real boon,' Richard persisted.

'Another couple of weeks and I'll be able to do away with these crutches. Once I'm using a stick then it will be no trouble at all to resume my normal routine,' Mary told him.

'In the meantime you are prepared to put up with Bill doing the washing up; even if he doesn't get things clean?'

'On the whole he does,' Mary defended. 'A tea stain on the inside of a cup isn't the end of the world.'

'Quite so, but if he leaves scraps of stale food on your dinner plate or dish, then that is another matter. You could end up with food poisoning,' Richard pointed out.

'You've been listening to Megan,' Mary said quietly. 'Forget about it, Richard. Thank you for your kind thought but I am too old to take on new-fangled appliances. I'll stick to the old-fashioned way of washing up in a bowl with hot water and detergent, if you don't mind.'

Richard shrugged. 'As you please, if you change your mind let me know.' He drained his cup and stood up.

'Are you going already?' Mary asked. 'I was hoping to hear

all about this holiday that you and Megan had at Christmas. She never said a word about it. Did you enjoy yourselves?'

'Yes, it was very good. It didn't feel like Christmas though because we were in hot sunshine.'

They fell silent again.

'Look I must go,' Richard said awkwardly as he checked his watch. 'I only came to see how you were and to make the suggestion about the dishwasher. I seem to have done both. When is your next hospital appointment?'

'Not for a while.'

The silence between them that followed was an uneasy one. Richard carried his cup through to the kitchen and came back for hers. She heard the tap running and her mouth tightened. She stayed in the sitting room and when he came back in to say his final goodbye he said with a dry smile, 'There won't be any tea stains on those!'

'I should hope not, seeing as we had coffee,' Mary said quietly.

Richard made no reply. He kissed her cheek and was gone.

Mary felt vaguely irritated as she heard the front door close behind him. It wasn't like Richard to try and run her life for her. She suspected Megan was behind the offer and she was afraid she had made it hard for Richard by refusing. Even so, she wasn't going to change her mind. If she wanted a dishwasher in the first place, then she would have bought one a long time ago. In the second, she didn't want to be under any obligation to them.

All she wanted was to be left to get on with her life in her own way without any interference whatsoever.

EIGHTEEN

Richard and Megan's visits made Mary more determined than ever to walk without the aid of crutches. Her progress satisfied her and a week before her hospital appointment she could think of nothing else.

'Thank goodness it's not until ten o'clock,' she commented

to Bill as they sat enjoying a coffee together, before he went off to do her shopping.

'I'll order a taxi for half past nine, that should leave plenty of time. All the office workers and shop workers will be at work, the schoolchildren safely in school and all the mums back at home, so there should be no holdups.'

'You don't need a taxi, I'll take you,' Bill offered. 'I'll be here at nine thirty and, as you say, it will be a straightforward run.'

'No, Bill, I'll get a taxi,' Mary repeated.

'Why? I've always driven you in the past?'

'Yes, I know but you do so much for me you have no time left for your own interests.'

'Taking you to hospital is one of my interests,' Bill told her with a wide smile.

With a little sigh Mary gave in gracefully. What was the point of arguing, she thought. She didn't want to upset Bill, he was so good to her and she knew that he was as sensitive about criticism as she was. It was because she was still feeling raw from Megan's comments that she didn't want to remind Bill that he now had AMD in both eyes and probably shouldn't be driving at all. He was a very careful driver, she told herself, the road would be very quiet at that time of the day so what was she getting so worked up about? Determinedly, she put it out of her mind. It was far more important that she concentrated on her walking, she told herself.

She really did feel that she was quite competent to do away with the crutches. She had tried walking around the house using only a stick and it had been very successful. She felt more confident with a stick than she did with crutches. Her leg felt stronger and she was able to put her full weight on it without feeling any twinges or discomfort.

The night before her appointment she set her alarm for seven, so as to give herself plenty of time to be up and dressed, have her breakfast and be waiting on the doorstep for Bill. Everything worked like clockwork. With five minutes to spare she was ready, so she checked that she had the details of her appoint-ment in her handbag, then locked the front door and stood in the shelter of the porch anticipating Bill's arrival.

Time ticked by but there was no sound of his car. She checked the time on her watch; he was five minutes late. She felt worried. That was unlike Bill. If anything he tended to be five minutes early. She waited for another five minutes then she began to feel really concerned. At this rate, she was going to be late and she wasn't sure what would happen if she was. They would probably put her to the back of the queue or, of course, they might even cancel her visit.

Frustrated, she checked her watch again. It was now quarter to ten. They'd never make it, she thought anxiously. She went back inside the house and phoned the hospital to try and let them know she would be late.

'I'm afraid my car hasn't turned up,' she told the receptionist. 'I'm afraid I'm going to be late for my appointment.' There was a further delay as she identified herself and waited for the receptionist to find the relevant papers.

'Thank you for letting us know,' the girl said, 'do you want to cancel?'

'Oh no!' Mary told her. 'It's most important that I see the surgeon today. Can you make it a little later?'

'How long will it take you to get here?' the girl asked.

'If I can get a taxi right away, I should be there before eleven,' Mary said hopefully.

'Very well, do that, but if you find that it will be later than that please phone in and let us know.'

Her heart in her mouth and her fingers trembling, Mary rang the taxi service she normally used. She had no idea what had happened to Bill and she was very worried, but she decided that at the moment her own appointment must take precedence. She would ring his number as soon as she got home again. It was unlike him to forget an arrangement, although, like her, he was getting older and things did slip from their memory from time to time. Surely not something as important as a hospital appointment though?

When the taxi arrived, she scrambled into the passenger seat as fast as she could and asked the driver to put her crutches into the back for her. Unsmiling, he did so. Then, without a word, started up and drove at excess speed to the main road.

'King Edward's Hospital?' he asked.

'That's right,' Mary confirmed.

After that they sat in complete silence. Mary was worried in case Bill had had an accident, while on his way to collect her, and that it had not been possible for him to let her know what had happened. She decided that the best thing to do was to concentrate on what lay ahead, get the examination over and done with first. Then, when that was over and before she phoned for a taxi to take her home, she would phone Bill and see if he was all right.

For the moment, it was important that she concentrated on what lay ahead. She must convince the surgeon that she was able to walk without the aid of crutches. The receptionist commented that she was very late and she wasn't at all sure that she could still see Dr Markham the surgeon.

'I phoned in and explained to one of your colleagues that my taxi hadn't arrived and so I would be late,' Mary told her.

The receptionist, a very young fresh looking girl, checked again on her computer and then nodded briefly.

'You're quite right,' she said apologetically. I'm afraid there might be a long wait though. Sit over there and we will call you.'

The wait seemed to last forever and Mary felt more and more frustrated. She wondered if there was time for her to phone Bill and find out if he was all right, but was afraid to do so in case she was called in to see Dr Markham. She was about to go back to the reception desk and ask if they knew how much longer she would have to wait, when her name was called. Slipping her handbag onto one arm, she grabbed the crutches in her free hand and hurried into his consulting room.

'I see, so when you're in a hurry you don't use the crutches,' the surgeon commented as she entered.

'I don't really think I need them any longer,' she said. 'My leg feels much stronger and I am sure I could manage quite well with a walking stick.'

'I'm sure you could,' he said with a dry smile. 'You rather made that point when you came in. Now, if you will just lie on the couch and let me examine your leg, please.'

Mary complied as quickly as she could.

He began to examine her leg and, although his face gave

nothing away, she could tell from his manner that he was perfectly satisfied with the results.

'Yes,' he said when she was sitting in the chair facing his desk once again. 'I think you're right, Mrs Wilson. I think you can now manage with a walking stick. I would like to see you again in three months' time just to make sure that you're progressing well.'

'Thank you, Dr Markham.'

'Take things very easy, Mrs Wilson. 'Don't try to hurry and be extremely careful when you're going up and down stairs or steps.'

'I will,' Mary said fervently. 'Not having to use the crutches is wonderful. What should I do with them?'

He looked at her speculatively. 'You can take them home with you as an insurance in case you find you do need them,' he said with a smile, 'or you can leave them in reception and they will return them to the appropriate department. Do you have a walking stick with you?'

Mary shook her head. 'I couldn't carry a stick and use my crutches,' she said with a smile.

'No,' he said. 'Even you would find that difficult. If you ask at reception they will arrange for you to have a strong walking stick before you leave the hospital and they'll make sure it is the right height for you. Understood?'

'Yes, and thank you very much,' Mary said, 'and I will come back in three months as you suggest.'

He turned back to his desk. 'Very good, goodbye.'

'Thank you for all you've done,' Mary said as she manoeuvred her way through the door.

Once outside she took a deep breath. She felt she would like to toss the crutches into the air, but decided that might not be advisable in a busy hospital corridor. Instead, she did as she had been directed, took the crutches along to reception and told them that she wanted to exchange them for a walking stick.

Again there was a considerable wait while they made sure that she was allowed to do this and then found a walking stick, which they measured to be the right height for her.

Feeling slightly nervous, Mary made her way to the hospital's restaurant. She needed a coffee and she was hungry. A sandwich or some biscuits with her coffee would set her up.

Above all, she needed time to sit and think about what she ought to do about Bill.

In the end, she decided that there wasn't really much point in phoning him until she got home. If he had remembered that she had an appointment then he would have gone round to her house and found she was already gone, and work out that she had taken a taxi. If he'd done that then surely he would have come along to the hospital to make excuses and to be there to take her home, she told herself.

No, it seemed far more likely that he hadn't felt well, not even well enough to telephone her and let her know. Or, much more probable, that he had had an accident of some kind and that worried her most of all. She finished her sandwich and coffee and phoned for a taxi. Now she must find out what had happened to Bill and she desperately hoped that he was OK.

NINETEEN

When she arrived home, before she even took her coat off, Mary phoned Bill Thompson's number. She let it ring for a dozen times then reluctantly returned the receiver to its place. It was obvious that he wasn't there. So where was he? She looked at the clock on the mantelpiece. Ten minutes past eleven. She picked up the phone again, hesitated and then put it down.

She felt exhausted. She needed a cup of tea. While the kettle was boiling, she phoned the police to see if they could help.

'Are you reporting him missing?' the desk sergeant asked.

'Well no, not really, or I don't think so.' Briefly she explained what had happened, that he had failed to pick her up that morning.

'He probably forgot or else overslept,' the man said.

'Yes, you could be right,' Mary agreed and rang off. She made some tea and tried to think of what the best thing to do next was. Should she call a taxi and tour all the hospitals in the area? No, that was probably pointless. If he had not felt well then he would have gone to the doctors and he would have been home again by now, she told herself. If he had been in an accident then the police would have known about it. Unless it had been a very minor accident and then he might have gone to A&E to have a cut stitched or something like that. She mused over this as she drank her tea. Then she phoned Wexham Hospital, but they had nothing on their records so they were unable to help.

She finished her tea and rinsed her cup out. Her mind was made up. She'd go round to his house. Perhaps he had had a fall and was unable to open the door. She had a key so she'd let herself in and look for herself. But, as she was about to shut her own front door, she hesitated. She no longer had her crutches and, as this was the first time she had been outdoors with only a stick, she wondered whether she would be able to walk that far.

'Better be on the safe side I suppose,' she muttered as she went back inside and phoned for a taxi.

When she reached Bill's house in Coburn Road she asked the driver to wait. She rang the doorbell and when there was no answer she took Bill's key from her pocket and let herself in. It was deadly quiet. She called out his name but there was no answer. She looked in the kitchen, everything was in order, she couldn't tell whether he had eaten breakfast or not. Apprehensively she slowly went up the stairs. His bed was neatly made, and again she had no way of telling if he had slept in it the night before or not.

He wasn't there! Convinced she made her way back down the stairs, carefully locked the front door and slowly made her way back to the taxi. She had no idea what to do next, except go home and wait.

As the taxi approached Silver Street she changed her mind. 'Could you take me to the police station first?' she instructed.

When they arrived there she asked him to wait.

The desk sergeant remembered her call earlier in the day and his face brightened. 'I've been trying to phone you,' he told her.

'You know what's happened to Mr Thompson?'

'Yes, we have him here on a charge of dangerous driving.'

'Oh heavens!' Mary said in alarm. 'What happened? Is he all right?'

'He's shaken up, but fortunately he isn't hurt and no one else is either. His car is badly smashed up and so are three others.'

'What!' Mary looked at him her eyes wide with shock. 'What happened?'

'He came round a corner, smashed into a parked car and shunted it into two others. Nasty little pile up. Fortunately, no one was hurt.'

'So why are you keeping him here?' Mary asked.

'Because we needed a statement from him,' the sergeant said. 'We also had to check him out for drink and drugs. Seems he was clear of those but he has admitted that he has AMD and we were waiting for him to have an eye test.'

'Has that happened?'

'Yes, and he shouldn't be driving. He has very poor sight in both eyes. We were about to send him home though, waiting for a car to be free to take him.'

'I can take him home with me,' Mary said. 'I have a taxi outside.'

The sergeant scratched his chin. 'Trifle irregular but if you give me your name and address I'll see if that's acceptable.'

Ten minutes later, Bill was in the taxi with Mary and they were being taken back to Silver Street.

'Wait until we get home before you tell me the whole story,' she told him.

He nodded then shook his head despairingly.

Mary reached out and touched his arm reassuringly. 'Try not to worry,' she said quietly.

The moment they were indoors Mary switched the kettle on.

'You go and sit down and I'll bring the tea through and then we can talk,' she suggested.

He nodded but followed her into the kitchen.

'How did you get on? You were late for your appointment, did they see you?'

'Yes, everything went all right,' Mary told him. 'I was able to leave the crutches there and from now on I can use a stick. Great news isn't it!'

He nodded. 'Yes, that's what you were hoping for, wasn't it?'

'I certainly was. Now, you go and sit down, I'll only be a minute.'

Mary put the tea and a plate of biscuits onto her trolley and pushed it through to the sitting room. She poured out the tea, placed his cup on a small table by the side of his chair and put the biscuits there as well.

'Help yourself,' she murmured, 'and when you are ready tell me what happened, the policeman said that your car was badly damaged?'

'Badly damaged!' Bill gave a dry laugh. 'It looks as though it will be a write-off. Anyway,' he added bitterly, 'I don't suppose it matters because by the sound of things I am not going to be able to drive anymore now that I have AMD in both eyes.'

It was on the tip of Mary's tongue to say: 'No, and if you had listened you would know that you should have given up driving some time ago. Then you could have sold your car as a going concern instead of having to send it to the scrapyard,' but the bitterness in Bill's voice stopped her from doing so. He looked so hangdog and miserable that her heart went out to him. She knew how he must be feeling.

There would be worse to follow, she thought sadly. It was so convenient to be able to jump into your own car and go off shopping or on a visit on the spur of the moment. Taxis were wonderful, but you had to phone for one, often wait anything up to half an hour for it to come and then you couldn't stop as the whim took you to look at something on route. And of course, you had to make arrangements for it to come and collect you and take you home again.

She had once worked out the actual cost of calling a taxi whenever you wanted to go anywhere and compared it with the cost of running a car. There wasn't a lot of difference over a year, not when you took in the necessity of repairs, MOT's, new tyres and so on.

Having your own car meant independence though and that was what became more and more important as you grew older.

That was what Bill was going to miss.

She would miss Bill's car too, she thought with a sigh. It had been wonderful to be able to go from front door to the shops and then back again, purchasing a weekly supply with such ease. From now on, it would mean visiting the shop two or three times a week and making sure that she didn't buy too much or it would be difficult to carry.

Of course, she could order a grocery shop by phone. Megan had suggested she should do this a long time ago and had looked at her with raised eyebrows, when Mary had said that you then had to accept whatever they decided to send you. When it came to fruit, vegetables and meat she liked to see what she was getting.

She'd have to get one of these shopping bags on wheels, she decided, or else a trolley. That way she could carry a lot more, but still nowhere near as much as she had done previously when Bill took her.

She waited patiently until Bill had finished his tea and began to look a little less grey and slightly calmer.

'Another one?'

He nodded and held out his cup.

'So what happened?' she asked as she took his cup from him and refilled it.

Bill shook his head from side to side. 'I took the corner too fast, I suppose. There was a car parked just on the bend and I went into it. That car went forward and shunted into the next one parked there and that one into a third.'

'Were the others badly damaged?' Mary asked.

'The first one I went into was pretty badly crushed and the other two not quite so bad.'

'Big bill for the insurance people,' Mary said dryly.

'That's what you insure your car for; in case of accidental damage,' Bill said shortly.

'You think your insurance company will cover the damage on your car?'

'No, as I said, it's a write-off,' Bill told her gloomily. 'Not that it matters all that much because as I've already said, I won't be able to drive in the future. The police will make sure of that.'

'You're lucky that they didn't charge you with dangerous driving.'

'I think they probably will. I've got to appear in court and then I'll probably be fined,' he said gloomily.

'Well that's better than them giving you a prison sentence,' Mary said consolingly.

Bill nodded and ran a hand over his chin. 'I suppose too that I'm lucky there was no one in any of the cars so there was no one injured.'

'Yes, you're very fortunate,' she agreed. 'You're also lucky that no one was crossing the road at the time.'

'Or on the pavement because the first car I crashed into ended up right across the pavement.'

Mary shook her head in despair. Bill was lucky that he hadn't been injured in any way although she suspected that he was badly shaken.

Bill finished his tea and stood up. 'I'd better be getting home,' he said resignedly.

'Wouldn't you sooner stay and have a meal here before you go home?'

'No,' Bill shook his head. 'Thanks all the same but I'm not very good company at the moment. The sooner I get going and work out what I am going to do from now on, the better.'

'Not having a car isn't the end of the world, you know,' Mary said sharply. 'You can still walk, just be thankful for that.'

He nodded. 'It's the end of our weekly trips to Maidenhead,' Bill said huffily. 'I won't be able to take you shopping each week either, you know.'

'I know, but we can always take a taxi when we want to do those things.'

'If you say so,' Bill muttered as he headed for the door. 'I'll phone you in a day or two. I'll be adjusted to being without my car by then.'

Mary smiled. She doubted it. If she knew anything about it he would take months to get used to not having a car sitting outside, ready to go anywhere he wanted to, whenever he decided to do so.

TWENTY

B ill Thompson felt utterly disgruntled and depressed. In fact, he had never been so fed up in his life. After his wife had died he had been irritated by all the things he had to do which he'd never even thought about before, but he had turned to and dealt with them. It was simply a matter of applying common sense and you could overcome most obstacles he thought, but now with poor eyesight and no car, life had reached a real low. It wasn't the money for taxis that he grudged having to pay out, it was the realisation that not having a car curbed his freedom.

He didn't drive very far these days but he loved his car. It was an old friend and it was always outside the door waiting to take him wherever he wanted to go, ready at any hour of the day or night he might want to use it. Taking Mary to the cinema in Maidenhead once a week and taking her shopping had become highlights of his week, but now all that would be finished. He knew she had said they could use a taxi but it wasn't the same somehow. He felt uncomfortable about it. He had been brought up to only use a taxi in an emergency, not for shopping trips or gadding about.

Every time he looked out of his sitting room window there was a great empty space where his car had always stood. Every time he looked it seemed to reproach him for being such a silly old fool. He'd been proud of the fact that he'd never had a mark on his license the whole time he had been driving.

He went through into his kitchen and switched on the kettle and made himself a cup of tea. As he sat drinking it he brooded about what else the police might do. They'd already banned him from ever driving again. They wouldn't simply leave it there though. He was bound to end up in court and then the magistrate would probably give him a hefty fine.

Even that would be better than a term in prison though, no

matter how short that might be. He didn't think that he would be able to endure the guilt he would feel if that happened.

'Pull yourself together, it's not the end of the world whatever the outcome is,' he told himself out loud as he rinsed out his cup.

He was still alive, he hadn't been hurt, except for it being a shock to the system and no one else had been involved. Cars were only lumps of metal and, although he was very sorry for the owners whose cars had been damaged, at least they hadn't been in them.

Over the next few days, as he came to terms with the situation, he realised that although he hadn't been hurt physically his confidence was extremely low and his ability to do things was more limited. A couple of times he was aware that when he reached out for something his hand trembled and whenever he decided to do anything, he had second thoughts before he did it. Or even abandoned what he had planned to do and decide to leave it for another day.

The other thing that troubled him was that he didn't want to go out or meet people in case they knew what a silly old fool he had been. He resolved not to let Mary know how he was feeling. It was his problem not hers. He was the one who must overcome it and doing it on his own would be better for him.

Three days later, however, when she called round to see how he was and find out if he had heard from the police or not, she found him so shaky and uncertain about what he was doing that she immediately took him to task. Within minutes he was telling her about all the uncertainty he was feeling.

'Of course you feel like that, your confidence has been dented,' she told him. 'Give it a week or two and you'll be back to normal.'

Bill stared at her, his eyes full of misery, and then shook his head.

'Do you remember how I was afraid to go outside the front door on those wretched crutches? Yet within a week I was managing to do so, even though I felt foolish and thought everybody was staring at me. I didn't really enjoy walking with them but after a couple of weeks my confidence was back and it no longer worried me. You'll be the same.'

'There's a bit of a difference between walking after a broken leg and what has happened to me,' Bill muttered. 'You didn't have a feeling of guilt hanging over you all the time, or sit there listening for a rap on the door and a policeman on the doorstep to take you into custody for careless driving.'

'You idiot,' Mary laughed. 'If they were going to do that they would have done so there and then! No, they thought you were careless but they know you can't repeat your crime because you have no car and anyway you have been banned from driving.'

Bill stared at her in silence for a long minute. Then, as if reading from the expression on her face that she meant what she was saying, he sighed and nodded his head.

'Perhaps you are right,' he admitted. 'I'll try and pull myself together.'

Although he had every intention of doing so, when he saw the report of his accident in the local newspaper that weekend he was mortified.

'Surely you expected that to happen,' Mary pointed out when he rang her and sounded very upset.

'They've even printed my name, address and how old I am,' Bill told her in high dudgeon. 'How on earth did they find all that out?'

'That's what reporters are paid to do,' Mary pointed out. 'Don't worry about it, by next week that newspaper will be in the recycling box and people won't remember half of the things they read in it, because they have more up to date news items and it will all be forgotten.'

Even as she said it, Mary waited for a call from either Richard or Megan because she was quite sure they would recognise Bill's name and address. When the call did come it was from Megan, who came straight to the point.

'I told you right from the start not to get involved with that old man,' she ranted. 'Do you realise that you could have been in his car and you could have been seriously hurt or even killed!'

'Yes, but I wasn't,' Mary said as calmly as she could.

'That's not the point, you've caused us a great deal of worry,' Megan stated.

'I can imagine Richard might have been a little concerned,'

Mary agreed quietly, 'I hardly think you would be too upset though, Megan.'

'Of course I would be upset if you were injured, you might end up unable to look after yourself . . .'

'And then I would have had to go into a nursing home,' Mary finished for her.

'Quite! What a waste of money that would have been!'

'Funerals are quite expensive too these days,' Mary commented.

'You are acting in a very strange way,' Megan told her. 'I think it might be best if Richard came round and discussed all this with you.'

Before Mary could answer Megan hung up.

Richard was obviously dispatched immediately, within the hour he was on her doorstep.

'Come on in, the kettle is boiling. Tea or coffee?'

'I haven't come on a social visit,' Richard told her. 'I needed to find out if you were all right. Megan said you were talking nonsense and she was worried about you.'

'I was talking nonsense?' Mary questioned with a desultory laugh. 'I think it was Megan who was doing that. Why has she such a dislike of Bill Thompson? She's only met him once and she was barely civil to him then.'

'Yes, well don't worry about that. I'm more concerned about how you are feeling. I'm sure you are very upset.'

'I'm sorry for Bill that it has happened. He's very upset and feeling very guilty about the whole matter. The only good thing is that there was no one in any of the other cars so no one was injured.'

'He wasn't hurt?'

'His self-confidence is dented,' Mary said with a wry smile.

'He hasn't heard any more from the police?'

'No, but I expect he will. If he is lucky, it will only be a matter of a heavy fine.'

'Yes,' Richard agreed solemnly, 'at his age I hardly think they will send him to prison seeing that no one was involved. He shouldn't have been driving, of course, not with AMD in both eyes.'

'We both know that, but if you remember your father was very reluctant to stop driving when he was diagnosed. Bill had only been told that his other eye was affected,' she added by way of explanation.

'That's really no excuse now, though,' Richard stated.

'Well, we all take chances. If someone hadn't parked so close on the corner it might never have happened,' Mary said tetchily.

'I was instructed to tell you that you are to stop seeing him,' Richard grinned.

'Knowing you, I hardly think you will take any notice.'

'No, I most certainly won't. I don't believe in abandoning my friends when they are in trouble. Look at the way he has helped me, do you think I'm going to desert him now?'

'In his hour of need?' Richard teased.

'He certainly needs a friend to boost his ego and help him to regain his independence,' Mary said in a serious voice. 'It's amazing how much he has taken this accident to heart.'

'Well, remember it has to be taxis from now on,' Richard stated.

'Of course. How else would we get to Maidenhead to the cinema or go shopping? His car is a complete write-off.'

Richard took her into his arms and hugged her. 'Bill Thompson is a lucky fellow to have such a stalwart friend,' he told her as he planted a kiss on her brow. 'You always come up trumps don't you, Mum.'

'I'm sorry if my decision is going to cause hard feelings with Megan but perhaps I should remind her that Bill has done far more for me than she has ever done.'

'I'm sure he has,' Richard agreed, 'but it would be easier for me if you don't say that to her.'

'All right, but don't you try to tell me what I should or shouldn't do,' Mary told him reprovingly.

'I wouldn't dare,' Richard said, his face creasing into a broad smile.

'Good! Now why didn't you bring little George round with you, does this mean I won't be seeing him this week?'

'Megan didn't think I should bring him because she didn't want him to be upset if we had a disagreement.'

Mary looked at Richard with raised eyebrows. 'Disagreement? Whatever is that? As far as I'm concerned, you are still a small boy and although I might listen to what you have to say I am not likely to take any notice. Well, not unless I think it will be to my advantage to do so,' she added.

There was a twinkle in her eye as she spoke and Richard merely raised his eyebrows and shrugged his shoulders. 'I know, I know . . . So shall we leave it there?'

'It depends. I still want a visit from George.'

'I'll bring him round tomorrow. Will that do?'

'Will Megan approve of you doing that?' Mary asked.

'Megan won't even know because she's off to New York for four days in the morning,' Richard said dryly. 'I'll come round straight after school.'

'Good! I'll be expecting you so don't let me down.'

TWENTY-ONE

Mary Wilson was extremely concerned about Bill Thompson. He was hollow-eyed and haggard and she wished that there were someone who could advise her. He had aged ten years overnight, not only in looks but also in his attitude to life. Since he'd lost his car and been told he would never be allowed to drive again, he had become increasingly withdrawn and lethargic.

Not only that, but he had let himself go as if he no longer cared how he looked. His hollow cheeks enhanced the lines around his eyes. He would go for days without having a shave and sometimes he looked so unkempt and dishevelled that Mary wondered if he bothered to have a wash. He certainly wore the same shirt day in day out. The state of his kitchen and the rest of the house reflected his loss of interest. Each time she called to see him, Mary tidied around but she was in no fit state to give it the thorough clean that it needed.

When she suggested that perhaps he ought to get someone in for an hour or so once a week to do the cleaning he merely scowled and said he didn't want strangers messing around the place. As far as he was concerned everything was as he wanted it to be. He had lost interest in most things, even going to the cinema in Maidenhead with her and he refused point blank to go shopping.

Hoping it was all talk and that when the time came he would comply, Mary made no comment but on her next shopping trip asked the taxi driver to stop at Coburn Road. When the taxi drew up outside Bill's house, the curtains were still drawn although it was mid-morning. Repeated knocking on the door and ringing the bell brought no response at all. They failed to rouse him, so in the end she had to go on her own.

When she took him to task about it Bill merely shrugged. 'I don't want to go out,' he muttered. 'Those days are over, the sooner I get to the end the better. I don't want to see people either. I've no time for ceaseless chatter about nothing. I just want to be left alone so that I can sit in my armchair and be quiet.'

'You mean doze, don't you,' Mary said with a laugh.

'No, I might be sitting there with my eyes closed, resting them, but it doesn't mean that I'm asleep. What is there to look at anyway? Everywhere is grey and drab and most of the time there's a fog or else it's raining. I've given up living by the clock. Night and day are much the same. Sometimes I sleep, sometimes I make a pot of tea or muddle around the place. I don't bother looking at the clock to see what time it is. When I'm tired I sleep.

'I've tried going to bed at eleven in the evening and I lie there awake for hours. In the end, I get up and potter around then I have a cup of tea and after that I sleep like a log.'

'Look at the state of your home,' Mary persisted. 'You say you potter around doing things but I don't know what they are, except make the place untidy. There was a time when you would have been ashamed to see it in the state it's in now. Everywhere and everything is grey with dust and you drop things where you leave them and your laundry basket it overflowing.'

'So what about it?' Bill muttered. 'You're the only one who comes in and sees it and if you go on nagging I won't open the door to you.'

'So what will you do for bread, milk and ready meals if I don't go and get them for you?'

'Manage without. I've no interest in food and if I want to have a drink then there's water in the tap.'

'You won't last long living on water and nothing else,' Mary retorted.

'Good. Then in that case I'll just drift off and that's the best thing that can happen to me. No one will miss me. Except you and that won't be much of a loss just one less thing for you to worry about.'

'Stop talking such utter rot,' Mary told him crossly. 'I thought you were a soldier, did you give up whenever things went wrong when you were in the army?'

'That was different. I was young and fit then, not an old has-been who can't even see to drive a car. Some days I can't even see where I've left my keys. I try to remember to keep them in my pocket, but even when I do that I can't always find them because of all the other things I have to keep there just so I know where they are.'

He turned out his pockets as he spoke and Mary saw what he meant. He was not only carrying his keys around but a screwdriver, tin-opener, potato peeler and an assortment of string and nails.

'You have AMD. You're not completely blind. You still have peripheral vision. You can see enough to get around, keep your house in order and do your garden when the weather improves. So stop feeling so sorry for yourself.'

'I still don't want to come shopping,' he muttered.

'I accept that for the moment. Let me know when you change your mind,' Mary told him quietly.

Although she invariably bought a selection of oven ready meals and fresh fruit for him, she often wondered if he bothered to eat them. She was so worried about his welfare that she even thought about contacting his son in Cardiff and seeing if he (or his wife) could pay his father a visit, and try to persuade him to pull himself together. She hesitated about doing this because it meant asking Bill for the telephone number. She knew he would probably guess why she was asking for it, and resent her doing it.

It seemed that, as far as Bill was concerned, his life was over. All he wanted to do was sit in his armchair and doze, or stay in bed until a call of nature got him up. She did her best to revive his interest in daily life, but it proved to be so ineffectual that in the end she gave up.

She had her own problems to contend with and felt that they must take precedence. Although her femur had healed and she was no longer in any real discomfort, she did find that her own confidence, when it came to going out on her own had diminished. She also found that she couldn't walk as far she had been used to doing and that she walked a great deal slower.

It irritated her when people thought that, by taking her arm, it would help her to walk faster. In actual fact, she found it did the reverse. It took away what confidence she had and in her efforts to comply and put one foot in front of the other more quickly, she invariably found herself stumbling. When she did this and they made conciliatory sounds, it irritated her even more and it took her all her will power to smile, or thank them and assure them she was all right.

She realised that it was all part of growing old and she resented her lack of energy but, unlike Bill, she was determined not to give in to depression or lethargy. As the days slowly lengthened, as the frosts and dull cloudy days disappeared and the daffodils waved golden heads to the sun, she felt her energy returning and her spirits stirring. She hoped that it would have the same effect on Bill and that once he saw that spring had arrived – and that there was new life in the garden – he would want to be out there digging in the soil, weeding and planting.

At first he remained unmoved. But one day early in April, she visited him and complained that one of the bushes in her garden needed trimming back and that if it was left any longer, it would be too late to do it without harming the plant. He volunteered to come and do it for her. She accepted this offer and the next morning, freshly shaved and looking much trimmer than she had seen him for a long time, he was at her back door with secateurs in his hand and asking which bush it was. When she next visited him a couple of days later, she found him tidying up the borders in his own garden. She was pleased to see that he looked brighter than he had for a long time.

'Can you get me some carnation cuttings next time you go into Maidenhead?' he asked.

Mary shook her head. 'No, if you want them then you'd better come with me. I'll be going there on Thursday. I'll call here about ten o'clock so be ready.'

Bill scowled but didn't answer.

When Mary's taxi drew up in Coburn Road on the Thursday morning, as she had promised, Bill was already waiting at the gate. He'd even put his suit on and looked his old spruce self. They found the cuttings Bill wanted, then they went shopping and when that was done, they went for a coffee before calling for the taxi to bring them home.

'Feeling a bit better?' Mary asked casually.

Bill nodded. 'Yes, I've shaken off the black devil. It had me in a real grip. I've never felt so down in my life. I wanted to curl up and die, there seemed to be nothing left to live for and I didn't care about anything. I don't know why you didn't just walk away and leave me to it.'

'I know what it feels like, that's why. Once you lose your independence it takes you a while to regain it.'

'Yes, I agree with that. I'm not quite there yet but I will be in a week two,' Bill said with a self-conscious grin. He was as good as his word. Two weeks later, he suggested that it was about time they went to the cinema in Maidenhead.

'I'll check and see what's on,' Mary promised.

'It doesn't matter what's showing, let's get back into the old routine again,' Bill said. 'I'm sure you've missed our trips and now that I'm back on form I'm missing them as well.'

Mary was delighted by the news. There was spring in the air, they were both reasonably well and fit and summer was ahead. She thought of all the outings they could have together. Neither of them could walk far but that didn't matter. They could take a taxi to Cliveden and stroll about the gardens, have tea in the Orangery and watch people enjoying themselves. They could take a taxi to Boulter's Lock, stroll by the river and then have afternoon tea there. They could go to Windsor and enjoy the shops, and take tea in one of the cafés. They might only be onlookers but it would a change of scenery and, of course, they could go to the pictures or shopping whenever they needed to do so.

No, Mary told herself, life was going to be good. They may be getting older but there was still a lot of things they could enjoy doing. They might even be able to persuade Lucia to come with them and bring George when they went to Cliveden. He would be in his element in the wonderful play area they had there, with swings, slides, climbing frames and the rest. They could buy a cup of tea in the little café near the playground and keep an eye on him so that he came to no harm. He would like the maze and, although she wasn't sure that either she or Bill would want to wander around, Lucia could take him.

All these outings would have to be fitted in between visits to the eye hospital for Bill's treatment and one or two more check-ups that she would have to make about her leg.

But, like all well-laid plans, things didn't work out as smoothly as she'd hoped.

This time she was the one with problems. Her ability to walk became less and less. It wasn't so much pain as sheer inability. She became exhausted so quickly. She had one or two scary moments when she placed her stick on something slippery and it let her down; she didn't react quickly enough so she stumbled and almost fell. The fear of having another fall and breaking a hip or her other leg scared her. That might mean ending up in a nursing home and she had a dread of that happening.

After a lot of thought and consideration she decided to buy a stroller; a three wheeled trolley with a shopping bag on it. It folded up quite well when the bag was empty so she would be able to get it into the taxi. It offered her stability and, at the same time, it was something to carry her shopping in when she was simply shopping locally for bread, milk and minor items.

'Must be like pushing a pram,' Bill commented. 'Would you like me to get you a little dog to sit in it?'

'No I would not!' Mary said sharply. 'I have enough trouble looking after myself without having a pet. What would I do with a dog! It would need taking for walks every day and when we were indoors it would probably get under my feet and I would fall over it.' She did find the trolley a great boon, however. She could walk faster, felt safer and had more confidence about walking.

'We could walk to the bus stop and take a bus into Maidenhead on some days, instead of using a taxi,' Bill said thoughtfully.

'We could. It would be all right going over there but not so good coming home if I'd done any shopping. How could I get it onto the bus with it full up? There are no conductors to help you these days and I don't see the driver wanting to do it.' Mary said.

'I could help you.'

Mary shook her head. 'I don't want you pulling your back and ending up unable to walk. A taxi is so much easier and it takes us right to the door, and all our shopping as well.'

'We could give it a try,' Bill persisted.

Mary shook her head. 'Let's leave things as they are. Everything is going fine; don't let's tempt fate by changing them.'

Mary's words were more prophetic than she knew. Less than a week later they had a new disaster to contend with; one which neither of them foresaw.

TWENTY-TWO

Now that spring had arrived and the primroses and violets appeared in the borders and glistening celandines along the edges of the road, Bill had quickly regained his normal optimistic outlook and Mary was relieved. There had seemed to be no way of lifting the depression that had had him in its grip. Now, once again he was alert, planning his garden, advising her about things she ought to do in hers and generally taking an interest in all that was going on around him.

In next to no time their routine was also back on track. Each week they paid a visit to the cinema in Maidenhead and spent one morning shopping, only this time they travelled by taxi. Bill still came round to Mary's house once a week for dinner and afterwards, weather permitting, they sat out in the garden chatting for an hour or so.

Megan still objected to Bill's presence but since she so rarely visited Mary, their paths didn't cross very often, and Mary really didn't care whether Megan approved of her friendship with him or not. Richard accepted him and George was particularly fond of him. Bill talked to him on a man-to-man basis. He listened

to George's prattle and tried to answer any question George
posed in a way the child could understand. He was so patient
when it came to explaining things to George that Mary often
found herself intrigued by his answers.

The spring and early part of the summer were so idyllic that
Mary thought it was almost too good to be true. With Bill's
help, her garden was looking like a picture, every bush was
neatly trimmed and the borders planted with flowering plants
that almost took care of themselves.

'They're like men; they don't want people fussing over them.
Give them a good drink every night and leave them alone,' Bill
advised.

It was the height of summer when trouble struck. Mary and Bill
had just finished dinner and were sitting out in the garden when
the phone rang.

'Now I wonder who that can be,' Mary murmured. She frowned
as she got up to answer it.

'I wonder if it's Lucia. I hope nothing is wrong with little
George . . .' Her voice trailed off as she hurried indoors. Bill
stayed where he was. He thought it probably was something to
do with George. He knew Megan was away in Paris and Richard
had gone gliding, so it was probably Lucia turning to Mary for
advice.

When Mary came back out ten minutes later he knew that
whatever was wrong it was something pretty serious. Mary's
face was devoid of colour, even her lips were white and they
were in a tight line as if she was trying to suppress her tears.

'What's wrong?' Bill said standing up and pushing her down
into his chair. 'Sit there, you look as if you've had a shock.'

'It's Richard,' she said and her lips trembled. 'He's in hospital,
he's had an accident.'

'In his glider?'

Mary nodded.

'What's happened?'

'They didn't say, except that he had already been taken to
hospital.'

'Didn't the paramedics say why he needed to be taken
to hospital?' Bill persisted.

Mary stared at him bewildered. 'That wasn't the hospital. It was the chief flying instructor from the gliding club.'

'How did it happen, did he say?'

Mary shook her head. 'Something about a crash on take-off but I was so upset that I didn't take it in properly.'

'Did you find out which hospital he is in?'

'Yes, the one at Stoke Mandeville.'

'Shall I phone them for you or would you rather we went there? They might let us see him.'

Mary looked at him blankly. 'I don't know. Would they let us see him . . . if he's really badly injured I mean?'

'Well, we don't know. Shall I phone them first?' Bill volunteered.

'Do you know the number?'

'No,' Bill frowned. 'It's bound to be in the telephone directory though.'

Mary hesitated. 'I think it might be better to go straight there. Could you phone for a taxi while I change my shoes and fetch my coat and handbag?'

'You sit where you are. You're shaking like a leaf and the next thing you'll be tumbling down the stairs. I'll phone for the taxi and then I'll fetch whatever it is you need. It will take the taxi a few minutes to get here so sit down and get your breath back. I'll get you a glass of water,' he added as he made for the back door.

Mary did as Bill suggested. Her mind felt numb. She couldn't even imagine what had happened but it must be something serious if he was in hospital. Just as they had done when Sam had been alive and gone gliding, a thousand and one possibilities went through her mind. In the past, she had imagined just such a phone call and being told that something serious had happened.

It never had, of course. Sam had never had a mishap the entire time he'd been gliding. He had landed out once or twice but he had always ended up safely in a farmer's field somewhere. Although there was often a long delay before someone could take a trailer out to pick him and his glider up and tow them back to Booker, it had never been anything to worry about. There had been accidents he wasn't involved in while he had been alive. She remembered that a glider had once crashed onto a main road and another time when . . . She stopped herself from thinking back. It didn't help. She must pull herself together and not anticipate what might have happened.

When Bill returned with her jacket and handbag, she was much more in control of herself. She was still trembling as he helped her into her jacket, but there was some colour back in her cheeks and she was no longer breathing rapidly as if she was short of breath.

The sound of a car horn made her jump and she grabbed hold of her handbag.

'That's the taxi. Wish me luck,' she said with a weak smile.

'Slow down, I'm coming with you,' Bill said.

Ignoring her protest that it wasn't necessary, he took her arm.

'I'm sure Richard's all right,' she affirmed as they reached the taxi. 'Taking him to hospital is probably simply a precaution and to make sure he hasn't got concussion.'

'Well, once you see him and he tells you exactly what happened, it will set your mind at rest,' Bill agreed.

'Do you think I ought to telephone Lucia and let her know what has happened?' Mary said as they reached the taxi.

'Yes, but not until after you've seen Richard. There's nothing she can do so why worry her?'

It would be about thirty miles to Stoke Mandeville Hospital and she struggled to pit all thoughts of what they were going to find at the end of their journey out of her mind. But before they climbed into the taxi, Mary's phone rang. For a moment she hesitated about answering it, but then hurried back into the house, thinking it might be the hospital again with more bad news about Richard.

TWENTY-THREE

It was a stunning July day, ideal for gliding. There was sunshine, a light warm breeze and a glorious blue sky, with just sufficient white clouds crossing it to provide the exact sort of lift Richard needed for a short evening flight. He had been watching it through the classroom window all day and hoping it would hold into the evening.

He had phoned Lucia during the lunch hour and explained he would be late home, to put George to bed at his usual time and tell him that he would come up and read him a story as soon as he got home. Then, the moment classes were finished for the day he was off, as eager as any of the children to be out of the claustrophobic classroom and free to do what he wanted to do.

He slung his light jacket into the back of the car and undid the top button of his shirt so that he could breathe more freely. He lowered the car windows and breathed deeply the balmy air as he drove up the M40 towards High Wycombe, and then on along minor roads to Booker airfield. When he arrived there he found it was a hive of activity. He was obviously not the only one eager to become airborne.

After parking his car, he strode over to the hanger where he kept his glider, exchanging greetings with other glider pilots, some who – like him – were taking advantage of the opportunity for an evening flight and others who had already spent several hours airborne and were now on their way home.

He manoeuvred his glider out from its place in the hanger, across the path that formed part of the perimeter track and onto the grassy field. Because it was summer the ground was firm and it was easy to push it single-handed to the launch point. He breathed deeply of the fresh clean air as he walked across the airfield. Already he was visualising the panoramic view of green oasis, swimming pools and wide-open spaces he could feast his eyes on once he was airborne.

He took his place in the short queue waiting to be taken up into the sky by the small tug plane. While he waited, he spent the next ten minutes doing the standard safety checks. Satisfied that everything was in order he climbed in, made himself comfortable and waited.

It was only a matter of minutes before the cable from the tug was being attached to the hook on the underside of his glider. He received the thumbs up; he was away, being taken up into the air at a surprising rate of knots. They were about sixty feet above the ground, just clearing the boundary fence when it happened. Richard had no idea why but the tug suddenly, and without any warning, released the cable and before he could collect his thoughts his glider was falling from the sky like a stone.

There was nothing he could do to avoid the crash that followed. He was too low to veer to the right or left. Before it had really dawned on him what was happening, the ground had rushed up and there was a terrific jarring that sent waves of pain right through his body.

Only much later would he learn that someone living near the airfield had launched a drone and that it had flown right into the windscreen of the tug – and that the tug had also crashed.

Immediately following the impact Richard was unaware of anything. As the pain became unbearable he drifted in and out of darkness. When he came to, he found a group of people encircling him. He tried to speak, to tell them he was in pain, but somehow they didn't seem to hear him, or if they did he wasn't sure that they understood what he was saying. Voices were calling his name and shouting across to each other. If he could hear them and what they were saying to each other then why didn't they hear what he was saying, he wondered. He couldn't fathom it out and once again he found himself in a dreamlike state, drifting away.

In a determined effort, he struggled to remain conscious of what was going on around him and ignore the waves of pain that swept through him whenever he breathed in.

From somewhere he could hear the sound of an ambulance approaching and it was become louder every second.

Suddenly Richard found uniformed men bending over him, telling him their name and that they were paramedics. He sighed with relief. They would know what to do. Expertly they ran their hands over his limbs and asked him questions. He tried to answer them but he was so dazed that his answers didn't make sense and weren't of much help. After consultation with each other, using words he didn't understand, they very gently lifted him on to a stretcher. The movement made him cry out in agony as pain shuddered through his back.

Once in the ambulance they administered gas and air and assured him that before they started moving they would give him an injection that would lessen the pain. Once more Richard found himself drifting into blackness. He tried to fight the feeling, to remain conscious of what was happening, but in the end he succumbed. By the time the ambulance left the airfield he was once more unconscious.

TWENTY-FOUR

Mary picked up the receiver just in time.

'Mrs Wilson?' The authoritative voice on the other end sent her heart pounding. 'Mrs Wilson? This is Stoke Mandeville Hospital.'

'Yes, yes, my son Richard has been brought in—'

'That is what I am phoning to tell you.'

Again Mary's heart thumped. This time it was so loud in her ears that she couldn't hear what the voice on the other end was saying.

'Could you repeat that please?' she asked.

'Richard Wilson has been taken to Wexham Hospital in Slough.'

'Oh. You mean he's there now?' she asked.

'Well, he will be very shortly. The ambulance left here about half an hour ago.'

'Why . . . why is he being moved?' she asked. She felt puzzled and was dreading the answer.

'He needs specialized surgery and the surgeon is already at Wexham Hospital, it's better for him to be there and remain under the direct care of Mr Dancer.'

'I see.'

She didn't see and she didn't understand.

'I was just on my way to Stoke Mandeville to see him,' Mary said. 'If I go to Wexham will they let me see him?'

'I'm afraid I can't tell you that. You will have to contact Wexham Hospital.'

'I see, well thank you for letting me know.'

There were so many questions she wanted to ask, but she

was sure from the clipped tones of the man on the phone he wasn't prepared to go into further details. Before she had time to sort out in her mind why they were making such a change, Bill called out her name; he and the taxi were still outside waiting for her. Pulling herself together, Mary hurried out, stopping only to lock the front door. She told the driver that they wanted to go to Wexham Hospital, not Stoke Mandeville.

The driver looked puzzled. 'You sure about that?' he asked.

'Yes, I'm quite sure. I had a telephone call minutes before you arrived to say my son had now been moved to Wexham Hospital.'

As Bill settled into his seat and had fastened his seat belt, Mary told him about the change of venue.

'Did they tell you why they were doing that?' Bill asked frowning.

'Yes, something to do with needing specialist surgery and that the right surgeon was based at Wexham and it was better for Richard to be there and in his care afterwards.'

Mary knew the taxi driver was listening to their discussion so she merely smiled at Bill and said no more. Mary found the journey a nightmare. She listened to Bill commenting on some of the places they passed on the way, but none of it meant very much to her. Nor did his talk dispel the disturbing thoughts racing through her mind about Richard and all the things that might have happened to him.

'Do you want me to wait?' the taxi driver asked as Mary paid him.

'No, I have no idea how long I'll be,' Mary told him. 'I'll ring your office when I am ready to go home.'

'Do you know which ward Richard is in?' Bill asked as they entered the reception area of the hospital.

Mary shook her head. 'No idea at all, I'll have to ask at the desk.'

The receptionist looked vague when Mary told her about Richard being transferred from Stoke Mandeville.

'Are you sure that he has already arrived here?' she asked.

Mary shook her head. 'Well, no. When they phoned to tell

me, they said that the ambulance had already left and that was about an hour ago.'

The receptionist pursed her lips. 'Well, in that case he may still be in the ambulance outside, waiting until there is a bed for him in A&E or reception,' she said. 'He certainly hasn't been admitted to a ward yet.'

'He's been seriously injured in a flying accident. Surely he would be admitted right away, not kept waiting? I was given to understand that he was sent here because he needs urgent surgery and the surgeon, Mr Dancer, is already here. I'm sure he has been told and is expecting him. Can't you ring his secretary or the head of his department and find out?'

'Why don't you go and have a cup of tea and come back again in ten minutes?' the receptionist advised. 'In the meantime, I will try and find out if he has arrived and where he is.'

Mary was about to argue but Bill took her arm, pulling her away from the desk. 'That sounds like a good idea,' he said. 'We'll be back in about ten minutes,' Bill told the receptionist, smiling at her.

'No point in antagonising the girl,' Bill said softly, as he steered Mary away from the reception desk and along in the direction of the hospital restaurant. 'Richards's details obviously haven't been entered yet so there's not a lot she can do to help you. Perhaps when we come back she will have some news.'

Mary took a deep breath and clenched her lips into a tight line. She knew Bill was right, but she felt so angry that the girl was so unhelpful that she wanted to scream. She left Bill to get their drinks and she found a small table at the back of the room, somewhere where they could talk without being overheard. She wanted desperately to see Richard and to reassure herself that his injuries were not serious. She also needed to find out whether or not he wanted her to get in touch with Megan, to let her know what had happened. As she sipped at the cup of steaming hot coffee, Mary tried to explain to Bill what might have happened.

Bill knew practically nothing about gliding except that he had always thought of it as madness to go up into the air in a machine that didn't have an engine. All the talk about riding the thermals meant nothing at all to him. What were thermals?

He knew they were air currents, but how did you find them and how did you know they were going to be strong enough to take a glider – and someone in it – up into the sky and for long distances? It simply didn't make sense to him.

Mary, on the other hand, knew a great deal about gliding because it had been something Sam had done ever since she'd first known him. In the early days, she had often gone up in a two-seater glider with him and could understand the exhilaration such freedom brought. Sam had been a very skilled glider pilot and had won trophies for long-distance flights. He was also a skilled aerobatic pilot and when he had tried to demonstrate his skills to Mary she had been so scared that she vowed never to go up again.

After that, he had only taken her on short flights, ready to return to base whenever she felt she had had enough. He had taken Richard up on numerous occasions and, as soon as he was old enough, he encouraged him to train as a pilot. Richard went solo on his sixteenth birthday, something both Sam and Richard felt proud about. Although Mary realised that it was a highly dangerous sport, she resigned herself to their enthusiasm.

All sports were dangerous, she told herself, motor racing, horse riding, football, rugby, golf, tennis and even walking was dangerous at times. She could never understand why people risked their lives climbing mountains or scaling rocks. Was it simply because they were a challenge or merely a case that they wanted to defy nature?

The minute they had finished their coffee Mary was on her feet anxious to get back to the reception desk.

'Slow down,' Bill told her. 'It will take time to trace him and find out where he is. This place is enormous, you know. They must be admitting and discharging people every second of the day.'

When they returned to the reception desk, the girl they had already spoken to greeted them with a bright smile.

'You know where he is?' Mary asked eagerly. 'Can I see him?'

The girls smile faded. 'He has been admitted,' she said cautiously, 'but he has been taken straight into surgery.'

'You mean I can't see him?' Mary said sharply.

'Certainly not at the moment and I have no idea how long

he will be in surgery. Or how long he will be in the recovery room afterwards,' the girl said cautiously.

'Can't someone tell you?' Mary asked agitatedly.

The girl shook her head. 'I don't think anyone knows for sure. Why don't you go home? We will phone you as soon as he is back in the ward and then you can come in and see him.'

Mary shook her head. 'No, I want to see him now. Where is the surgery, if I go along they might let me have a quick word with him before they operate?'

The girl shook her head. 'I'm sorry, that is out of the question.'

Mary refused to be turned away. She put forward every plausible argument she could but the girl remained firm.

Finally Bill took her arm. 'I think we had better do as suggested and go home and wait for a telephone call. It could take several hours before Richard is in a fit state to see you or anybody.'

Mary shook his arm away. 'I don't mind waiting; I've nothing better to do.'

'Well do it in comfort then,' Bill said firmly. 'I'll ring for a taxi and we'll go home. There's no point in hanging around here. There's nothing you can do and Richard wouldn't want you to be waiting here.' Before Mary could protest, Bill added, 'We must let Lucia know, she must be worried stiff. She probably doesn't know what to say to little George. He will be wondering where his Daddy is, so we can at least set their minds at rest.'

Mary sighed but agreed. As they left, Bill thanked the receptionist for her help.

There was a taxi available for them. Mary was silent on the way home.

'Do you want to go straight home or shall we call in on the way to let Lucia know what's happening?' Bill asked.

Mary hesitated. 'We'd better do that, I suppose,' she agreed reluctantly. 'We'll ask the taxi to wait. I don't think I have the strength to walk home from there.'

'Have you decided what you are going to tell her?' Bill asked.

'What is there to tell her except that Richard is in hospital and we can't see him?' she said hopelessly.

'True,' Bill agreed, 'but what about telling Megan? It's going to be quite a shock for little George when Lucia breaks the news to him that his Dad has had an accident.'

'Yes, I'm sure it will be.' Mary agreed.

'Well, he might need his mother to comfort him when he hears it,' Bill warned.

Mary was quiet, thinking it over. As the taxi drew up outside Richard's house she said, 'I'll ask Lucia for Megan's phone number and ring her later this evening.'

'The school will also have to be informed as well,' Bill reminded her.

'Yes, and I'll do that tomorrow morning. By then I might have some real news to tell them.'

TWENTY-FIVE

Megan was very abrupt when Mary phoned her later that evening.

'I am getting ready to go out so I haven't time to stand chattering,' she said very ungraciously.

'I'm not ringing for a chat. I have some bad news to tell you,' Mary said in a quiet voice.

'Bad news? What sort of bad news?'

'Richard has had an accident.'

'In the car?'

'No, he was in his glider.'

'Oh, the damn fool,' Megan exclaimed irritably. 'I've been on at him for years to give it up. I knew he would have an accident sooner or later.'

'Well this is the first time in almost thirty years,' Mary said dryly.

'Such a senseless pastime. If you want to fly then go in a proper plane with an engine and let someone experienced fly it,' Megan ranted. 'When did it happen? Has he hurt himself badly?'

'It happened only a few hours ago. He has hurt his back. He is in Wexham hospital and at the moment is having surgery.'

'This evening! What was he doing up at the gliding field this evening? He should have been at home supervising Lucia and making sure she was putting George to bed.'

Mary didn't answer.

'Well, is that all?' Megan asked.

'It's all I can tell you at the moment.'

'Have you been to see him?'

A lump came into Mary's throat. 'No, they said I would have to wait until after the operation was over,' she said gulping back her tears.

'Ridiculous. They should have let you see him so that he could tell you what happened.'

'Don't worry, I'll be at his bedside as soon as they will let me,' Mary told her forcefully.

'Good. Well, let me know how he is getting on. You can tell him that I have no intention of cutting my trip short to come home.'

Before Mary could make any comment, she heard the receiver go down at Megan's end. She stood motionless for a second until Bill, who had obviously been able to hear one side of the conversation and had surmised what was being said on the other end, commented.

'Heartless bitch!'

'Bill!' Mary looked shocked.

'Well she is. Most wives would have caught the next plane home. What is she doing? She's going out to a party.'

Mary wiped away the tears that were flooding her eyes. Bill was so right. Megan was heartless. She hadn't sounded the least concerned, only angry with Richard for having had an accident.

'Try not to let it get to you,' Bill said gruffly. 'I'll make us both a drink. Tea or coffee?'

'Thanks Bill, that's just what I need. Let's have coffee and put a spoonful of whisky in it,' Mary suggested, trying to smile.

'Whisky! I didn't know you liked the hard stuff,' Bill teased.

'I don't but I keep a bottle of it in the house for emergencies. A drop in hot water with a spoonful of honey at bedtime is wonderfully soothing, if you have a cold or a sore throat.'

'We don't have either,' Bill pointed out.

'No, but it's soothing all the same and will help me get some sleep tonight.'

Bill gave her a quizzical look but said nothing.

He stayed with Mary until almost ten o'clock, both of them hoping that there would be a call from the hospital with news about Richard.

'Surely they've finished operating on him by now,' Mary said anxiously.

'He's probably still in the recovery room and they won't telephone you until he is fully conscious,' Bill commented.

'You mean not until tomorrow morning.'

'Does seem to be that way. I'm off home but I'll come round tomorrow morning about eleven?'

'Why don't you phone first and I can tell you what's happening?'

Bill hesitated. 'All right, but promise you'll phone me if you hear from the hospital. Don't go there on your own, I'll come with you.'

'Thanks Bill, that's good of you.'

Mary saw Bill to the door, then returned to the living room. She had no intention of going to bed. Despite what Bill said, she was sure they would call her before morning and she wanted to be near the phone. She settled herself into her reclining chair and draped a light throw over her legs, in case it became chilly later in the night. She didn't think she would sleep but the long arduous day, coupled with the hot toddy, took care of things. Half an hour later she was asleep.

It was ten o'clock the next morning before the phone call came. Mary was so relieved that for a moment she couldn't understand what the woman on the other end was saying.

She took a deep breath to calm her nerves and asked the woman to say it all again.

'That is Mrs Mary Wilson?'

'Yes, yes. I'm sorry. I was so relieved to be getting some news that—'

The woman didn't wait for Mary to finish. 'It's about your son, she said more slowly.

'How is he?'

'He has regained consciousness and is in Intensive Care. If

you wish you can come and see him, but you will only be allowed to do so for a few minutes. We don't want him stressed or excited.'

'I'll be there, probably within the hour,' Mary told her. As soon as the line was clear, she phoned Bill and told him the news.

'Are you going to pick me up?' Bill asked.

'Very well, I'll phone for the taxi in about twenty minutes. I need to get properly dressed.'

'Phone for the taxi now and tell them to pick you up in twenty minutes,' Bill advised. 'I'll be ready and waiting.'

Mary tried to concentrate on what she had to do next. She had never felt so relieved, so anxious, or so flustered in her life. She phoned for the taxi as Bill had suggested and then started to get herself ready. The face that was reflected back at her as she put on her make-up was so lined and drawn that she shuddered. She must stop worrying. Richard would be worried if he saw her looking so anxious. She forced herself to lighten up and smile as she completed putting on her make-up. Then she picked up her light summer coat and handbag, locked the front door and walked down the garden path to the gate to wait for the taxi.

The warm July air refreshed her. She tried to console herself that the worst was over now and Richard would probably be sitting up in bed, ready to relate all the details about his crash by the time she arrived at the hospital. The taxi arrived on time and she asked the driver to go via Coburn Road in order to pick up Bill. He was waiting at his gate and climbed into the taxi greeting her with a wide smile. The journey was uneventful; along familiar roads and lanes to Wexham Hospital, which was on the outskirts of Slough.

As they went into the hospital, Mary headed straight for the reception desk and to her relief found that the same girl they had seen the previous day was attending her. The girl recognised them immediately and smiled brightly.

'You've come to see your son, Mrs Wilson. Well this time I can tell you where he is. He has just been moved into ward six. If you follow the signs along the corridor turn left, then turn left again and you'll see more signs guiding you directly to the ward.'

'Thank you,' Mary said. 'Thank you for arranging for them to phone me and for all your help yesterday.'

'Just doing my job,' the girl said brightly, but she looked pleased that someone had recognised her hard work.

Their footsteps clattered along the tiled corridor as they made their way in the direction she had told them. When they finally reached it, Mary stopped and took a deep breath. She was so relieved that everything was all right. She didn't want to look anxious when she met Richard. Bill took her arm and propelled her forward, pushing open the double doors to let her through and smiling at her encouragingly.

Mary stood just inside staring round the ward looking for Richard. She had expected to see him sitting up, waiting to see her, but all the patients seemed to be lying down. Perhaps it was their afternoon siesta. Bill was also looking around, searching for Richard.

A nurse came hurrying up to them frowning slightly. 'Yes who are you looking for?'

'Richard Wilson.'

The nurse looked at her rather doubtfully.

'You're not going to stop me seeing him are you?' Mary said sharply.

'No, you can see him but only for a few minutes and only one at a time.'

'That's all right I'm just a friend,' Bill said quickly. 'I'll wait here.'

The nurse nodded and indicated a chair in the corner. 'Perhaps you wouldn't mind sitting there or out in the corridor?' she said.

Mary noticed that all the time she spoke she kept her voice quite low and she wondered why. Perhaps it was because all the men appeared to be asleep, she thought as she followed the nurse down the ward. They stopped at the first bed, which had screens around it and Mary took a quick deep breath to try and stop her heart racing. This couldn't be Richard!

The person lying prone in the bed was white faced and his shallow breathing was strained.

Once again she thought this can't be Richard. She had expected to find him sitting up ready to welcome her and laughing about the silly thing that had happened to make him crash. The man lying there looked almost a shell. Tentatively, she approached the bed and she could see from the man's hair colouring and features that it was Richard. There was no mistake about that, but he looked so ill and so fragile.

The nurse looked at her watch. 'Right I can give you ten minutes and please don't say anything to upset him or excite him.'

'No, of course not. I understand,' Mary said in a low voice. She sat down in the chair at the side of the bed, reached out and took one of the limp hands that were lying on top of the covers. The man in the bed didn't even stir. 'Richard, Richard,' she said softly. Then when it had no effect she repeated his name again this time a little louder, bending her head so that her lips were quite close to his ear

Slowly his eyelids fluttered then gradually, very gradually, he opened his eyes. He stared at her for a moment, then recognition lightened his features.

'Mother,' he said but his voice was weak and little more than a whisper.

'Richard, I didn't expect to find you like this,' she said sadly.

'No,' he said his voice so weak she could barely hear him. 'It was a nasty accident. I'm not sure what happened but I am sure that someone will tell me. I had only just taken off when it happened. I'd done all the checks on my glider beforehand so I don't know what it was . . . I'm not even sure if my legs will work.' He added in a despairing whimper.

'Richard, don't say that please. I'm sure the operation will have put everything right. It's simply a case of resting and recovering.'

He gave a faint smile. 'I hope so. At the moment I feel completely washed out.' He closed his eyes again and seemed to sink into unconsciousness. Mary didn't know what to do. She squeezed his hand and once more his eyelids fluttered then he looked up at her.

'Is George all right?'

Mary nodded. 'Yes,' she said positively, George is all right. We told him that you had an accident and that you were in hospital. He wanted to come and see you, of course, but we had to tell him he would have to wait a day or two until you were stronger.'

'Good. Does Megan know?'

Mary hesitated. How could she tell him how Megan had received the news? Yet somehow she had to do so. She took a deep breath.

'Yes, Megan knows. I rang her last night and told her you had an accident. I couldn't give her any details because I didn't have them.'

'She's coming home?'

'Well, yes, but not immediately. She said it was impossible to do so.'

Mary didn't know how to explain, but it didn't seem to matter because Richard had drifted away again. She bent closer, trying to see if she could rouse him when the nurse appeared. This time there was a man with her.

'Good afternoon, Mrs Wilson. I am Mr Dancer, the surgeon who operated on your son last night. He has quite a nasty injury. It may be some time before he's up and back to normal.'

'He will walk again?' Mary said anxiously

Mr Dancer looked thoughtful. 'We hope he will. With skilled nursing and also plenty of physiotherapy, exercise and a determination to get better he should be all right,' Mr Dancer stated.

'Try not to worry,' he added as he turned and pulled aside the curtain and left.

'I think you've been here long enough; you've had your ten minutes and we don't want to tire him do we,' the nurse said briskly. 'Your son needs every ounce of strength to get better.'

Mary stood up, 'Yes, of course. I understand.' She hesitated. 'Can you tell me a little bit more about what happened? As far as I understand his glider crashed on take-off.'

'So we were told when he was brought in,' the nurse affirmed. 'He has damaged a couple of the vertebrae in his back, they will take time to heal but as Mr Dancer explained, with plenty of physiotherapy he should regain full use of his legs in due course.

'You don't know why his glider crashed?' Mary persisted.

'I'm afraid not. I am sure someone who witnessed the accident will be able to tell you more about that,' the nurse said dismissively.

TWENTY-SIX

Mary Wilson felt in a daze as she left Wexham hospital. She couldn't put the sight out of her mind of Richard lying prone in his hospital bed and the fear that he might never walk again. As she sat alongside Bill Thompson in the taxi taking them back home, she tried to sort out in her head how badly injured Richard was. Sam had never had an accident in the whole of his flying career and she had no idea what actual damage Richard had done to his back.

The nurse had said something about damage to some of the vertebrae, which she knew meant the bones in Richard's spine. In that case he might not be able to walk again. The thought of that terrified her. How on earth would he earn a living, look after George and generally lead a normal life if that was the case?

Bill sat beside her, holding her hand and saying nothing; there was really nothing he could say. He understood to a degree what had happened to Richard and he was extremely worried. Richard was a comparatively young man and to be incapacitated to such an extent as not being able to walk was unthinkable. Did it mean he would be in a wheelchair? These days, of course, there were all sorts of mechanical means of getting around other than a wheelchair, so perhaps he would be able to adapt to that type of substitute for walking. It was still a dreadful burden for a young man to bear. He might easily live for another thirty or forty years. He didn't know what to say to Mary.

He'd taken several sideways glances and each time he could see that the news had greatly disturbed her, from the deep furrows down either side of her cheeks and the way she kept dabbing at her eyes, although she was not actually crying. Someone would have to tell Megan and he didn't think that that she would respond in a very conciliatory way. He was sure that she would only be concerned insofar as it affected her life. She was elegant and beautiful on the outside but hard as a dried up nut on the inside.

Lucia had to be told exactly what the situation was and probably have arrangements made so that she could manage to run Richard's home in his absence, so they called on her on their way home. Lucia accepted the news stoically, but little George's reaction brought tears to Mary's eyes.

For a moment she couldn't answer when he asked 'Is my daddy with you?'

'No,' Mary told him her voice shaky with emotion, 'your daddy is in hospital.'

'Oh!' George looked taken aback. 'Will he be coming home soon?'

'No, dear, I'm afraid he will be in hospital for quite a long time.'

Georges face crumpled. 'I want him home now,' he protested. 'He always reads me a story when I go to bed before I go to sleep.'

'Well I expect Lucia will read you a story,' Mary said with a gentle smile.

'She does but it's not the same as when Daddy reads it. When he reads to me I fall asleep as soon as he has finished. I don't do that when Lucia reads to me. Her voice is different.'

'What about if I came round and read you a story before you went to bed?' Bill volunteered.

George looked at him in astonishment. 'Can you really read stories?'

'Oh yes,' Bill assured him 'I am very good at reading stories.'

George looked at him doubtfully 'It won't be quite the same as when Daddy reads to me,' he said, his voice trembling.

'Well shall we give it a try,' Bill suggested.

George nodded. 'I suppose so.'

'Well, in that case, shall I come around tonight?'

Bill looked at Lucia as he spoke and she nodded her head in agreement.

'Good! You had better tell me what time you want me to come round and I'll be here, and you can choose whatever story you want me to read.'

'OK. I go to bed at seven o'clock, can you be here at seven o'clock?'

'I will do my very best,' Bill told him.

Mary smiled gratefully at Bill and then looked at her watch and drew in her breath sharply as she said, 'We must be on our way home; the taxi is outside waiting. We've been out most of the day what with one thing and another.'

She kissed George goodbye and told him to be a good boy and said she would make sure that Bill came round to read to him that night.

'That was very kind of you to offer to read to George,' she said as they got back into the taxi. 'Are you sure you're going to be able to manage to do it? If it is successful he may expect you to read to him every night!'

'Well, I suppose I can manage to do that until Richard comes home if it helps,' he said gruffly.

Mary squeezed his hand. 'Thank you, Bill.'

'It will probably be a lot simpler than dealing with Megan,' he mumbled.

'I think telling Megan is going to be very difficult indeed,' Mary admitted.

When they reached her house and she had paid the taxi driver and he'd driven away, Mary braced her shoulders as they walked up the garden path.

'Job number one is to ring Megan,' she stated as she unlocked the front door.

'I don't think it is going to be very easy,' she commented as they went inside.

'I'm sure it won't be,' Bill agreed, 'so why don't you have a cup of tea first and prepare yourself for what you are going to say to her.'

Mary's call to Megan was every bit as difficult as she had imagined it would be. Megan was still very annoyed that Richard's accident had been as a result of him going gliding.

As Mary relayed what Mr Dancer had said Megan grew increasingly annoyed.

'He really should listen to advice. He acts like a spoiled boy,' she said snappily. 'If I have told him once I've told him a dozen times to give it up. If he had done as I asked this would never have happened.'

'No but he may well have had some other kind of accident,' Mary defended.

'Possibly, but certainly he wouldn't have broken his back. How long is it going to take to get better? Were you told?'

'No one knows,' Mary said. 'Mr Dancer the surgeon who operated said it may take a considerable time. He also advocated careful nursing and plenty of physiotherapy.'

'He won't be getting any nursing from me I can assure you on that point,' Megan said quickly. 'When he comes out of hospital he will have to go into a nursing home,' she added sharply.

'Don't you think it would be better to wait and see what condition he is in when he does come home?' Mary argued. 'I am quite sure that they wouldn't send him home from hospital until he is capable of walking. It may be with the aid of crutches or something, but I am sure they will not send him out of hospital in the condition he is in now. If you saw him—'

'I'm not likely to see him for quite a while. I am certainly not coming home just to look at him lying in a hospital bed! Nor do I intend to sit by his side and hold his hand,' Megan interrupted. 'The very fact that he is in hospital is his own fault not mine.'

'Do you want me to tell him that?' Mary asked in a shocked voice.

'You can tell him what you like, or whatever you think he wants to hear. You can certainly tell him that I am not changing my plans just to accommodate him.'

'Shall I give you the address of the hospital so that you can write to him?'

'Good heavens no! What is the point of me doing that?'

'You could express sympathy and tell him how sorry you are that this has happened. I am sure it would make him feel better.'

'I am much more likely to tell him how stupid he has been.' Megan said scathingly. 'For years I have told him to stop gliding, so I am unlikely to be sympathetic. He has behaved like a fool and I have no patience with him for such foolishness, especially when I have asked him countless times to give it up.'

Before Mary could make any retort the phone went down at the other end. With a sigh of regret, Mary hung up. There was nothing else she could do. Poor Richard would have to be told that Megan wasn't coming home, but that could wait. The important thing was to get him better and, at the moment, he was barely conscious so what on earth could a piece of news like that do to him except set him back? For the next few weeks it would be up to her, Bill, and Lucia to do whatever they could to boost his morale, and encourage him to have patience and do whatever the hospital told him to do.

Bill listened in silence when she told him what Megan's reaction had been.

'Did she ask after George? He asked.

Mary shook her head. 'No, come to think about it she never mentioned George or how Lucia was going to manage. I'll leave it a day or two and then ring her again. By then we might have some fresh news.'

Later that week there was news, but not the sort of news that Mary expected.

TWENTY-SEVEN

Mary felt that Richard's progress over the next few days was agonisingly slow. Bill told her to have patience.

'The doctor and nurses seemed quite satisfied by his progress and they're the experts,' he pointed out.

Mary knew he was right but nevertheless she was impatient to see Richard sitting up and talking. As it was, each time she went in to see him he was still lying prone and although his eyes were open and he appeared to be looking around he said very little. Finally, she spoke to the nurse about it, telling her that she thought he ought to be sitting up by now.

'Good heavens, no!' the nurse said with a smile. 'The longer he remains lying flat the quicker the damaged vertebrae will heal. He is doing extremely well, Mrs Wilson, and you must be patient.'

Mary shook her head. 'So everyone tells me but I can't help feeling anxious about him. He says so little.'

'He is probably feeling extremely exhausted and remember that whenever he moves, no matter how slight it may be, he feels pain. We are as careful and as gentle as we can be when we wash and feed him, but we know it is still a trauma for him.'

She patted Mary's arm. 'Now don't worry and try and be patient, Mrs Wilson.'

Mary knew the nurse was right and she really did try over the next couple of days to control her own feelings. She was concerned that she still hadn't had a call from Megan and wondered if the time had come to ring her again.

'Leave things as they are for the moment,' Bill advised. 'Time is dragging for you but she probably doesn't realise that it's been nearly a week since Richard had his accident. After all, she is working and her mind will be on what she is doing. She hasn't seen Richard so she probably can't envisage how poorly he is.'

Two days later she had a fresh problem. When she called in to see Lucia and to see how little George was she found her looking very worried.

'Is something wrong, Lucia?' she asked. 'It's not George, is it?'

'No, Mrs Wilson. George is fine. It's about money.'

Mary frowned. 'What do you mean?'

'I have none left,' Lucia said and shrugged helplessly. 'No money for food or for anything else. No money for me,' she added with a deep sigh.

'I'm sorry, Lucia, but I don't quite understand,' Mary said.

'Aah! I will try and explain,' Lucia said. 'All the payments for things like mortgage, rates, lighting and heating are paid for straight from the bank account, I am told, and nothing at all to do with me. Mr Wilson takes care of those. Madam provides all the money that I need to buy food for us all, and cleaning and odds and ends once a month. I have had no money from her since she went to America, in fact, none for a long time before she left. Now I have used all this money, the petty cash as she calls it, and I am having to buy the things we need from my own wages.'

'So, you have been receiving your wages,' Mary said with relief.

Lucia shook her head. 'No, that is the problem. You see they come out of the petty cash and there has been none from Madam since weeks before she went away.'

'You just told me that you had been paying for things out of your wages,' Mary frowned.

'I can explain,' Lucia said quickly. 'I always save part of my wages to send money home every month to help my mother.'

'Your mother?'

Lucia gave a sad little smile. 'My mother has been a widow for many long years and I have a sister only two years younger than me, who has been sick all her life and needs to be cared for by my mother.'

'Does your mother work?'

Lucia shook her head. 'No, she is too old to work; she is in her eighties.'

Mary stared at Lucia as if seeing her for the first time. She was of middle stature, with jet dark hair and an olive complexion. Her dark eyes were bright and she looked extremely healthy. There must be some mistake; her mother couldn't be that old.

'You are only in your twenties so how can your mother be in her eighties?'

Lucia laughed dryly. 'I am not in my twenties. I am in my forties.'

'In your forties! I don't believe it. You certainly look in your twenties . . . twenty-nine possibly but not in your forties,' Mary protested.

'I was forty-one on my last birthday,' Lucia told her, 'and my sister is thirty-nine. My mother claims she was an accident. She thought she was far too old to have any more children. She married late and expected that I would be her only child.'

'Has your sister been incapacitated all her life?' Mary asked

Lucia looked away as if too embarrassed to explain. Then, tightening her hands into fists at her side she looked directly into Mary's eyes.

'Yes,' she said gravely. 'Ever since her birth.'

She took a deep breath and Mary waited patiently for her to go on.

'It was a difficult birth and my mother says it was because

she was far too old for childbearing. She felt it was a punishment for saying she didn't want any more children.'

'I hardly think so,' Mary murmured.

'As a young child, Maria was different from my friends and me, but not so bad that it made any real difference. We accepted her and played with her, and she played with us. We made allowances for her because she was my sister. She was always the last no matter what game we were playing, but we accepted that because she was the baby of our group.'

'So, when did . . .' Mary hesitated not sure how to ask. 'When did you become aware that she was different?'

'My mother always suspected it, but it was pointed out when she went to school. At first the teacher said she was backward but, by the time it came for her to leave school, it was obvious that she would never be able to hold a job down. She had no idea of time or purpose. You could show her how to do something but five minutes later she'd forgotten all about what she had learnt. She was pleasant, smiling and happy as a child. As she grew older, and realised that she couldn't work or enjoy herself in the same way as I did, she became rather morose and eventually very depressed.'

'Didn't your mother take her to a doctor or someone who could have advised and helped? Someone who knew about these things?'

'We were very poor, my father had died and my mother had to work to keep us. My mother left her at home and told her of the jobs she wanted her to do, but very rarely did Maria remember to do any of them. When my mother returned from work she would have to prepare a meal and then do the chores that my sister should have done, but had forgotten how to do.'

'And you? Were you working?'

'Oh yes, I worked from the day I left school. I was training to care for children and when I got home I then helped my mother and took care of Maria.'

'So, your mother has worked all her life,' Mary said reflectively.

'Yes, until she became crippled with rheumatism and was unable to work anymore. You see because she was unskilled all she could do was menial jobs, like scrubbing or washing and cleaning. When her rheumatism became very bad such work was impossible.'

'Oh dear, she has had a hard life. Why did you leave home and come to work here in England?' Mary asked curiously.

'It was the money. I earn so much more here than I was earning at home. Right from the beginning I send money home to help my mother, because she couldn't manage on her meagre pension.'

Mary nodded understandingly.

'Trying to keep one person on the pension is difficult, to keep two is impossible. It is only because I can send her money regularly that she manages. Now I have heard from her that she is desperate. They are short of food and soon the winter will be upon us again, and she has no money put aside to buy warmth.'

'I understand,' Mary said consolingly. 'Now don't you worry about it Lucia, I will arrange something.'

Lucia dabbed away the tears that had sprung into her eyes. 'Madam you are so kind, so understanding,' Lucia said huskily as she flung her arms around Mary's waist and hugged her.

'You say Megan normally supplies the cash from which you take your wages?'

'That is right.'

'She provides money on a regular monthly basis and you are told to take your salary from that?'

'Yes, that is so, and then I send part of my salary home to my mother,' Lucia said with a watery smile.

'Right. I'll arrange something,' Mary promised, 'I will ring Megan tonight and see what she is proposing to do about it.'

When Mary got home from the hospital that night, she told Bill about her conversation with Lucia and he was aghast.

'I wouldn't have thought Lucia was that old,' he agreed. 'She looks so young! She must be very worried about her sister, what a terrible problem.'

'Yes! It appears that the sister, Maria, is two years younger than Lucia,' Mary said.

'I can see now why she puts up with Megan's harsh ruling, tries to obey her every whim and is so secretive about bringing

George to visit you,' Bill said. 'It's because she is afraid of losing her job.'

'True,' Mary agreed. 'She needs the money and if she loses this job she will have to go back to Italy and hope to get work there. It would not be easy for her. But, at the moment, there is no question of losing her job. We need her to look after George while Richard is in hospital, and probably afterwards because I shouldn't imagine he will be capable of doing very much for quite some time.' Mary hesitated for a moment then added, 'There is also this other problem to be confronted and I am not at all sure if I am handling it as I should be. As well as not receiving her wages, Lucia is running out of money for running the household. All the main bills, the rates and things of that nature are already covered by standing order and paid directly from Richard's bank account. But apparently, from what Lucia has said, the day-to-day running costs for food and cleaning materials and any other monies was supplied by Megan.'

'So you're going to ring Megan tonight and find out what the situation is?'

Mary nodded. 'You know, Bill,' she said, 'if Sam had had an accident I would have been spending every moment at the hospital hoping they would let me see him.'

'Things are different these days,' he told her. 'Married couples seem to live their own lives. They have different interests, and Megan, remember, is a very ambitious lady.'

'She's certainly a very heartless one, in my opinion,' Mary said crossly, 'in the meantime, I'm having to give Lucia some money from my savings, so that she can send some home to her mother, then I will try and organize things with Megan. If she says things will have to wait until she comes home, then I will have to make further inroads into my savings.'

The plans sounded feasible and Mary spent time thinking it through while she was washing up, clarifying in her own mind what she was going to say to Megan.

Before she could pick up the phone, however, it rang and it was Megan on the other end.

TWENTY-EIGHT

'I was on the point of calling you,' Mary said. 'There are one or two problems that need to be sorted out.'

'Then you had better discuss them with Richard because I am not interested,' Megan said sharply.

'It's about money,' Mary persisted, ignoring Megan's tone. She felt angry; Megan hadn't asked how Richard was or even if little George was all right.

'Lucia tells me that she hasn't received her wages and that she is running short of money to deal with other expenses she has to meet right away.'

'Then tell her to ask Richard for the money,' Megan said shortly.

'Richard is in hospital still and he is certainly in no fit state to be worried over household matters.'

'Yes, well I'm not interested,' Megan said abruptly. 'It's his own fault that he's in there.'

'You want me to tell him that?'

'Of course I do and give him this message at the same time: tell him that I will not be coming back to England. I will be phoning Lucia and telling her to send on my clothes and other possessions.'

'What are you talking about?' Mary asked. 'How long do you intend to be in New York?'

'Permanently. I am leaving Richard for good. I have no space in my life for a man who will be a cripple.'

'What!' Mary gasped, unable to believe what she was hearing. 'You say you're leaving Richard? Oh Megan, isn't that rather a heartless decision. Richard is very ill at the moment; he will find such news very distressing.'

'This is as good a time as any to tell him,' Megan said callously. 'The fact that he is in hospital is his own fault. I would have been telling him anyway, but the fact that he is now going to be a cripple has helped me decide to make the break sooner.'

'What are you going to do about little George?'

'He's Richard's son so it's up to him to look after George. I'm divorcing Richard, he will be hearing from my solicitor very shortly.' The phone went down with an ominous clatter before Mary could say anything else.

Slowly, she returned her own handset to its cradle, then she sat down heavily on the nearest chair. The full impact of Megan's words and all the consequences that would follow, filled Mary's mind like an enormous black cloud blotting out the sun. How on earth was she going to break the news to Richard? He would be devastated.

Then there was poor little George. How would be react when he learnt that he would never see his mother again? She simply couldn't imagine how hurt he would feel. She hoped he wouldn't feel it was his fault. She understood that children often did blame themselves when their parents split up. Thank heaven Lucia had not threatened to leave. She understood George and would know the best way to comfort him. She must make things as smooth as possible for her after Megan told her the news, especially over her wages and money problems. Mary needed to ensure Lucia did stay on, Mary thought worriedly.

Richard's unfortunate accident was now rapidly becoming a nightmare for them all.

She would have to think very carefully about how to tell Richard, that was the part that worried her the most and it was the first thing that she must do. She would talk to Bill; he was usually very level handed and might be able to offer some suggestions on the best way to handle things. She could listen to his advice, even if she didn't take it.

She was about to pick up the phone to ring him and ask him to come round, when it rang. She hesitated. Could it be Megan to say she had changed her mind, that she wasn't deserting Richard after all?

'Mrs Wilson?'

The voice on the other end of the line was faintly familiar but it wasn't Megan. It was an authoritative voice yet much softer than Megan's.

'Yes, who is it?'

'This is Wexham hospital. Your son is asking for you.'

'Is something wrong, has he had a relapse?'

'No, nothing like that, but he does seem to be upset about something and he won't tell us what is wrong. He says he needs to talk to you.'

'I see. Well of course I'll come right away. Has he by any chance had a telephone call?'

'Yes, as a matter of fact he has. It was about twenty minutes ago and he seemed to be very distressed afterwards.'

'I understand. I'll be there as soon as I can, be so kind as to tell him I'm on my way,' Mary said quickly. Of course he was feeling upset, Mary thought angrily. Megan had not given her the chance to break the news gently; she had phoned him direct herself. Mary could imagine the brutal way she would have told him that she was leaving him. Suddenly she hated Megan. She had always tolerated her and tried to be friendly towards her. She had never uttered a word of criticism about what she thought of as Megan's unreasonable behaviour in neglecting her husband and child all these years.

Mary didn't think she could face all this on her own. Picking up the phone again she rang Bill.

'Are you doing anything or can you spare the time to come to the hospital with me?' she asked the moment he answered.

'Why? Is Richard worse?'

'No, not really, but he's asking for me.'

'Why? What's happened?'

'Look I'll tell you all about it on the way there. I'll phone for a taxi and pick you up as soon as possible.'

Once Bill was in the taxi, Mary told him about Megan's phone call. She kept her voice low and hoped the driver couldn't hear what she was saying. Bill's mouth gaped when she said that Megan was leaving Richard.

'What a thing to have to tell him when he is lying on his back in hospital,' Bill gasped. 'It takes me back to the war years. I was a very young trainee hospital orderly and soldiers who were seriously injured frequently received such calls from their wives or girlfriends, because they couldn't bear to think of spending the rests of their lives with a cripple. We used to call them "Dear John" letters and the poor devils seemed to lose heart for weeks after they got one.'

'That's what I am afraid has happened to Richard,' Mary said sadly. 'Although Megan told me to tell him, I think she may have already telephoned the hospital and told him herself, and that is what is upsetting him so much.'

'She is a heartless bitch,' Bill muttered. 'Fancy getting news like that when you are lying helpless in hospital and feeling as low as a snake's belly.'

Mary shook her head from side to side, biting her lower lip to hold back the threatening tears.

Bill was right; Megan was heartless. She did seem to have no feeling for anyone other than herself. Mary wondered if there was another man involved. If there was, then he was probably a tycoon of some sort. Megan loved money and position. Mary could never understand why she had married Richard, except of course he was very good looking and always ready to do everything he could to let her further her career.

'And what about little George?' Bill asked cutting into her thoughts.

'Megan said he's Richard's responsibility and it's up to him to bring him up. She doesn't want him and has made it clear she won't be making any claim on him, so there's nothing Richard needs to worry about on that account.'

Bill let out a long whistling breath. 'Most mothers fight tooth and nail to keep their children when the family split up,' he said shaking his head from side to side in disbelief.

'I don't think that Megan had a very strong maternal streak. She has never been very motherly,' Mary said sadly.

'Nevertheless, very few women would give their child up like that. I know some very young unmarried mothers do it the minute the child is born because they know they won't be able to bring it up on their own. Even then, from what one hears, they regret it for the rest of their lives.'

'True, very true,' Mary agreed. 'Megan is only interested in her career though. She has never really had time for George. I imagine that, once he was old enough, she would have wanted to pack him off to boarding school and let someone else shoulder the responsibility of bringing him up.'

'So, what are you going to tell him?' Bill asked. 'It's not a job I'd like to have to do.'

'No,' Mary sighed heavily. 'It's certainly not one I relish. I'm not sure how he will take it.'

'I imagine George will be very upset,' Bill told her.

'I don't know, he may not be. He sees very little of her, in fact, he sees more of Lucia than he does of his mother.'

'Perhaps you should leave it to Lucia to tell him,' Bill suggested.

Mary shrugged her shoulders in a despairing way. 'I simply don't know what to do for the best.'

'Or let Richard tell him. He might accept the news better if it came from his father.'

Mary shook her head. 'No, Richard is in no fit state to deal with it at present and the sooner George is told the better. Supposing someone at school said something to him about it!'

'Not very likely, is it?' Bill frowned. 'It's not as though Megan was friendly with any of the other mothers and I don't think Richard's close to any of them.'

'No, but Lucia may be.'

'Tell her not to say anything. I would think she would know better than to gossip about the family to anyone.'

'I don't know. I simply don't want to take chances. You know how people overhear things and then repeat them. That's how rumours spread.'

Before Bill could answer the taxi came to a stop outside the hospital.

'What about having a coffee first, before you face Richard?' Bill suggested after Mary had paid off the taxi and they were inside.

'No.' Mary shook her head. 'I think I would prefer to get this over with first and I am sure I will need a coffee afterwards,' she added as she squared her shoulders and started to walk towards the ward she knew Richard was in.

'Do you want me to come with you?' Bill asked frowning uncertainly.

'Mary hesitated. 'No, perhaps it would be better if I saw him on my own.'

'Right. Well I'll wait for you in the restaurant,' Bill said quickly before she could change her mind.

He felt sorry for Mary, for having to break such terrible news

to Richard and for Richard, for having to receive it. He couldn't
start to imagine what it would do to him when he was in such
low spirits anyway, but he felt that it was such a personal
matter, that it was better for the two of them to be alone. It
might only upset Richard even more if he felt everyone knew
about it before he did, Bill mused as he headed towards the
hospital restaurant.

TWENTY-NINE

Mary's spirits lifted slightly as she walked into the ward
and saw that the green curtains were no longer drawn
around Richard's bed. Even more encouraging was the
fact that, supported by four or five pillows, Richard was sitting
propped up in bed. He was watching the door and the moment
she entered he raised his hand weakly in greeting.

'How are you, my dear?' she asked as she bent down and
kissed him on the brow. He reached up and squeezed her hand,
but shook his head without actually replying to her question.
As she sat down in the chair beside his bed, she saw the deep
frown that creased his forehead and the tension around his eyes.

'You've spoken to Megan,' she stated, having decided that
the sooner it was said and out into the open the better.

'Yes,' he said quietly. 'She's already phoned you and told
you the news?'

'That she is not coming back from America. Yes, she told
me that.'

'Not coming back *for good*!' he said bitterly as he ran a hand
over his hair until it stood on end. 'I tried to reason with her,
for George's sake but she wouldn't listen. Can't you make her
see sense, Mother?'

Mary shook her head sadly. Much as she disliked Megan and
thought her unbelievably heartless, she would have done
anything in her power to have her back if it kept Richard happy.

'I'm afraid, Richard, that I am the very last person she would
listen to.'

He stared at her hopelessly for a minute.

'Can't you persuade her to do it for little George's sake. What is going to happen to him?' he said in a strangled voice.

'You will have to look after him and I will do all I can to help, of course,' Mary told him. She could feel her tears coming and she swallowed hard. She mustn't cry, she told herself. She must be strong for Richard's sake. 'It's a good thing we still have Lucia. George is very close to her and she cares for him deeply.' She paused, hoping that what she was about to say wouldn't upset him further. 'We are lucky to have Lucia because George sees more of her than he does of Megan,' she said gently.

He looked at her blankly as if he didn't understand what she was saying. Then he shrugged rather dismissively.

'I suppose we are,' he said in a flat, toneless voice. There was an uneasy silence for a few minutes and then Richard said, 'I really don't understand why she is leaving me. I've always let her lead her own life, what is she gaining from us divorcing? I've never stood in her way. I know her career has meant a lot to her, but she has always been free to travel whenever it was necessary to do so.'

'Yes, I know, dear,' Mary murmured consolingly. She wondered whether she should tell him that one of the reasons was that Megan thought he might be a cripple, but since she couldn't see that there was anything to gain from doing so, she kept quiet.

When Richard next spoke she was glad that she had held her tongue.

'I told her that the surgeon was pleased with my progress and that I'd be walking again in a couple of months, but it didn't seem to interest her. In fact,' he added, looking at Mary, 'he seemed to think that, by the time the new school year started I would be, more or less, back to normal. Doing physiotherapy every day is not much of a way to spend the school holidays, of course,' he grinned, 'As far I was concerned it was brilliant news.'

'Oh, it is, it's wonderful news,' Mary said smiling.

'Well, you might think so but it didn't impress Megan. She never even commented on it,' he said bitterly. 'No, all she said after I told her was "George is your son so it is up to you to look after him. I don't want anything more to do with him." Can you understand that, Mum? She doesn't want anything more to do with her own child.'

In Megan's case Mary could understand it, because she had already revealed herself as callous and heartless. A child might hamper her progress in her career and she wasn't prepared to take that chance.

Mary bit her lip and then said, 'Don't let it upset you, Richard. It is a relief to know that you won't have to go to court to establish your rights. There is no doubt that he will be looked after far better if he lives with you than with her.'

He still looked gloomy so once again she reminded him how lucky they were to have Lucia looking after George.

'I know, but who is going to tell him that his mother isn't coming home and that he will never see her again?'

Mary didn't answer. She didn't know what to say or to suggest. She could understand Richard not wanting to be the one to tell him because she knew how she felt about doing so. She didn't really feel that it was right to expect Lucia to do it and Mary worried she would tear up whilst telling him, which wouldn't help at all. Yet who else could be asked?

Suddenly an idea came to her but she wasn't at all sure how Richard would react if she voiced it. She pondered on her idea for several minutes, then hesitantly she suggested, 'What about letting Bill tell George?'

Richard looked at her startled. 'Bill?'

'Yes, Bill Thompson. George likes him and trusts him, and Bill is very good with him.'

Richard was quiet as if contemplating what the outcome might be. 'It's hardly fair on Bill to ask him to do a momentous thing like that, is it? He mightn't want to do it but he might not want to upset you by refusing.'

'I don't think that's a problem. Bill is very pragmatic. He will turn the idea down if he doesn't think it's a practical solution.'

'You know him better than I do, but don't forget that friendships can be like marriages and easily broken,' Richard said bitterly.

'Bill is waiting for me in the hospital restaurant. I'll go and proposition him over a cup of tea and let you know how he feels about it.'

'Are you sure?'

'Oh, he'll be there. He promised to wait for me,' Mary told him guilelessly.

'I didn't mean that and you know it,' Richard said with the trace of a smile. 'Go on then and ask him. Tell him I will be eternally grateful to him if he will do it.'

THIRTY

Mary waited anxiously for Bill to return from reading a bedtime story to George. He had promised to call in and let her know how George had reacted to the news about Megan. She felt guilty, perhaps she should have been the one to tell him. After all she was his grandmother; Bill was not even related to George. The moment she heard Bill's footsteps coming up the path she switched on the kettle then went to open the front door.

'Did you tell him?'

Bill shook his head, avoiding her eyes as he came into the hall. 'No, the time wasn't right.'

'What on earth do you mean?' Mary frowned. She felt annoyed. He had volunteered to do it and now he had chickened out. She should have known this would happen. How could you expect a man to tell a young child that his mother had left him and that he might never see her again?

Mary turned her back on Bill and went back to the kitchen. The kettle had switched itself off, so she poured the water into the teapot, which was standing there ready with the teabags already in it. She was so perturbed by Bill's news that she hardly watched what she was doing, until she missed the pot and the scalding hot water went over her hand. With a shriek, she put down the kettle and rushed to hold her hand under the cold tap to ease the burning.

'Are you all right?' Bill asked solicitously.

'No, I'm not all right,' Mary said in a tight voice.

'Here, let me take a look at it,' he reached out to take her hand but Mary pulled away.

'My hand will be all right in a minute,' she said tetchily. 'It's George that I'm upset about.' She took a deep breath. 'What am I going to tell Richard?'

'He'll understand when I explain,' Bill said quietly.

'Explain? Her brow furrowed. 'What do you mean by explain.'

'Here let me finish making the tea and then, while it is brewing, I'll explain,' he told her. Mary watched in silence as he finished pouring the water into the teapot. Her hand was throbbing, but it was nothing compared with the turmoil she felt because George still had to be told the news.

'I didn't tell George,' Bill explained 'because I felt it was too much for him to take in. I wanted to prepare him for it first.'

'How can you do that?' Mary asked.

'By telling him a story related to such an episode,' Bill told her. 'Tonight, I told him one about small boy whose friend had moved far away to a foreign country and he would never see him again.' Bill piled all the tea things onto a tray. 'Let's take these into the other room and sit down,' he suggested. He waited until they were both sitting in armchairs and then he poured out the tea and passed a cup to Mary.

'How is your hand now?' he asked.

'Stinging, but that will wear off,' Mary said quickly. 'What did George say when you'd finished the story?'

'He was quiet for a minute or two and then he said, "Why can't he get on a bus and go and see his friend?"'

'You managed to explain?'

'Yes, a rambling explanation about how long it would take and how much it would cost to do that.'

'George accepted that?'

'After he'd thought about it.' Bill smiled. 'George said if that happened to him he'd get another best friend.'

'Sensible, but it won't be the answer when you tell him about his mother leaving him,' Mary said dryly.

'No,' Bill agreed.

He was quiet for a moment, sipping his tea and looking thoughtful. 'No,' he repeated, 'there's no easy solution is there.' He put his empty cup back on the tray and stood up. 'Now don't worry and look after that hand. I bet it's sore,' he added as he headed for the front door.

'So, when are you going to tell him?' Mary asked again.

'Tomorrow night,' Bill promised.

'Can I put Richard's mind at rest on that point when I go in to see him?'

'Yes, you can do that,' Bill nodded. 'You can also explain why I've delayed. I'm sure he will agree.'

'I hope so,' Mary said. 'I know he's very worried about how George is going to react to the news.'

'I understand,' Bill said quietly. 'Now don't worry. I'll call in on my way home from seeing George tomorrow night and let you know how things are.'

Mary spent the day worrying about little George. Would he understand and be able to accept that he was never going to see his mother again? Or would he brood on it? When she went to visit Richard later that day, her heart thudded as she saw the hopeful, expectant look on his face. She dreaded having to tell him that George still didn't know. Richard took the news stoically. His mouth hardened and the tiny lines underneath his eyes creased as he listened to what his mother was telling him.

'He said he would definitely tell him tonight?'

'Yes, he assured me on that point. He felt it would be the ideal time. George had had time to think about the boy in the story losing his friend, so it wouldn't be too much of a shock for him when he told him that his mother was moving away to another country and he wouldn't be able to see her.'

'I can see his reasoning but I'm not sure about it,' Richard sighed. 'Still, I can't tell him and it's not fair to ask Lucia, so we will have to hope for the best.'

Mary bit her lip. She felt guilty, too. She knew that she ought to be the one to tell George, but she felt she wouldn't be able to stand the sight of his little face crumpling and that once it did, her tears would mingle with his, even if it was for a different reason.

Mary didn't stay at the hospital as long as usual. Richard

kept closing his eyes and no matter what she said to him he only mumbled 'yes' or 'no.' He complained that he wasn't feeling too bright and said he wanted to sleep so Mary took her leave. She promised to call in the next day and let him know if Bill had told George.

She found it difficult to get through the rest of the day. She went to the shops and bought some cake and chocolate biscuits to offer Bill with his cup of tea. She knew he would have preferred homemade cake, but her heart wasn't in it and she couldn't concentrate. She had everything ready and waiting, and the moment she heard his step she brewed the tea so that there would be no delay. She waved him to his armchair the moment he came into the hall and poured out his tea almost before he could sit down.

'Well?' She looked at him expectantly. 'Have you told him?'

Bill sank wearily into the armchair. 'Yes,' he said. 'He knows.'

Mary waited while he took a sip of his tea.

'He took it quite well,' Bill said, then gave a chuckle. 'He listened to what I had to tell him then looked me straight in the eye and said, 'I don't mind, I don't know her very well.'

Mary's hand flew to her mouth to cover her gasp of dismay. 'Oh, poor child,' she said shaking her head from side to side. 'Was that all?'

'No.' Bill took another gulp of tea then put his cup down on the saucer. 'He said, "My daddy hasn't gone as well, has he?" So I quickly reminded him that his daddy was in hospital. Then George said, "Will he go when he is better?" I assured him that his daddy would be coming home and staying with him, just as soon as he was better. He thought about it for a couple of minutes then he asked if Lucia was going away and I was able to put his mind at rest on that point as well. You should have seen his little face when I told him that. It lit up and he said, "So everything will be the same as it is now," and snuggled down in bed to listen to the story he wanted me to read to him.'

'So all is well,' Mary said. 'Richard will be so relieved. I am as well and so very grateful to you for telling him,' she added reaching out and squeezing his hand.

'He's a tough little guy,' Bill said. 'There were no tears, no scene.'

'Well, you had prepared him in a way,' Mary said thought-fully. 'You really do understand children, Bill. You should have been a schoolteacher.'

'It's much too late now for thinking of anything like that,' Bill laughed. 'I must say, though, I am very fond of little George.'

'He likes you,' Mary said. 'Look how he's wanted you to be the one to tell him a bedtime story.'

'That's true. Nevertheless, I shall be glad when Richard is back home and able to resume his duties.'

'You are finding it exhausting?'

'The last couple of nights have been pretty trying.'

'I'm sure they have,' Mary agreed solicitously. 'I hope he won't be asking you too many awkward questions about his mother leaving.'

'I don't think he will mention it again,' Bill told her. 'He's accepted she's gone and that he won't be seeing her again. All he wants now is for Richard to come home.'

'Yes,' Mary said thoughtfully. 'I wonder if I ought to ask if I can take him in to see Richard. I know they don't allow young children in as a rule, but the sister in charge of the ward seems to be very understanding and if I tell her the reason I am sure she would let me do it.'

'It is certainly worth a try,' Bill agreed. 'Although George accepted it when I said Richard would be home as soon as he was better, hearing it from his Dad's own lips would really set his mind at rest.'

'Perhaps you should also have a word with Richard, so that it doesn't come as too much of a shock for him when he sees George at his bedside.'

'Oh,' Mary's face fell, 'I thought it would be a lovely surprise for him.'

Bill shrugged. 'Maybe, or he might think that he is worse than he is and that the hospital have told you to bring George in to see him.'

'Oh dear! I never thought of that. You are right, of course. Richard is still rather fragile and he might draw the wrong conclusions. Thanks Bill, you really do think of everything.'

THIRTY-ONE

Sister Delia Cook was of medium height, tubby, with straight brown hair. She was plain but very efficient. When she smiled her whole face was transformed, and there was a warmth and interest in her brown eyes, as though she really cared about what the other person was telling her.

All the other staff liked her because, although she ran her ward with a firm hand and expected everything to go like clockwork, she was fair in her dealings. Patients adored her because she always had their interests at heart. There were no shortcuts when she was on duty, she never raised her voice, yet nurses jumped to attention when she spoke and carried out her orders to the letter. Mary liked her but, nevertheless, she felt apprehensive about approaching her to ask if she could bring George in to visit his father.

'How old is he? Sister Cook asked.

'Five. He's at the end of his first year at school,' Mary said. 'He's very quiet and well behaved and no one will know he's here.'

Sister Cook smiled gently and shook her head. 'We have strict rules about children as young as that coming into the ward.'

'Yes, I know but this is an emergency,' Mary said.

'An emergency?' Sister Cook frowned. 'Your son is out of danger and making good progress.'

Mary bit her lower lip. She didn't want to parade family problems to the whole world but it looked as though she was going to have to tell Sister Cook why it was so important for George to see his father.

'It's a family matter.' She stopped and hoped that Sister Cook would accept that and not ask any further questions but, as usual, Delia Cook needed to know the details before she would make a decision. There was an uneasy silence. Then Mary looked round quickly to make sure no one else was within earshot. 'It's to do with my son's marriage,' she said in a voice that was little above a whisper.

'Shall we go into my office?' Sister Cook suggested. Without waiting for a response, she led the way towards the small room set aside for her use. 'Now sit down, take your time and tell me what the problem is.' She listened without interruption as Mary told her that Richard's wife, Megan, was a high flying career woman and that at the moment she was in New York and that she had phoned to say that she wouldn't be coming home again. She was leaving Richard for good.

Sister Cook's eyes widened when Mary told her that Megan had said that George was his responsibility and she didn't want to hear from any of them again.

'Does the little boy know that his mother has left them?'

'He was told last night. His big worry was that his father had already left him as well because of course he hasn't seen Richard since he had his accident and was brought in here. I thought that if he could just come in and see his father for a few minutes it would set his mind at rest,' Mary explained.

'Yes, I understand your problem,' Sister Cook said, laying a hand on Mary's arm.

'So, can I bring him in?'

Sister Cook hesitated for a brief second then she nodded her head. 'Yes, of course you may. I can't allow him to stay very long, but he can certainly reassure himself that his father really is in hospital and that he will be home again as soon as he is better. You had better bring him in today while I am on duty,' she added as she stood up and indicated that their chat was over.

Mary thanked her profusely. 'I'll bring him in this afternoon. Will that be all right?'

'Fine. I'm on duty until six o'clock,' Sister Cook told her with a gentle smile.

Mary could hardly wait to tell Bill the good news.

'Do you want me to come with you?' he asked.

Mary hesitated. 'I'm not sure that they would let you in as well,' she said frowning.

'That's all right. I'll wait in the restaurant and you can come along there afterwards and tell me how you got on. I'm sure George would enjoy one of their fizzy drinks and a cake.'

Mary phoned Lucia and explained she would come round and collect George as soon as he came from school.

'I'll bring him straight round to your house,' Lucia volunteered.

'I can't offer to take you with me, they wouldn't allow you into the ward,' Mary explained.

'That is all right. You telephone me when you rerun home and I will collect him,' Lucia said cheerfully.

'No need, I'll drop him off at your door,' Mary promised.

Richard was propped up in bed with his eyes closed the same as he had been the day before when Mary had gone in to see him.

'Richard.' She said his name softly. 'I've brought you a visitor.'

He opened his eyes slowly, almost as if he was too weary to do so. Then when he saw who was there he struggled to sit more upright, which brought a flash of pain that contorted his face for a moment.

'George! Hello, son.' He said in delighted surprise.

George went to fling himself into his father's arms.

'Careful,' Mary whispered. 'Your Daddy's hurt his back remember.'

George hesitated and nodded. Richard put out a hand and drew him closer. 'It's great to see you,' he said ruffling George's hair affectionately.

George stood there wide eyed and nodding, but obviously uneasy.

'Are you all right, son?' Richard asked.

George nodded. Then in a burst he asked, 'You're not going to go away and leave me, are you Daddy?'

'Of course I'm not,' Richard reassured him. 'I've got to stay here until my back is mended but then I'll be home again, don't you worry.'

'I won't, as long as you are coming home again. I don't want you to go and live in America as well,' George told him.

'Now why would I do a thing like that?' Richard said with a tight crooked smile.

'That's where Mummy has gone and you usually go with her when she goes away.'

'Not this time,' Richard promised.

'She's going to stay there for good.'

'Yes, I'm afraid she is,' Richard said.

'I don't mind, I don't like her very much. She always

pushes me away when I try to give her a kiss. I knew she didn't like me.'

'George! You mustn't say things like that, or think them.'

'It's the truth,' George said stubbornly fighting back his tears. 'When are you coming home then?' he asked, in a choked voice.

'I told you, just as soon as my back is mended.'

'How long is that going to take?'

Richard looked away from him to speak to someone who had quietly approached his bedside. 'You'd better ask Sister Cook that question; she might be able to tell you.'

Delia Cook stood at the bottom of the bed studying them both. 'So you are George,' she smiled. 'I'm sure your daddy is very pleased to you.'

'I'm pleased to see him because I miss him,' George told her seriously. 'Can he come home soon?'

'I certainly hope so,' Sister Cook replied. 'It won't be for a while though. His back still has to get better.'

'Can I come in again to see him?' George asked.

Sister Cook hesitated. 'Yes, but not every day. Your daddy has to lie very quietly, but perhaps once a week?'

'That's not very often,' George sighed. 'It's lonely at home without him.'

'Well the more he lies quiet and isn't disturbed the sooner his back will be better,' she told George.

'I suppose so,' he nodded.

'I'm afraid I've come to tell you that you must go now,' Sister Cook went on, 'so say goodbye to your daddy.'

She waited while George kissed Richard and then she took him by the hand and began to walk towards the door with him, leaving Mary to have a few quiet words with Richard.

'I hope Daddy can come home soon,' George said. My mummy's gone away and isn't coming back. I don't mind that so much but I do miss Daddy.'

'I'll try and make him better as soon as possible,' Sister Cook promised as Mary joined them.

Mary thanked her for allowing George onto the ward and asked Sister Cook whether she had meant it when she said George could come in once a week.

'Yes, but try and make it when I am on duty. I'll give you a copy of my rota next time you come in.'

'That's very kind of you,' Mary said gratefully. 'It has meant a lot to be able to put George's mind at rest.' Then, taking George's hand, Mary said. 'Come along, I've another surprise for you. We're meeting Bill in the hospital restaurant.'

While George sat immersed in a chocolate cake, a glass of lemonade and a comic, Mary told Bill what happened. She saw him smile when she mentioned what George had said about Megan.

'It's shocking but, in a way, it is better that he feels as he does because it makes the separation less traumatic for him,' he said gravely.

'Yes, I'm sure you are right,' Mary agreed.

'That Sister Cook is very kind and understanding,' Bill added thoughtfully. 'Richard's in very good hands there.'

They took George home and while Bill read him a story from his comic, Mary explained the situation to Lucia.

'I don't think you are going to have any problems because I don't think George is too upset by what has happened.'

'It certainly doesn't sound like it,' Lucia agreed. 'Children are so honest, aren't they?' she said with a relieved laugh. 'We would try our best not to let other people know how we felt, but he comes straight out with the truth.'

'Yes, and the important thing now is to keep life to his normal routine.'

'Except that he will be able to visit his father.'

'Yes, Sister Cook said he can visit Richard once a week. When I see her tomorrow, I will try and find out if she has any idea at all about how long Richard will be in hospital. I understand he is being seen by Mr Dancer, so she may have some definite news. In the meantime can you manage on your own?'

'As long as I have money for food and household bills I can,' Lucia assured her.

'Don't worry about that, I will make sure that you have what is needed and I will pay your wages regularly as well,' Mary told her.

'Thank you! That is a great relief, you make me very happy,' Lucia told her smiling broadly.

'In a way it is a pity that George is just starting on his school holidays. It means you will have to care for him all day and every day.'

'I understand and that is no problem,' Lucia assured her.

'I will have him some of the time, of course, so that you can have your time off each week,' Mary promised.

'That will be very nice, but only if it fits in with your visits to see your son,' Lucia insisted.

'We'll manage something, so don't worry,' Mary promised. 'I'll come and see you tomorrow and we can work out something that suits us both.'

THIRTY-TWO

Seeing George was the highlight of Richard's day. It was against hospital rules, so it was a secret between Richard, Sister Cook and George. Mary only brought George in when she knew Sister Cook was on duty. To try and make sure that no one on the ward knew, Sister Cook always drew the green curtains around Richard's bed. George loved that.

'It's like going camping and living in a tent,' he said. If any of the other nurses happened to peep inside the curtains to check that everything was in order, George would hold a finger to his lips and shake his head at them. Most of then found it hard to keep from laughing, but they knew that would give the game away, so they nodded back at him and held a finger to their lips, before making sure that the curtains were closed tightly and no one could see in.

George and Sister Cook became great friends. He loved talking to her and asking her questions. She never seemed impatient and he was careful to be very quiet and not to talk as she hurried him down the ward to his father's bedside. Mr Dancer, the surgeon who had operated on Richards's back was both pleased and surprised at the excellent progress he was making.

'It's the special tonic I receive from Sister Cook,' Richard told him.

Mr Dancer frowned, 'Special tonic?'

'She allows my little boy in to see me and that acts like a tonic,' Richard smiled.

'It's certainly working,' Mr Dancer smiled genially.

'The swelling and inflammation around the damaged vertebrae has diminished and fortunately there has been no damage at all to your spinal cord,' he told Richard 'Another two or three weeks and you should be fit enough to be discharged.'

'You mean I will be able to walk?'

'Yes, but you will need to use crutches at first and you will have to attend a clinic for physiotherapy as an outpatient for quite some time,' Mr Dancer warned.

George's school holidays were almost over when Mary was told that Richard was being discharged.

'He will have to come back as an outpatient twice a week for physiotherapy,' Sister Cook told Mary, 'and of course he will need a great deal of rest, because he will tire quiet easily. Are you going to be able to manage that, or do you want him to go into a nursing home?'

'No, I am sure Lucia can cope with all that and I will do all I can to help too,' Mary said.

She knew Richard would hate having to go into a nursing home. He would consider that as an extension of being in hospital. She had already talked things over with Lucia and she was confident that they would be able to nurse Richard.

'Perhaps we should arrange for a carer to come in to help him shower and dress in the morning and to help undress him and get him into bed at night,' Sister Cook suggested.

Mary thought about it and agreed. That would lighten Lucia's work considerably.

The day Richard came home was a day for celebration. With Bill's help, Lucia had managed to bring a single bed downstairs, so that Richard wouldn't have to climb the stairs, and she had made the room as comfortable as possible. George spent the day standing by the front door waiting for the ambulance to arrive. When he saw it coming down the road he ran down the path to the gate, waving wildly so that they wouldn't go to the wrong house.

George danced up and down in excitement, as the back doors of the ambulance were opened and Richard was lowered onto the platform, and then down onto the road in a wheelchair.

'Daddy, Daddy can I ride on your lap?' he called running over towards Richard.

The paramedic pushing the chair put out a hand to stop him.

'It would be too heavy for me to push if you were on it as well,' he said laughing down at George.

Before George could protest, someone took his arm and he looked up in surprise to see that it was Sister Cook.

'I've come to make sure that your Daddy settles in,' she said. 'Can you show me where he will be sleeping?'

'Yes,' George said importantly. 'I helped Lucia get the room ready for him.'

Mary made tea for them all, while Delia Cook explained to Lucia about Richard's medication and the best way of caring for him. Then, together with the paramedics, she went back to the ambulance to return to the hospital.

'I wonder if she accompanies all the patients when they are sent home . . .' Mary mused.

'I doubt it,' Richard said with a smile. 'I think she wanted to see George again.'

Mary doubted that. She felt sure that it was to make sure that Richard was settled in, but she merely nodded and said nothing.

Settling in took Richard several days. He woke early in the morning as he had been used to doing in hospital and Lucia found she had to adjust her own routine to suit his, because he always wanted a cup of tea when he woke up and she had forbidden him to attempt to make one for himself. The carer arrived somewhere between half seven and nine o'clock to shower and dress him, so breakfast was often interrupted.

The routine for the rest of the day depended on how Richard was feeling. George would hover near, ready to accompany him if he wanted to take a walk in the garden or along the street. Twice a week, usually in the mornings, the ambulance came to pick Richard up to take him for a physiotherapy session. When he returned home, he was usually exhausted and wanted to have a sleep.

Mary came to sit with him most days and while she was there, Lucia would nip out and do whatever shopping she had to do. Bill also came and sometimes he would read aloud to both Richard and George, while the two of them lay on Richard's bed curled up together.

George looked forward to the visits from Delia Cook. Usually she was out of uniform when she came to visit and she would sit and play board games with George, and sometimes Richard would join in.

Before Mary left she would check on Richard's progress and encourage him to use his crutches to walk around the house, and to sit out in the garden if the weather was fine. Occasionally, she encouraged him to go for a short walk down the street, but she always went with him, because she knew he still felt nervous about using his crutches. At first, he had found them difficult to use, but with regular practice he gained confidence and, accompanied by George or Delia, he would even walk down the street to the corner of the road and back again.

Mary was delighted and very relieved at the steady progress Richard was making, but when he talked about going back to school – when the new term started – she was doubtful.

'I think you should wait a bit longer, you would find it difficult to cope in the classroom on crutches,' she pointed out.

'By next week I should be able to walk around indoors without them,' Richard told her.

'I would have to use a stick,' he said quickly when he saw the doubt on her face.

Mary shook her head. 'I think we should let Sister Cook be the judge of whether or not you should do that,' she said quietly. 'You don't want to undo all the good you've achieved so far.'

The next time Delia Cook called to see them Mary posed the question about Richard going back to work.

Delia shook her head. 'No, I don't think so. Another month at least, and then only part time. A full day of teaching would be very stressful and might do some harm,' she warned. When Richard started to argue, she said, 'You have an appointment to see Mr Dancer again in a week's time. Why don't you wait until he has assessed you and find out what he says about it?'

'I'm going back to school next week,' George, who had been listening to their exchange, told her proudly.

'Are you! Will you be going into a higher class?'

George nodded. In an excited yet serious voice, he told her all about the new class he would be in and the new teacher he would be getting and Richard's problems were temporarily pushed to one side. George going back to school posed fresh problems for them all. Although Richard maintained that he would be quite all right left on his own while Lucia walked George to school, Mary wouldn't agree.

'No, you're not being left in the house on your own,' she said firmly. 'Supposing you had a fall? If there was no one here to help you then you wouldn't be able to get up.'

'I could simply stay where I was on the floor until Lucia came home. It wouldn't be for very long,' Richard pointed out.

'No!' Mary was adamant.

'So, are you expecting George to go to school on his own?' Richard asked.

'Of course not! I will come round and take him and collect him again in the afternoon when school ends,' Mary said. 'Bill will help. We'll take it in turns. Now don't worry, everything will be organised.'

'I think you are making work for yourself,' Richard argued but Mary refused to listen.

George enjoyed having different people come to meet him each day. His grandmother usually brought a biscuit or some sweets in her handbag, and Bill would tell him stories on the way home. Best of all, though, he liked it when Lucia came, because that meant that Sister Cook was at their house taking care of his Daddy while Lucia came out. Sister Cook always stayed for tea and sometimes she stayed with him and Daddy all evening, while Lucia went out on her own. They would have a wonderful time because Delia Cook would play board games. She had bought him several new ones and showed him how to play them, so that he could play with them when she wasn't there. Most of the time his daddy said he was too tired to play, but Bill always played when he came to collect him from school.

George didn't understand why his daddy was always too tired when they were there together, but not when Sister Cook was there as well. He wondered if they went on playing after he was sent up to bed at seven o'clock. Somehow he didn't think they did, because once he had crept down the stairs to find out and saw they were sitting on the settee holding hands and just talking. He'd been disappointed and scuttled backup to bed before they found him.

Richard continued to make good progress, although he tired very easily. He was still using his crutches whenever he went out of the house, but managed to get around indoors with a stick.

His hopes of going back to work after the half term break were dashed by Mr Dancer who said it would be detrimental for him to do so. Richard was very disappointed, but Delia explained the complications that could arise if he did too much too soon. Although he was still frustrated, her quiet reasoning made him accept the situation. Delia had now become a firm family friend. Bill thought she spoke a lot of sound sense, Mary liked her calm, firm approach when dealing with George and the way she persuaded Richard to be reasonable, when either of them became argumentative or stubborn.

She knew she could never have dealt with them like that. Richard's accident and the extra work it had entailed had made her feel her years. There was another problem that worried her. She was quite sure that Bill had not been attending the eye clinic as often as he should have done and she felt quite guilty about it. She knew she had been devoting more time to Richard and his needs, and overlooked Bill's AMD and had stopped checking with him whether or not he had received an appointment.

She knew he hated having to go there and suspected that he had ignored any letters from the hospital. She wasn't at all sure that he would confess to having missed appointments and she wondered what was the best way of dealing with the matter.

THIRTY-THREE

It was Bonfire Night and they were all gathered in Richard's garden. Over the past week, with Bill and George doing most of the work, they had built an enormous bonfire. There was a guy perched on the very top, dressed in an assortment of Bill's old clothes. Mary had spent the day baking and she had brought along sausage rolls, rock cakes, bread pudding and gingerbread for them all.

Before she came out into the garden, Lucia laid up a tray of mugs ready to make coffee as soon as it was needed. There was also beer for the two men and lemonade for George. George was dancing around excitedly. Sister Cook was there as well and George knew she had a brought a box of fireworks, because he'd met her at the gate and she'd let him carry them for her. Richard was playing safe and using his crutches, because he felt more confident on them in the dark than merely using a stick.

The air was thick with smoke from neighbouring bonfires and George let out a whoop of delight when Richard put a light to theirs. After a couple of minutes, the flames were leaping up into the sky, licking around the bottom of the guy. Richard and Bill were in charge of the fireworks. George had a sparkler which he was holding in his gloved hand and waving around enthusiastically. They had just let off the last firework; a rocket that went high into the air and exploded with a great bang, sending a thousand coloured stars showering into the air, when they heard the phone ringing.

'Surely no one is ringing to complain,' Richard frowned. 'Everybody else is letting fireworks off.'

Lucia went to answer it and when she came back she was shaking so much that Mary couldn't understand what she was saying.

'Calm down, Lucia,' Delia said and placed an arm around the trembling figure. 'Who was it on the phone?'

Lucia shook her head from side to side. 'My mother, she has had a heart attack,' she gulped back her tears, 'they say I must go to her fast because she is in hospital, desperately ill.'

'Oh Lucia! I'm so sorry,' Delia said, holding her closer, in an effort to calm her. 'Of course you must go, we understand. I'll call the airport and see if we can get you a flight.'

Lucia shook her head. 'I don't know what to do. I can't leave here, Mr Richard is still not well enough to look after himself and George.'

'We're here and can take care of him, Lucia,' Mary said, 'so of course you must go to your mother right away.'

Lucia shook her head. 'You are very kind but it will be too much for you to do,' she protested.

'I'm here as well,' Delia said. 'I have just started a fortnight's holiday and I have no plans to go away, so I can stay here and look after Richard and George.'

Lucia was speechless. She hugged Delia and then went over and hugged Mary.

'Come on indoors, Mary said. 'I'll help you pack a bag while Delia phones for a taxi. Richard, you check the time of the next flight and see if you can book a ticket on it for Lucia. Bill, will you and George start tidying up out here and make sure George doesn't get too near the fire?'

For the next hour they were all busy carrying out Mary's orders. When the taxi arrived, Delia said she would go to the airport with Lucia to make sure she boarded the plane safely, because she was in such a state that she didn't think she would be able to cope.

'I hope she will have calmed down and can manage at the other end,' Richard said. 'She seems almost as worried about her sister as she is about her mother.'

'That's because her sister is not able to look after herself, she is retarded,' Mary explained.

'I didn't know that,' Richard said in surprise.

'Apparently, she has been since birth. Lucia sends part of her wages home each month to help her mother to manage.'

'Whew!' Richard gave a low whistle. 'What will happen to the sister if their mother dies then?'

'I have no idea, Mary told him. 'I suppose they have care

homes over there, but I'm not sure if Lucia would be able to afford to put her in one of those.'

Richard shook his head but said no more.

'Shall I make us all another hot drink?' Bill suggested.

'That might be a good idea,' Mary agreed. 'We'll come inside and have it. I think we can finish clearing up out here tomorrow.'

'I'll come round in the morning and deal with the ashes from the bonfire,' Bill said.

'I think it is time George was tucked up in bed,' Mary said. 'As soon you've had a hot drink,' she added as she saw he was about to protest.

'Can I have some bread pudding as well?' George asked.

'Not at this time of night, you wouldn't be able to sleep afterwards. You can have a small piece cake or a biscuit,' Richard told him. George knew from the sound of his father's voice that if he didn't accept that he might be sent to bed with nothing, so reluctantly he agreed.

'Will you save me some for tomorrow?' he asked, looking pleadingly at his grandmother. 'You make the best bread pudding in the world.'

George was safely in bed and already fast asleep before Delia came back from the airport. She reported that Lucia had caught her plane and she seemed confident that Lucia would be able to cope after landing. She had euros for the taxi at the other end and would be able to get one right outside the airport. She had promised to phone the next day after she had seen her mother and let them know how things were.

'This is going to cause problems,' Mary said shaking her head.

'Not at the moment,' Delia told her. 'I really am starting my holidays and I can move in and take care of Richard and George, until we know what the situation is.'

'That's very kind of you,' Mary said gracefully 'but surely you had plans? When you are working as hard as you do you must look forward to your holiday more than most people.'

Delia smiled and her brown eyes softened as she looked at Richard. 'No, only to visit Richard and George, so it will be easier for me if I move in,' she murmured.

*   *   *

The next day, Mary was glad that she had agreed to Delia's suggestion. Lucia phoned as she had promised to do, but the news was not good. Her mother was unlikely to recover from her heart attack and for the moment Lucia felt she had to stay with her sister. Three days later, Lucia phoned again to say that her mother had died.

For the moment, it looked as though Delia would be spending her entire holiday looking after Richard and George, which was a relief for Mary. She was concerned, however, about what was going to happen when Delia's holiday was over, because normally she lived in the nurses' quarters at the hospital. Delia solved the problem by saying that she was moving in permanently to take care of Richard and George. She would be keeping her job at the hospital, of course, but Richard was now so much more mobile that, between them, they would be able to manage as long as either Bill or Mary took George to school and collected him in the afternoon.

The new routine worked well, until Delia went on night duty. Mary worried because Richard was alone with George all night.

'Delia's home before we get up in the morning,' Richard laughed. 'She gets our breakfast and helps me have George ready for when you collect him for school.'

'What happens if George wakes up in the night?' Mary asked.

'He either takes himself to the toilet or comes in to me,' Richard told her. 'He's six now, he's not a baby.'

'I know that but children sometimes have bad dreams,' Mary murmured.

'He rarely has one but if he does then he comes in to me,' Richard repeated. 'Stop fussing, Mother, I am practically better and I will be going back to school in the new year.'

Things didn't go quite so smoothly for Delia. Living out, away from the hospital, meant she wasn't available if there was an emergency.

'I can leave you a telephone number to contact me and I can be here in twenty minutes,' Delia told Matron when she took her to task about living out.

'Twenty minutes!' Matron said in a frosty voice. 'The emergency will be over by then, Sister Cook.' It became a bone of contention between them and, although no one ever phoned Delia and asked her to come in for an emergency, her availability was always being brought up at staff meetings. Usually, Delia stayed quiet, although she knew quite well who the sister was, who had absented herself whenever Matron brought the matter up. Finally, however, she cracked and when Matron made her allusions to "staff who were out of reach" Delia said, 'Why don't you say my name, Matron, so that everyone knows who you are talking about?'

Matron stiffened and her eyes narrowed. 'You must be feeling guilty, Sister Cook,' she snapped.

'No, I don't feel guilty,' Delia responded. I have left a telephone number with you, but you have never contacted me, so I don't know that there has been an emergency until I come in the next day and hear people talking about it.'

'Precisely! You don't even know about it! Sister Cook, your first duty is to your patients and not to your relatives. I think it is time you reconsidered your living arrangements.'

Delia was incensed. In the heat of the moment she retorted, 'Very well, and I'll reconsider my working arrangements as well.'

Matron seized the opportunity. 'I accept your resignation, Sister Cook.'

Before Delia could say that she hadn't meant that, Matron had swept her out of the room and Delia was left feeling flustered and disconsolate. She knew everyone else in the room was looking at her and one or two were exchanging whispered comments. Head held high and without a word to anyone, she stormed out. She wished she did still have a room she could go to, but there was nowhere to go except the cloakroom. Holding back her tears she went straight there, collected her coat and an umbrella she had left several days before, and walked out of the hospital heading for Richard's home.

He was still trying to tidy up and he was very surprised to see her in the middle of the morning.

'On holiday again?' he quipped when she walked in the door. Then he saw the look on her face and realised that something traumatic had happened.

With her head on his shoulder, he smoothed her thick dark hair and tried to calm her as she gave way to her pent-up feelings. When she told him what had happened he felt stunned.

'What are you going to do?' he asked, when she had calmed down and was sitting with the cup of strong coffee he'd made for her.

'I don't know.'

'Will Matron forgive and forget and take you back?' Richard asked.

'I shouldn't think so. Too many people witnessed our spat.'

'What about if you apologise?'

'Apologise! I wouldn't dream of doing that. That would put me in her power even more. No, I have left and that's that. I can get work as an agency nurse.'

'Agency nurse!' Richard raised his eyebrows. 'You are a fully qualified Sister.'

'I think nurse is the most I can hope for, if I am working for an agency,' Delia told him dryly. 'The only way to retain my Sister status would be to go to another hospital, and I'm pretty sure if they asked Matron for a reference, she would make sure they wouldn't take me.'

THIRTY-FOUR

Mary was very worried about Bill. No matter when she asked him if he'd had an appointment from the hospital about further treatment for his eyes, he always denied it. He wasn't very convincing though and she suspected that he was ignoring the letters and not keeping the appointments.

There were so many signs that Bill's eyes were getting worse. He constantly bumped into things; he often missed the curb or the bottom step and he had started knocking things over, like cups and glasses. Mary didn't know whether it was because he didn't see them or because he misjudged where they were. She wasn't at all sure whether it was safe for him to be taking George to school, because she didn't think he could see cars were approaching and she was afraid the pair of them might get knocked down crossing the road.

She kept going over things in her mind, wondering how she could find out, because she was sure he wasn't telling her the truth. Finally, she hit on a plan; she phoned the appointments office at the hospital and asked when Mr Thompson's next appointment was.

'Next appointment? Well, we haven't made one because he hasn't attended the last three,' the woman on the other end said in an annoyed voice.

'I'm sorry about that but I'll make sure he comes to the next one,' Mary promised.

'Well he's at the very bottom of the waiting list now, of course, so it may be months before we can see him.'

'Oh dear, I hope not,' Mary said sweetly. 'He really is having trouble. Haven't you any cancellations?'

There was a long silence then the woman said, 'Tomorrow morning at ten o'clock.'

'Fine, he'll be there,' Mary promised.

When she told Bill he looked very taken aback. 'How did you know I hadn't been keeping them?' he asked in surprise.

'I know the routine. Sam had AMD remember, so I know that the longest you wait between appointments is a month or six weeks.'

Bill looked glum. 'It's pointless going,' he muttered.

'No it's not and I'm coming with you. Come straight to my place after you've taken George to school and we'll have a cup of tea while we wait for the taxi.'

The eye department at the hospital was very busy and they had to wait for almost half an hour before Bill's name was called. Mary waited while they put drops in to enlarge the pupils, to check how far down the chart he could read and test the pressure in his eyes. As she expected, when he came out of that surgery they had to move to a different waiting room. That waiting room was also very full, but they managed to find adjacent chairs and sat waiting for Bill's name to be called. This time he had to go into a small office, and sit in front of a machine while the operator took pictures of the back of each of his eyes.

That done he returned to the chair by Mary to wait to be called to see the specialist. When his name was called again, Mary stood up as well.

'I'm coming with you,' she said when he stopped in surprise. 'I want to hear what they tell you.'

She thought Bill was going to argue and make a scene but he shrugged resignedly and let her go with him. The news was not good. As Mary had suspected, the AMD was bad in both of Bill's eyes and the fact that he had not been having regular treatment had made things worse.

'If you had come back sooner, then I would have been able to treat your eyes and minimise the damage. As it is, most of the central vision has now been damaged. I am going to make an appointment for you to have those injections as soon as possible.' He looked across at Mary, 'will you ensure he attends?' he said sternly.

Bill was very quiet when they went to the hospital restaurant afterwards for a cup of tea, while they waited for the taxi.

'I suppose it looks as though I've been rather foolish, but I didn't think it was all that important and you had so many other problems that it seemed selfish to bother you.'

'Stop making excuses. You could have attended without me,' Mary said crossly.

'I know, I know,' Bill admitted. 'I'll attend the next one, I promise,' he assured her.

'Good, and I'll come with you.'

'Thanks, but you don't have to do that,' he mumbled.

'I rather think I should. You won't be able to see very well afterwards.'

Bill reached out and took her hand and squeezed it. 'I don't know how I would manage without you,' he murmured. 'For that matter, I don't know any of us would,' he added thoughtfully as he stirred his tea and took a biscuit from the packet Mary had bought. 'It's getting more difficult for you. It was bad enough that Lucia had to leave so suddenly, but now Delia's lost her job, because she was trying to help out, and that is something else which is going to cause difficulties.'

'Yes, that is a shame,' Mary agreed. 'You've done your share though, Bill, and we are grateful. George thinks you are his hero and he's always talking about you. He looks forward to his bedtime story so much, but I think we will have to call a halt to that. Richard can read to him himself now and it must be a strain on your eyes trying to read in the evening.'

'I enjoy story time as much as he does,' Bill told her. 'We usually have a chat as well as a story.'

'You can have your chat on the way to school in the mornings,' Mary smiled.

'Oh don't worry we have one then as well. He's a fine lad and I'm sure Richard is proud of him.'

'I think you are probably right,' Mary agreed. 'It would have broken his heart if Megan had taken him away.'

'Have you heard from her since?' Bill asked as he drained his cup.

'No, not a word. Her solicitor has been in touch with Richard's solicitor, but I'm not sure at what stage things are. There's definitely going to be a divorce though.'

'The sooner it's all settled the better,' Bill agreed.

Mary smiled and said nothing. She had spent so many sleepless nights worrying about what the outcome was going to be that she didn't want to stir up all her uneasy thoughts again. At the moment, she had managed to push them to the back of her mind, but she was well aware that it would only take a chance remark to bring them all flooding back. Her greatest fear was that Megan might change her mind and decide that she wanted George after all.

So far, George had remained unperturbed by the fact that he hadn't seen his mother for weeks and that he had been told she wasn't coming back. His days seem to be filled with helping to take care of his father and his excitement in having Delia staying with them. He still liked Bill to read him a story at night, but if Bill felt he couldn't make it then George listened to Richard telling him a story quite happily. He had also accepted Lucia's absence. Delia had more than amply filled her place in his life. School took up a lot of his time, of course, and he enjoyed learning. Every afternoon, he came home eager to tell them what he had been doing or to tell them about something he had learned. He had been given quite a big part in the end of term Christmas play and so he

had his lines to learn. They had all promised to be there on
the big night.

'You won't know who I am because I will be dressed up,'
he told them, forgetting that he had already told them the name
of the character he was playing.

He was also excited about Christmas. He had written so many
letters to Santa Claus and asked for so many different things,
that even Richard was confused about what to get him.

'We don't want the house cluttered up with presents he never
looks at or isn't interested in playing with after Christmas Day.
I'm in favour of one really big present, and then a stocking and
perhaps a present at the dinner table.'

'You can't limit him like that,' Delia told him. 'We all want
to give him a Christmas present. I know Bill has a book of
bedtime stories in mind, probably ones he wants to read,' she
added with a smile. 'Mary will want to give him something
and I know she has been knitting away for weeks, making
him something special to wear on Christmas Day. I certainly
want to give him a nice present and, as you have just said, so
do you.'

'That's four special presents for a start,' Richard grumbled.

'Yes, and he'll probably get small ones from friends at school.'

'Does that mean we will have to take him shopping, so that
he can buy presents for his friends?' Richard frowned.

'It certainly does, and I think that perhaps this Saturday might
be as good a time as any. If we leave it any later all the good
things will have gone, the shops will be packed and there will
be queues a mile long.'

'Well good luck to you,' Richard grimaced. 'I'm glad I'm not
fit to come.'

'Rubbish!' Of course you are,' Delia told him. 'Being in a
crowd will be good practice for when you go back to school
in January.'

Richard tried to argue, but Delia was having none of it and,
to his annoyance, when his mother called in later that day, she
agreed with Delia when they told her about the proposed
shopping trip.

'With so much happening before Christmas he will be tired
of things before the big day,' Richard stated.

'Not a bit of it,' Delia told him. 'He still has to help put up the decorations at home and I know he is planning to come round here, to help your mother to make paper chains to go up in her living room,' she added giving Mary a wink.

'Where are you planning to go?' Mary asked. 'There's not very much of a selection of toys in the village. We used to have a toy shop here but, like so many of the other small independent shops, it didn't pay so it was closed down.'

'We thought of going to Windsor,' Delia said.

'What a splendid idea. George will love seeing the castle, all the bright lights and the wonderful window displays in the town.'

'Would you like to come as well?' Delia asked her. She felt a little guilty and wondered how Mary felt about her organising the trip, when in the past Mary could have been the one to do so.

'No thank you!' Mary shook her head. 'I'm not walking too well at the moment and I find Windsor a little bit hilly and its cobbled streets rather difficult. I think the three of you will do very well on your own. George will love seeing the castle, but walking up the hill to see it would be too much for me.'

'If you are sure,' Delia said.

'Yes, I am quite sure,' Mary said with conviction. 'Why don't you all come back to my place for tea afterwards? I will invite Bill for tea as well and then George can tell us all about it and show us all the things he has bought for his friends.'

The idea of them enjoying tea together did not work out as well as Mary had hoped. George was overexcited, Richard was tired and Delia was exhausted.

'You were quite right,' she told Mary as she sank into an armchair and eased her shoes off. 'Windsor is rather hilly and those cobbles certainly make your feet ache. It's been years since I was there and I had forgotten how tiring it could be.'

'At least you weren't trying to walk with a stick,' Richard pointed out. 'The number of times it twisted or slipped, it's a wonder I didn't fall.'

'No, you did very well,' Delia told him. 'It proves how much progress you've made. Perhaps you could try very short walks without your stick,' she suggested.

His handsome face brightened for a moment and all signs of tiredness vanished. 'Only if you are with me, so that I can grab your arm if I need to,' he told her.

'I could walk with you,' George said. 'I can walk like a soldier.' He wriggled out of his chair and began marching up and down the room, stamping his feet each time he turned, imitating the soldiers he had seen on guard duty at Windsor Castle.

'Stop that, you'll wear the carpet out,' Richard said grabbing his arm. 'Tell your grandma about the presents you bought for your school friends.'

George shook his head and pulled himself free. 'No, they're a secret,' he said. 'All the presents I bought today are secret,' he said stubbornly.

'Don't be cheeky!' Richard said crossly.

'Well, they are,' George persisted defiantly.

'In that case then, I think it is time for us to go home,' Delia said quickly before an argument could start between George and Richard.

'Thank you for tea Mary, sorry to leave you with all the washing up, but I think these two boys have had a long day and need their bed.'

THIRTY-FIVE

The morning that Bill was due at the eye hospital, Mary woke up with a cold. She made a cup of tea and took it back to bed, but she knew she couldn't stay there, because they had to be at the hospital by ten o' clock. As she showered and started to get dressed she felt terrible. Her head ached and she could hardly breathe. She didn't feel like making porridge, so she put a slice of bread into the toaster.

As she sat eating it, she wondered what she ought to do. Was it fair to go to the hospital with Bill when she might pass it on to sick people, or even to Bill? But if she didn't go with him, could she trust him to go on his own? He didn't need much of an excuse not to go, she thought gloomily.

Since he was having injections in both eyes and would struggle to see afterwards, she didn't think he could manage on his own. She took a couple of paracetamol tablets to try and ease the pain in her head and hoped that, if that went, she could work out what to do for the best. She wondered if Richard was fit enough to go with him. After all, it was only a case of seeing him from the taxi into the hospital and then phoning for a taxi to bring them home again afterwards.

When she phoned Richard it was Delia who answered the phone. Mary told her what the situation was and Delia immediately offered to take Bill.

'I'm sure Richard could manage but he isn't up yet and I am up and dressed.'

'It means leaving Richard on his own,' Mary said worriedly.

'Richard will be fine. As I said, he isn't even up yet, and if I take up the newspaper to him and another cup of tea, he'll probably stay where he is until mid-morning and I'll be home again by then.'

Mary glanced at the clock and knew she had to make a quick decision. 'If you wouldn't mind, Delia.'

'Of course I don't mind,' Delia told her.

'I'll phone for a taxi then and ask them to pick you up first, and then Bill.'

'You go back to bed, I'll arrange that,' Delia told her briskly. 'Now, don't protest, there isn't time. You make yourself a hot drink and go back to bed for a couple of hours.'

Bill was surprised to find that it was Delia, not Mary, in the taxi when it stopped for him.

'Is she all right?' he asked and his brow furrowed as he heard Delia's explanation that Mary had a cold starting.

'Well it's best she stayed home,' he agreed and it's good of you to take her place. I could always have phoned the hospital and tell them that I wasn't coming,' he added.

'That's exactly what was worrying Mary,' Delia told him, hiding a smile, 'she was afraid you might do that if she left you to go on your own.'

Delia took a deep breath as they want into the hospital. The familiar smells and the sight of nurses in their crisp uniform were like coming home after a long absence. Her eyes shone with interest as she accompanied Bill to the eye department reception desk. Bill knew the routine and showed Delia where to wait for him while he went for tests and drops to prepare his eyes for treatment.

When he was called into the surgery for his injection, he shook his head when Delia offered to accompany him and told her he would rather she waited for him outside. She was sitting there, deep in thought, reminiscing about her own nursing days, when someone spoke her name. Surprised she looked up, then gasped when she saw a familiar face, a woman wearing a sister's uniform, standing at her side.

'Peggy? Peggy Bristow? Heavens, we haven't seen each other for about ten years,' Delia exclaimed staring into the green eyes that locked with her own and showed equal surprise.

'That's true,' Peggy smiled. 'So how are you and what are you doing here? Not eye trouble, I hope?'

'No, no,' Delia said quickly. 'I have brought an elderly man in for treatment.'

'I see!' Peggy's eyebrows went up. 'So why aren't you in uniform?'

'He's not a patient, he's a family friend,' Delia explained.

Peggy nodded understandingly. 'You are still nursing though?'

Delia shook her head, her eyes lining with tears.

'Oh, why ever not?' Peggy asked in surprise.

Delia hesitated for a moment and then in a sudden need to tell someone who would understand, she found herself telling Peggy the whole sad saga of how she had been forced to leave her job as a sister.

'Whew!' Peggy whistled softly. 'That was tough. So what are you doing now?'

Delia shrugged. 'Nothing at all,' she confessed.

'So how are you living? If I remember, none of your family is still alive. Your mother died while we were still training.'

'That's right,' Delia acknowledged, 'and of course my dad died several years before that.'

'So however are you getting by? You're not married are you?'

Again, Delia shook her head. 'No, I'm looking after a friend who has been sick.' She related the story of Richard's accident;

how his wife had left him and his housekeeper had been called away, because her own mother died and she had to go back to Italy to care for her sister.

Peggy listened in silence. 'Is this Richard recovering from his accident?' she asked.

'Oh yes, he's going back to work after Christmas. He's a schoolteacher so he should be able to manage to do that without too many problems.'

'So you will be redundant again,' Peggy mused.

'Well, not exactly. He has a child, a boy of seven, so he still needs someone to be there when the child comes home from school.'

Peggy frowned. 'If this Richard is a teacher then surely he will finish work around the same time as the child comes out of school?' she commented.

Delia looked at her startled. She hadn't thought of that.

'Anyway,' Peggy added, 'because both parents are usually working these days, they seem to have after-school clubs to keep the children occupied, until one or other of the parents can come and collect them.'

Delia stared at her in silence. She hadn't thought of that either, but now the possibility that her help might no longer be needed by Richard alarmed her.

As if reading her thoughts, Peggy said, 'We have a vacancy for a staff nurse, so why don't you come here. I know you were a sister and it would be a bit of a come down, but it is better than nothing and it would get you back into circulation again.'

Delia looked doubtful. 'I was thinking of applying for agency work,' she admitted, but working here would be ideal. The only thing is, I don't think my old Matron would be willing to give me a reference.'

'Don't worry about that,' Peggy told her. 'If you are interested then leave it with me. It might take a few weeks to organise, but I'd say the job is as good as yours.'

'Really?' Delia looked both pleased and surprised.

'Very much so,' Peggy assured her. 'Look, I must go, I have work to do, people to organise, you know how it is. Sit tight where you are at the moment, give me your details and I'll be in touch. As I said, it may take a week or two to organise.'

When Bill came out of the surgery half an hour later, Delia was still feeling bemused by what had happened. She and Peggy Bristow had trained together and shared a room. As well as confiding in each other about all their fears and sharing grumbles about what was expected of them, they had become firm friends. After they had qualified, they had both been disappointed when they had been sent to different hospitals, which were so far apart that they knew visiting each other was out of the question. They promised each other that they would keep in touch, but they never did apart from sending each other cards at Christmas and on each other's birthday. Even this had stopped about five years ago.

Delia pushed aside thoughts of Peggy and the past from her mind. She hoped something would come out of Peggy's promise to get her a job whilst Bill, on the arm of a nurse, was brought over to where she was sitting.

'Wait at least ten minutes to make sure he is all right before you leave,' the nurse told her. She handed Delia some drops and gave her careful instructions about putting them in. 'We will make an appointment to see him again in four weeks' time,' the nurse told her.

'It will only be a check-up next time, Mr Thompson,' she said patting Bill's arm reassuringly.

Delia waited ten minutes, as she had been told to do, then she asked Bill if he was ready to go.

'You don't feel giddy or anything, do you?' she checked.

'I'm fine, stop fussing,' he mumbled and stood up.

'Good.' She took his arm and led him through the reception area towards the exit. 'Sit here while I arrange for a taxi,' she said indicating a seat.

'Aren't we going to the restaurant for a cup of tea first?' he asked.

'Do you feel up to doing that?' Delia questioned.

'Of course I do. Mary and I always have lunch here when she comes with me,' he insisted.

Delia hesitated. She thought he was probably referring to the times when he came for a check-up, not when he'd had an injection.

'They do wonderful jacket potatoes,' he told her. 'And they have all sorts of different fillings, there's bound to be something you like.'

'I wanted to get you home before the anaesthetic wears off and your eye starts hurting,' she told him.

'Don't you worry about that. It will hurt far more if I have to try and get myself some dinner when I get home.'

She had to admit the menu sounded tempting so, reluctantly, she agreed. She could see his point that it would be far easier for him to eat now, rather than having to make something for himself when he got home. He was quite right too; the jacket potatoes were the best she'd ever tasted and were served with a crisp salad, as well as the filling of their choice. The moment they had finished eating she insisted on calling the taxi. Before they left the hospital, Delia had requested a pair of dark glasses for Bill and now insisted that he should put them on.

'The sun is really bright and it's so low in the sky at this time of year that you won't be able to stand its glare. These will protect your eyes,' she told him.

'I'm not wearing those things,' he said, getting increasingly grumpier as the anaesthetic wore off and his eyes felt increasingly gravelly.

'No, I think you should wear them. Mary said you found them helpful when she brought you for the injection,' Delia asserted.

He pushed her hand and the glasses away irritably.

'Come on,' she insisted. 'I did what you asked and had lunch at the hospital, so now you do what I am asking and wear them,' she said firmly.

Bill gave in and, by the time they were half way home, he admitted that he found the glasses were a great help in the bright sun.

'Can I hang on to them for a couple of days?' he asked when he reached home.

'Of course you can,' Delia told him. 'In fact, you can keep them for good. You might find them very useful when your eyes are tired as well as when you are in bright sunshine.'

THIRTY-SIX

Delia Cook hummed happily to herself as she tidied the sitting room in Richard Wilson's house, in readiness for putting up the decorations when George came home from school.

This was going to be to be the best Christmas any of them had ever known, she told herself. George was happy at school, Mary's cold was better, Richard would be starting back at work when the new school term began in January and Bill didn't have to go back to the hospital for a check-up for his eyes until the end of January. Above all, there was every possibility that she would be back working in a hospital again in the New Year.

Although she was looking forward to being back in the heart of things, she tried not to be too optimistic about it. A sister didn't have the power to hire and fire and, although she knew Peggy Bristow would do all she could to persuade whoever did have the authority to do so, there was only a slim chance that they would listen to her. She knew hospitals too well, after working in one for over ten years, and she knew there would be raised eyebrows when they heard that an experienced sister was applying for a job as a staff nurse.

It didn't make sense and they would delve into her background to discover what her misdeed had been to cause her to be sacked. When they heard the reason, that it had been because she had insisted on living out so that she could care for a friend, they might doubt her loyalty and decide it was too much of a risk to employ her. She cleared a corner of the sitting room so as to leave enough space for Richard to put up the Christmas tree that he had already bought and which was still in the garage. He said they already had lights for it, so he would put those on and then leave the rest of the decorating for her and George to do. Yes, this really was going to be a good Christmas for them all, she thought happily. January would be the start of something new for all of them. She went out to the garage to see how Richard was getting on.

'Almost finished,' he told her. 'I can never understand it; all the lights were working when I packed them away last year and now when I go to put them on the tree again there are three broken bulbs.'

'Have you got new ones or do you want me to go the shop for some?' Delia asked.

'No, I've replaced them and now I'm going to bring the tree indoors. Have you made a space for it?'

'I have in the sitting room.'

'Good! What about a coffee then?' he said in a pleading voice. 'A workman needs his coffee to keep going, you know.'

'It's already on,' Delia told him. 'I'll help you get the tree inside and then we'll have it.'

They had just erected the tree to their mutual satisfaction when the doorbell rang.

'Who on earth can that be?' Richard frowned.

Delia went to answer the door and stared in astonishment when she saw their visitor.

'Peggy! This is a surprise. Come on in.'

Peggy hadn't waited for an invitation; she was already in the hall. She must have found Richard's house from the details Delia had given her, to apply for the staff nurse job.

'Can I smell coffee?' she asked sniffing appreciatively.

'Yes, have you time to stay and have one with us?'

'Too true I have,' Peggy said unbuttoning her coat.

'Who is it, Delia?'

Peggy's green eyes widened with interest as she heard Richard's voice. 'You have a man friend here,' she grinned accusingly.

'Yes, come and meet Richard. I look after him and his little boy George.'

'Of course, I remember you telling me about him,' Peggy enthused. You're the man who had the gliding accident,' she said holding out her hand to Richard.

Delia turned away, wondering how Richard would feel at finding out that she had been talking about him, especially the fact that she had discussed his accident with an outsider.

'Why don't you two go through to the sitting room and I'll bring the coffee in?' she suggested.

'Good idea, this way,' Richard said, leading Peggy towards the sitting room.

Delia took her time to fill a plate with biscuits and poured out the coffee. She wasn't at all sure whether Peggy took milk and sugar or merely milk so she put the sugar bowl and an extra spoon on the tray. What if she likes it black? She thought as she reached the sitting room door. She smiled brightly as she went in; ready to make inconsequential chatter, but neither of them looked at her. They were deeply immersed in a discussion about gliding tactics. Delia listened for a moment in silence; she didn't understand what they were talking about. She placed the coffee in front of them and handed out the biscuits. Peggy waved the plate away; Richard took two and sat munching in between his earnest conversation with Peggy.

'I didn't know you ever went gliding,' Delia said loudly and pointedly, determined to draw their attention from each other.

'Oh, I don't *go* gliding,' Peggy admitted, 'but I am often up at Booker. I use one of the helicopters.'

'You do!' Delia looked amazed. 'What for, joy rides?'

Peggy didn't answer, she was once more deep in a discussion with Richard about thermals, cumulus clouds, wind speed and so many other things that Delia didn't understand.

Delia sat back and sipped her coffee, studying Richard and Peggy. They were obviously interested in each other and she felt a sudden spasm of jealousy. Up until now, she had regarded Richard as a patient, someone she was looking after. The fact that she was living in his house, or that he had a small boy, was simply part of the baggage that went with his care. She had never thought about him as a man who might be interested in women.

Perhaps it was because she knew all about Megan, Delia thought, and because of that she felt sorry for him. But why should she? It was Megan who had chosen to leave and, as far as she could understand, there had been no argument other than the fact that Megan didn't want a husband who might be a cripple for the rest of his life. What if Megan saw him now and realised she had been wrong in her assumption, would she

change her mind and want to come home? From what both
Mary and Bill had said, Richard had been an exceptionally
tolerant husband, never complaining when Megan took off for
Paris, Milan or New York at a moment's notice and left him to
be responsible for George. True, Lucia had been there in those
days but, even so, not many husbands would have tolerated
such a lifestyle. Did that mean he was a doormat?

Looking at him now, in animated conversation with Peggy,
she hardly thought so.

Suddenly another spark of jealousy shot through her. Why
was she sitting here letting Peggy arouse his interest like this?
If she wasn't careful, Peggy might move in and take Megan's
place. Delia shook herself. She was being fanciful. Peggy was
a visitor, it was the first time she had met Richard and she
was only being polite by showing an interest in him. Peggy,
standing up and holding out her hand to Richard, stirred Delia
out of her uneasy thoughts.

'I must go Mr Wilson, I am on duty at the hospital in half
an hour.'

'Call me Richard, please,' he protested. 'I've enjoyed meeting
you, you must come again soon.'

'Thank you, but I must go now,' Peggy repeated, 'after I've
set Delia's mind at rest about the job.'

'Job?' Richard looked bemused.

Peggy turned to Delia. 'You've got it. Starts in January,
I'll see you again soon and tell you what the hours are and
so on.'

'Really!' Delia felt her antagonism towards Peggy melt.
Peggy really had managed to get her taken on. She had refused
to let herself think she would be successful and yet it was hers
after all.

'Yes, you start as a senior staff nurse,' Peggy told her. 'Brilliant,
isn't it?'

After she had left, Richard said, 'Nice woman, but what was
all that about a job?'

'I met her when I took Bill to the eye hospital,' Delia said,
'she's a sister there and she was saying that they had a vacancy.
When I told her the story of how I was no longer nursing she
asked me if I was interested.'

'Working as a staff nurse? That's lower than a sister, isn't it?'

Delia shrugged. 'Yes, it is, but I don't mind. It will be good to get back into uniform and the hospital routine again.'

Richard looked at her quizzically. 'I thought you were happy here with us.'

'I am. I'm very happy,' she affirmed.

'Then why do you want to leave?'

'You will be back at work next month, so you won't need looking after anymore. You can walk now without a stick.'

'What about George?' he frowned.

'What about George? You will be able to look after him with the help of your mother and Bill.'

'He's used to you being here though, he'll be heartbroken.'

It was on the tip of her tongue to say that George hadn't missed either his mother or Lucia, but she felt that was rather underhand, so she merely smiled and gave a little deprecating shrug. Richard stood up and, hands in his pockets, paced the room.

'I don't want you to leave,' he sighed, shaking his head from side to side. 'I'm used to having you here as well. I've never felt so settled and contented. Can't you rethink the matter?'

Delia felt her colour rising. He'd said he would miss her, yet she had always thought that he barely noticed her presence and that when he did he took it for granted. Remembering how animated he had been when he was talking to Peggy, she felt confused. She had felt jealous of the rapport there had been between the two of them, she reminded herself. She had even been worried that Peggy might muscle in and become attached to Richard. What on earth was the matter with her!

She was conscious that Richard was looking at her, and that there was a pleading look in his eyes, something deeper that she couldn't fathom.

'I could go on living here and looking after George, I suppose,' she said slowly.

'Will you!' The eagerness of his reply took her by surprise. Richard held out a hand. 'Shake,' he ordered.

She hesitated, then laughing she took his hand; he grabbed her arm with his free hand, and pulled her towards him.

'We'd better seal that with a kiss,' he told her, shrewdly.

Suddenly she found his lips were on hers and, for one blissful moment she allowed herself to relax, and felt his arms tighten around her.

'You can't break your promise now,' he whispered, 'so don't even think about doing so.'

Delia was conscious that Richard was still holding her in his arms. She liked the feel of his body and it was only with a supreme effort that she pulled away from him as they heard a key in the front door.

'Anyone in?'

At the sound of Mary's voice, Delia felt both relief and exasperation. As Richard hurried out into the hall to greet his mother, Delia smoothed her hair back into place and tried to see in the mirror if her lipstick was smudged. Mary's arrival put a stop to what they were saying.

'I've brought along a whole bag of Christmas decorations,' she told them. 'I've decided not to bother putting them up this year since we're all coming here for Christmas Day.' She handed the bag to Delia who looked inside at the collection of baubles and garlands in red, gold, green and silver.

'Lovely,' she murmured, 'but I don't think you are going to manage to get away with no decorations at your place, because George is planning to make paper chains with you.'

'He's welcome to come and make them, but I am certainly not going to put them up,' Mary said firmly. 'He can bring them home and put them up in his bedroom. I'm too old for all that palaver. I'm planning on having a quiet Christmas and letting you two do all the work,' she told Delia firmly.

THIRTY-SEVEN

They were putting the finishing touches to the Christmas tree. Richard and Delia were both standing back, giving words of advice and encouragement to George who was trying to fasten the last few baubles onto the tree, when the doorbell rang. It was Peggy and, the moment the door was open, she walked in brandishing a gift-wrapped parcel and asking for George.

'He's in the sitting room helping to decorate the Christmas tree,' Delia said, but Peggy was already ahead of her, bursting into the room and greeting both Richard and George with enthusiastic kisses and hugs as if she had known them all their lives.

'George, this is for you,' she said holding out the parcel.

George looked at his father; as if uncertain about what to do, but the moment Richard nodded his head and smiled he darted forward and took the parcel from Peggy.

'Thank you,' he said turning it over in his hands and trying to feel what it was. 'Shall I put it under the tree?' he asked, looking from Delia to his father and back again.

Before either of them could answer, Peggy said, 'Oh, I was hoping you would be allowed to open it now! I wanted to see the look on his face when he saw what it was,' she said guilelessly to the other two, 'and I won't be here when he opens his presents on Christmas Day.'

'Well,' Delia said hesitantly, 'he did ask a few minutes ago if he could open one of his presents, but we told him he must wait until Christmas Day.'

'One won't matter, will it, George?' Peggy said with a smile.

George hugged his parcel but said nothing, still looking hopefully from Delia to his father.

'Well, I suppose one won't matter,' Richard agreed. 'After all, Peggy is right; she won't be here on Christmas Day, will she?'

George was elated. He tore off the brightly decorated paper and found a box inside; he stared at it looking puzzled. There was a picture of a helicopter on the outside.

'Can I help you?' Peggy said.

George nodded and handed her the box, watching with intrigue as she opened it and drew out a lovely model of a helicopter. She placed it on one of the small side tables. He looked on in delight when, using a remote control, she made the helicopter rise up in the air and do a complete circle before crash landing on the carpet.

'Would you like to see if you can do better than me?' she asked George.

He nodded eagerly and took the remote control from Peggy's hand. His first attempt was not very successful, but he seemed to get the hang of it quite quickly and managed to fly the helicopter around room twice before it collided with the curtains and fell to the floor.

'Can I have a go? It looks very exciting,' Richard said.

George handed over the remote and watched enviously as Richard achieved three circuits of the room, making the helicopter rise and fall in impressive style, then slowly landed it safely in the centre of the carpet. Eyes shining, George reclaimed the remote and again flew the helicopter around the room, this time crashing it into the wall and almost into a picture.

When it crashed to the floor this time, no amount of pressing the controls would get it to fly again. George was very upset.

'I didn't mean to break it,' he said, trying to keep his voice steady as he brushed away the tears that sprang into his eyes and were sliding down his cheeks. He ran to Delia and she put her arms around him and hugged him.

'I'm afraid you will find that you have to constantly keep charging it up, Richard, that's the only problem,' Peggy explained and produced from the box another wire, this one with a plug on the end of it. She put the plug into one of the wall sockets and then showed Richard and George where the lead fitted into the helicopter.

'How long will that take?' Richard asked.

'It may take a couple of hours; or overnight. Something like that,' Peggy said vaguely. She picked up the book of instructions and began looking through it. She found the right page and Delia watched as she leaned in to Richard, reading the instructions so close to him that her cheek was almost touching his.

'I think you should wait until you can practice flying it outside,' Delia said as she tried to comfort George.

'Outside!' Richard exclaimed. 'What on earth are you talking about, Delia. Fly this outside and it might rise, heaven knows how high, and you might lose control of it and cause an accident. That's what caused my accident, remember? And look what the result of that has been.'

'I thought you said it was a drone that flew into your glider.'

'It was, but what's the difference?'

'Well this is nowhere near as big as a drone,' Delia argued.

'Maybe not, but it could still cause an accident. Someone out walking, or on a bike, or even in a car. If the window was open it could fly right inside.'

'Oh Richard, how very thoughtless of me,' Peggy said contritely. She put out a hand and touched his shoulder. 'I forgot about what happened to you. Oh dear, what a silly mistake.' She picked up the helicopter, detached the wire from it and started to put it back in its box. 'I'll buy you something else, George, perhaps a car that has a remote control. OK?'

George burst into tears at the thought that she was going to take his present away. Sobbing, he ran from Delia's arms to his father's, begging him to let him keep the helicopter.

Peggy put her arms round both of them, telling Richard how sorry she was. Richard patted her shoulder.

'Not your fault Peggy. It was a lovely thought and a most unusual present.'

'Can I keep it, Daddy? Please, please, please,' George begged.

Richard looked perplexed as he stared at George. His face was red and blotchy, and tears were still running down his cheeks. He wanted to say no, and that he must let Peggy replace it with a car, but he couldn't bear the anguish in his son's eyes, so reluctantly said, 'Only if you promise me that you will never fly it outdoors.'

'I promise, I promise,' George agreed, hiccupping between each word as he wiped the back of his hand across his eyes to wipe away his tears. He hugged Richard and then turned and hugged Peggy. 'You are the two people I love most in the whole world,' he told them sternly.

Richard hugged and kissed him. 'Now, don't forget, you've promised us that you won't fly the helicopter out of doors,' Richard reminded him.

'I won't, Daddy. I promise,' George said earnestly.

'Right, well we'll say no more about it. A coffee or a cup of tea would be nice after all that,' he added looking across at Delia.

'Yes, of course,' she said and stood up to go and make it. 'Lemonade or milk for you, George?'

'Lemonade, please,' he said.

From the kitchen, Delia could hear the sound of Richard and Peggy's voices and catch the odd sentence or two as they laughed and joked together. Once again, a pang of jealousy went through her. He never laughed and bantered with her like that, she thought crossly. When they talked, no matter what it was about, Richard was always so serious. He was polite, considerate and would usually see reason, but he was never what she would call light-hearted.

Was that because he saw her as a servant rather than a friend? she wondered. To him, was she just someone who looked after him and George, ran the house, did the shopping and had even nursed him when he had come out of hospital?

Well, she asked herself, isn't that what she did? He was her patient, not her friend, so perhaps that was why he was so impersonal towards her – apart from that one kiss that could be brushed off as a one-off burst of playfulness, or worse, as merely an attempt to make her stay caring for him, rather than anything more . . . She supposed she should have been pleased about his reserve, seeing she was alone in the house with him so much of the time.

She didn't make any attempt to take part in Richard and Peggy's cheerful exchange as they drank their coffee. They were comparing the different advantages of helicopters, small power planes like Cessna's and gliders, something she knew so little about that she knew she would probably say the wrong thing anyway and make a fool of herself.

When Peggy drained her coffee cup and said she must be going, Delia felt a sense of relief. She knew that Peggy was on duty over Christmas, so at least they would be able to celebrate the festive holiday with Mary and Bill, without Peggy being there. As Richard helped her put on her coat, Peggy clapped a hand over her mouth and pulled out a wedge of papers from her pocket.

'Heavens, I almost forgot about this,' she said as she handed them to Delia. 'This is the rota if you decide to start with us after Christmas,' she said. 'Any queries simply ring me.'

'After Christmas?' Richard frowned. 'Are you still seriously thinking of going back to nursing?' he said, staring at Delia in dismay.

'I certainly hope she is,' Peggy said, as she placed a hand on the door latch. 'Don't worry Richard, I'll pop round on my days off and keep you company when Delia is working,' she promised with a cheeky smile.

THIRTY-EIGHT

Christmas Day started very early for Delia. George awoke while it was still dark and crawled down to the end of his bed, in the hope that Father Christmas had been. When he found the bulging stocking hanging there his excitement knew no bounds. He was out of bed and into Richard's room, hugging the sock full of goodies, eager to open it and share all the wonders with his father. Richard was in a deep sleep and unresponsive to all George's pushes and pulls.

'Go back to bed or come in here with me,' he growled, without even opening his eyes.

George had another go at waking him, but when he found it was impossible to do so he raced off to Delia's bedroom to show her what Father Christmas had left for him. Delia was a lighter sleeper than Richard and he was able to rouse her fairly easily. He clambered into bed beside her and began to unpack his treasure trove. He was thrilled with everything. There was a packet of his favourite sweets, a comic, an apple, an orange, chocolate, an assortment of hazelnuts and walnuts still in their shells, a packet of marbles and a yo-yo. By the time he had emptied his stocking and Delia had made the appropriate noises of amazement, she was wide awake.

Having eaten some of the sweets and half the small bar of chocolate, George was ready for a nap. He drifted off to sleep in the warmth of Delia's bed. She felt wide awake.

She looked at her watch; it was only seven o'clock but she didn't feel sleepy. She crept out of bed and went down to the kitchen to make a cup of tea.

When she opened the fridge to get the milk out there was the turkey, already prepared for the oven, so she decided that, before she went back up to bed, she might as well turn the oven on and start cooking it.

Mary arrived just after half past nine, laden with presents that she asked George to put under the tree.

'When are we going to open them?' he asked.

'After we've eaten the wonderful Christmas dinner that I am going to help Delia to prepare,' she told him.

'Is everything under control?' she asked, turning to Delia.

'Yes, I think so. George woke me very early so the turkey has been in the oven on a low heat since seven o'clock. The only problem I have is that I haven't enough pans to cook all the vegetables, not unless I either put several kinds together in one saucepan, or cook them and put them in the oven to keep warm. They're all prepared and in bowls of water in the fridge.'

'Why don't you parboil the root vegetables, drain them and put them into a dish with a little seasoning? If you then pour some cooking oil over them, you can put them in the oven alongside the turkey to roast. Then you have the saucepans free to cook the greens.'

'What a great idea!' Delia smiled.

'Don't throw away the water you cook them in, we will use that along with the juices out of the turkey to help make the gravy.'

Bill arrived at midday with another bag of parcels. Once again, George was told to put them round the tree for later.

'We can't open them until we have eaten our Christmas dinner,' Bill told him.

It was almost two o'clock before they sat round the table that, with George's help, Delia had laid with cutlery, glasses and red and gold serviettes the night before. The meal was a great success, with both men asking for a second helping of turkey.

'Leave room for the Christmas pudding,' Mary warned them.

Richard and Bill cleared the table and helped with the washing up. Then they all went into the sitting room. Richard brought out a bottle of port and Mary made the coffee, while Delia made sure that the mince pies were hot before she handed them round.

'Now can we open the presents?' George asked hopefully as he looked at the pile under the Christmas tree longingly. George acted as Father Christmas, taking each parcel to Richard first so that he could make sure it was going to the right person. The rustle of paper and the exclamations of surprise and delight as they unwrapped them lasted almost an hour.

Everyone seemed to be very pleased with what they had received and George was ecstatic. He had everything from board games and books, to a glider model making kit.

'Will you help me do it, Daddy?' he pleaded, but Richard shook his head.

'No, not today, son. Perhaps we can do it tomorrow. Don't open the box because if you lose any of the pieces we won't be able to make it at all.'

'Why don't you come out to the kitchen with me and we'll make everybody a cup of tea?' Delia suggested.

'Tea, we don't want tea,' Richard said. 'We need another drink.'

'You and Bill have your drink, I agree with Delia, a cup of tea would go down really well,' Mary told him. By the time they'd made the tea and brought it back into the sitting room, George had persuaded Bill and his father to play one of his new board games with him.

Mary and Delia watched. They didn't want to join in. They were both feeling pleasantly tired and were enjoying relaxing in front of a glowing log fire.

'One of the best Christmases I've had in years,' Bill commented.

'It has been wonderful,' Mary agreed.

'Now it is time for George to go to bed,' Delia stated.

'Not yet, please,' George pleaded. 'It is Christmas, you know.'

'Well, perhaps you can stay up for another ten minutes,' Richard agreed, as they all laughed.

'Why don't you let your daddy read you a story from one of your new books,' Bill suggested. 'I feel too tired to tell you a bedtime story tonight.'

George considered for a moment.

'It's that or straight up to bed right now,' Delia told him.

'OK,' he then took a further five minutes to select the story he wanted Richard to read. That decided, he curled up on Richard's lap and they all fell silent, listening to the story with him. By the time Richard was halfway through the story, George's head was nodding and he was struggling keep his eyes open. When Mary suggested that he might like to hear the rest of it in bed, he shook his head repeatedly.

'No, I want to stay here,' he said firmly.

'Oh, that's good,' Bill said. 'I want to hear the end as well.' They all settled back, and Richard started reading again, when there was a ring of the doorbell.

'Who on earth?' Richard said, frowning in Delia's direction.

'I have no idea,' she told him, as she stood up to answer it.

'Probably Father Christmas come to see if you are in bed, George,' Bill joked.

They heard voices in the hall, then Delia opened the door and Peggy Bristow rushed in. Peggy was looking very warm, yet glamorous. She was wearing a cream suede coat that had a wide fur collar and, when she undid it as she entered the room, they could see that it was lined with the same fur. Under it she was wearing a bright red wool dress and knee high cream boots also trimmed with cream fur.

'Happy Christmas, everyone,' Peggy murmured, her eyes fixed on Richard.

'I'm sure you remember Bill Thompson from our trip to the eye hospital recently, but I don't think you have met Richard's mother, Mary Wilson,' Delia said, introducing her.

'Hello Peggy,' George was already scrambling down from Richard's lap and running over to give her a hug.

She bent and kissed him and ruffled his hair. 'I hope I'm not interrupting anything,' Peggy said and once again her eyes were fixed on Richard.

'Peggy gave me a helicopter for Christmas,' George announced to them all. 'Can I show it to them, Daddy? Please, please,' he said quickly when he saw Richard hesitate.

Delia saw Richard and Peggy exchange looks, sending signals, so she wasn't too surprised when Richard said, 'Very well, but you are simply to show it, not demonstrate it.'

George let out squeals of happiness as he darted upstairs to his bedroom to fetch his precious helicopter. When he returned, he walked all around the room, displaying it to them all and explaining different points to each of them.

'Right, that's it,' Richard said. 'Put it back in its box and take it back upstairs.'

George obediently picked up the helicopter, carefully put it in the box, and then walked towards the hall. As he reached the door he turned and, lifting the lid of the box, said, 'Say goodbye to all the people, helicopter, you're going to bed now.' As he went to close the box he accidentally touched the remote. The helicopter was fully charged and before he could do anything, except gasp in surprise, it came out of the box and soared high into the air.

'George!' The shouts from Richard and Delia were simultaneous and startled George even more, making him press down harder on the remote. The toy zoomed and spun all over the place, until it finally crashed and bounced off the wall behind Bill, narrowly missing his ear. Pandemonium followed. Richard was shouting at him, Delia remonstrating, his grandmother saying how dangerous it had been and Bill assuring everybody that he was all right. George didn't seem to know what to do for the best and, sobbing loudly, he threw himself in Peggy's arms since she was the only one who wasn't telling him off. Richard and Mary were fussing over Bill.

'Are you sure you are all right?' Mary said anxiously. 'It did hit your face, are you quite sure your eyes are all right?'

'They're fine,' Bill asserted gruffly, embarrassed by all the fuss. He had been quite shaken by what had happened, but he was sure George hadn't meant to do it deliberately. He simply pressed the remote accidentally when he was putting the toy back into its box, but Richard wouldn't accept that.

'He did it deliberately, he was defying me,' he said angrily. 'I'm so sorry, Bill, you must have been scared to death.'

'It all happened so quickly I didn't have time to think about it,' Bill mumbled.

'Well George can apologize to you.'

He pulled George unceremoniously from Peggy's arms and marched him over to Bill.

'Now say how sorry you are for being so disobedient,' he ordered. 'You know Bill has to go to the hospital for treatment for his eyes, well, you could have made them far worse. You might even have blinded him if that helicopter had hit his eye and not his ear!'

In a flood of tears, George said how sorry he was.

'I know you didn't mean to do it, that it was an accident,' Bill said, shaking George's hand in a man-to-man fashion. 'Now don't worry about it, no harm done at all.'

Richard was still angry.

In a flirtatious, teasing voice, Peggy said, 'Didn't you ever do anything naughty when you were a boy, or were you always a goody-goody like you are now?'

Richard coloured up, but didn't answer.

'Come on, I'll take you up to bed and daddy can come up and tuck you in,' Peggy said, taking hold of George's hand and leading him towards the hall. 'Let me carry the box, it might be safer,' she added, taking the helicopter from George. 'Don't be too long,' she told Richard raising her eyebrow suggestively, 'we'll only be five minutes undressing and getting into bed.'

There was an awkward silence in the room after they'd left, then they all began talking at once as if an attempt to forget what had happened. The atmosphere had been ruined though. Mary was concerned about Bill and kept squeezing his hand reassuringly. Richard was still angry about George disobeying him and, a couple of minutes later, he rose from his chair muttering that he was going to tuck George in.

'Don't say anything else to him about what happened or the poor little devil will be having nightmares,' Bill warned. Richard didn't reply and he was gone so long that Delia kept wondering what was going on upstairs.

As if sensing her unease, Mary said, 'I expect he is reading George a story to try and calm him down.'

He might manage to calm George down but he certainly wasn't doing anything for her blood pressure Delia thought, as she strained to hear his or Peggy's footsteps on the stairs.

Finally she said, 'Shall we all have a coffee?'

Mary and Bill assented and on her way through to the kitchen, she called up the stairs,

'Coffee time you two,' in the hope that it would bring them back down immediately.

THIRTY-NINE

After they had eaten lunch on New Year's Day, Delia began taking the Christmas decorations down. She asked Richard to dismantle the lights from the Christmas tree and pack them away.

'What's going on? You don't need to pack these away until twelfth night and that's not for ages,' Richard told her. 'What's the hurry?'

'We both start work tomorrow or have you forgotten?'

'Of course I haven't forgotten!'

'We might not have time to do it when we get home or we might be too tired,' Delia told him.

'Are you still going ahead with the idea of taking that job?' Richard frowned.

'Yes, I am,' Delia said firmly.

'Will you be able to cope after this length of time away from nursing?' Richard asked dubiously.

'Of course.'

'Well, you will have Peggy there to guide you and tell you what to do.'

'Peggy! I don't need her or anyone else to help me,' Delia said indignantly. 'I have been a sister longer than she has.'

'You mean you were a sister. Don't forget you're going back as a staff nurse. I would imagine a demotion like that makes quite a difference.'

'You don't have to remind me,' Delia said sharply.

'Yet you still want to do it?' He stared at her with a puzzled look on his face.

'You want to go back to work, don't you?'

'That's rather different, I'm going back to the same job as I had before and I will be holding the same rank as before.'

'Do they have ranks in schools?' she asked sarcastically.

'You don't have to be obtuse, Delia. I am going back to my old job and it is highly unlikely that it has changed in any way.'

'Well I hope you enjoy it,' she told him as she reached up and flicked a long gold glittering chain from on top of one of the pictures.

'So are you going to help?' she asked again.

'I will do what I can. I will certainly pack the lights away, because you would probably make a hash of it and then next year I'd have to get all new ones,' Richard said resignedly.

'You had to get new ones this year and you were the one who took them down and put them away last year.'

Richard didn't answer and went over to the tree, pulled out the plug and began systematically to unwind the lights from it.

They worked in silence for about ten minutes, then Richard asked, 'Are we doing a complete spring clean?'

'No but I do want the place to look tidy when your mother comes round to look after George.'

'I think that's all she is going to do, look after George, not make a tour of inspection,' Richard said smugly.

Delia scowled. 'Will you help me to get the rest of the decorations down or not?' She asked him.

'Very well, if you will go and make me a coffee,' he told her.

'I'm too busy,' she told him.

'You make the coffee and I'll clear the room while you're doing it,' he compromised.

'In ten minutes flat! I think you will find that takes rather longer than that.'

By the time she returned with two steaming cups of coffee Richard had removed all the decorations from pictures and odd places she had put them, and even taken down the Christmas cards she had fixed on the doors with blue tack. He had meticulously removed it from the back of each one and rolled it into a single ball. Everything was piled up neatly on the table.

'We'll drink our coffee and then if you find the boxes, we can pack all this stuff away and I'll put it back up in the attic,' he told her.

On returning to the house after her first day at work, Delia found Richard trying to get George to eat a sandwich he had made for his tea. George was shaking his head adamantly, tears creeping down his cheeks.

'If you don't eat that sandwich then you can go hungry. I've been dealing with awkward kids all day and I don't want to come home and find another one,' Richard ranted.

'What's the problem?' Delia asked.

'He is,' Richard muttered. 'He is complaining that he is hungry, so I've made him a banana sandwich and he won't eat it.'

'He doesn't like bananas when they're mashed up, he likes to eat his banana whole in between bites of bread and butter,' Delia told him.

Richard looked exasperated but said nothing. Delia went to the fruit bowl and picked out a banana, peeled back the skin a few inches and handed it to George who took it eagerly.

'I'll cut you some bread and butter in just a minute, so don't eat it before I've got that ready for you,' Delia told him. 'What sort of day have you had?' she asked, turning to Richard.

'Absolutely lousy! My head aches, my back is killing me and all I want to do is go and lie down for half an hour.'

'Go on then, I'll bring you up a cup of tea in half an hour, after I've got our meal ready. I'll finish feeding George first.'

Richard grunted acceptance of the plan.

'What was your day like? Good?' He asked as he headed for the stairs.

Delia smiled but said nothing. She slipped her coat off and went to cut George his bread and butter. When she came back with it, Richard had vanished and she could hear him padding around upstairs. With a sigh she slipped off her own shoes and sank down on a chair.

It had been anything but a good day. Peggy had picked on her from the moment she had arrived. Under the pretence of 'showing her the ropes' Peggy had lectured her as she would have done a first-year student nurse. Afterwards, she had followed her around, making points and finding fault with everything she did. Some of the other nurses were exchanging amused glances and, as the day went on, Delia felt that any authority she had because of her senior staff nurse status was rapidly diminishing. To add to Delia's chagrin, Peggy had said at the end of their shift, 'Not too bad for your first day. Give my love to Richard when you get home.'

Give her love to Richard, Delia thought defiantly, that was the last thing she was going do. She wasn't even going to mention Peggy's name unless he asked after her.

Richard did ask. He wanted to know if Delia had enjoyed her first day back at nursing.

'Of course you had Peggy to put you right,' he said. 'How is she?'

'As efficient as a sister can be,' Delia said dryly.

'Friendly?'

Delia shrugged. 'Personalities don't come into it when you're working,' she said evasively.

Richard laughed. 'You should try being a teacher. You would have thought that I had just arrived from Outer Mongolia and knew nothing at all about the curriculum, from the way some of the new teachers acted. I wasn't off for all that long but there were three new faces and they looked quite hostile.'

'What about the old guard?'

'Oh, they were OK, except they kept ribbing me about trying to fly a plane without an engine.'

'I suppose you have to expect that,' she sympathised.

'I don't see why,' Richard said huffily. 'After all, it's the nearest thing to pure flying. Birds don't have an engine.'

'True,' Delia admitted. She knew he expected her to say something more intelligent than that but she was too tired to think of anything, so she quickly went on to another topic.

'Did Bill and your mother say they had managed all right?'

'Mother looked tired and I agreed with Bill that, since he was picking George up in the afternoon, I would read the bedtime story, so that Bill wouldn't have to trek back here again at seven each night.'

'That sounds sensible,' Delia agreed, smothering a yawn as she spoke.

'You found your first day tiring as well did you?' Richard smirked. 'Not used to being on your feet all day.'

Delia was about to defend herself and tell him that cleaning his house, doing the washing and the shopping, and running after George, meant that she didn't have a lot of time to curl up with a book, but she decided not to. Instead she began to clear away the debris from their meal and carried the dishes through to the kitchen. She waited hopefully for Richard to come and see if she needed any help, but he had already sunk down in his favourite armchair with the evening paper.

'I thought you were going to go up and read to George as soon as you had finished eating,' she reminded him.

'I did say I would but he's probably asleep by now,' Richard said not looking up from the paper.

'I'll go up and take a look,' Delia said resignedly.

Richard was right. Not only was George in bed and asleep, but he was still clutching the book open at the story he wanted his father to read to him. Gently Delia removed the book, pulled up the covers, and tucked him in.

Their first day at work hadn't been an overwhelming success for either of them, she reflected. It was going to be necessary to ask Mary to oversee a snack for George each afternoon. Delia would also have to devise meals in advance, so that all she had to do when she came home was pop them in the microwave or ask Mary to put them in the oven before she left.

Another thing she was going to have to give some thought to was the cleaning, washing and shopping. True she was only planning to work part-time, but could she fit all those jobs in when she wasn't at the hospital? If she felt as tired when she came home as she did today, then she wasn't at all sure that she could. She would have to plan a detailed schedule. Perhaps ordering online might be the answer, but then what happened if they delivered and there was no one at home to take them in?

She was too tired to think about it tonight, she told herself. Well, it was early days. Once she had organised things better, it would be no problem at all. Many wives did a part time job, managed to look after their husband and several children, and still have time to go out and enjoy themselves.

Or perhaps Richard had been right after all and it wasn't going to be possible to work, run his house and look after him and George all at the same time . . .

FORTY

Delia struggled to overcome the exhaustion she felt at the end of each day, trying to convince herself that it was less and less each day. When she arrived home the following week, feeling not only tired but also irritable – Peggy had been particularly trying that day – she found not only Richard and George, there but also Mary and Bill.

'Hello, what's going on, are we having a party?' she greeted them in what she tried to make a cheerful voice.

'No, we've got a problem,' Richard told her.

'Oh yes?' she looked at him enquiringly.

'Bill has a hospital appointment tomorrow and it's at three o' clock in the afternoon. So it is unlikely that he and my mother will be able to pick George up.'

'I see . . .' Delia frowned.

'I can go on my own, there's no need for your mother to come as well, Richard,' Bill told him.

'I know, but she feels she ought to be there,' Richard stated.

'Yes, I do,' Mary said firmly. 'He is having an injection and he will need someone to look after him afterwards. Someone to make sure he doesn't leave the hospital too soon, that he manages to phone for a taxi and someone to help him into it and out again when he gets home.'

'Yes, of course he does,' Delia agreed.

'The trouble is I can't take time off tomorrow,' Richard said. 'We have an inspector doing his rounds so I must be there.'

'So, you mean it is up to me to take time off.' Delia frowned. There was a long silence while she considered whether this would even be possible. She rather thought Peggy would be furious and tell her she was only working part time hours as it was. She braced her shoulders. So, what if Peggy did? Perhaps it would be an excuse to give up nursing and to stop feeling so exhausted each day.

'Don't worry,' she smiled brightly, 'I'm sure I can arrange

something. We really must try and get friendly with some of the other parents,' she added as an afterthought.

'What for?' Richard asked in a puzzled voice.

'So that we could ask one of them to bring George home from school, when there is an emergency like this, of course. After all,' she added when she saw the scowl on Richard's face at her suggestion, 'it would only be for about half an hour, because you are usually home just after George, aren't you, Richard?'

'I'm sure Peggy will understand when you explain everything to her,' Richard said. 'It isn't as if it happens every other week. Bill won't have another appointment for at least a month, will he mother?' he asked looking at Mary.

'Possibly even longer if they use this new injection, instead of Lucentis,' she agreed.

'There you are then, Bill, all solved,' Richard smiled.

It might be solved as far as they were concerned, Delia thought, but she still had to face Peggy. She spent a restless night, constantly waking up to go over in her mind what would be the best way to ask Peggy. When she arrived at the hospital, all her prepared speeches went out of her mind. When the opportunity came for her to ask Peggy, she felt as awkward as a schoolgirl facing her headmistress. Peggy's face was expressionless as she listened to Delia rambling on about Bill having to attend for eye treatment and not being able to pick George up from school.

'I wouldn't need to leave here until three o'clock.'

Peggy frowned.

Delia clenched her hands into fists until her nails bit into her palms. Surely she's not going to say I can't, Delia thought desperately. Instead, she was completely taken by surprise.

'It won't be necessary for you to take time off, Delia,' Peggy said, 'I am off this afternoon. I'll pick George up from school. Give me a door key and I'll take him home and look after him until Richard gets home.'

Delia felt at such a complete loss for words that she found herself stuttering as she tried to thank Peggy. She wanted to refuse her offer, but she realised she had no choice. She either had to accept, or defy Peggy and take the time off whether it was granted or not.

'Don't worry, George knows me well enough by now, he will be quite happy. Go and get me the door key.' She looked at her fob watch. 'I will be leaving in twenty minutes,' she added as she walked away. Delia stared after her. What would Richard think about her giving the door key to a stranger? She thought worriedly. Well, Peggy isn't a stranger, she thought. She'd visited them several times, she knew Richard, she knew Bill and Mary, but could she be classed as a family friend?

Delia knew that her worries were groundless. The only reason she was asking herself all these questions was because she didn't want to think of Peggy being in the house alone with Richard.

She wouldn't be alone with him, she reminded herself, George would be there as well.

FORTY-ONE

Two weeks later, the problem of Bill having to go to the eye hospital occurred again.

'I don't believe it!' Delia groaned. 'Mary said that it would be at least a month before he would have to go back.'

'Grandma said that it was for his other eye,' George, who was curled up on the settee with a book, told them.

'That's right,' Richard agreed, 'this time it is for the other eye apparently and they've given him very short notice.' They looked at each other in despair. 'I don't think I can ask for time off,' Richard said apologetically, 'how about you?'

Delia shrugged. 'I can try.'

The next day, when she asked for time off, she saw the knowing look on Peggy's face.

'Don't worry, I'll take care of things,' she said without any preamble. 'When is it?'

'The day after tomorrow.'

Peggy nodded. 'I am off so it will not be a problem.'

*   *   *

Later that day, when Delia thought about it, she wondered if Peggy had deliberately doctored the list so that she could see Richard again. Then she scolded herself for being so suspicious.

Jealousy will get you nowhere, she told herself, with an inward smirk. Yet, in her heart of hearts she was positive that it was true and wondered how she could find out for sure. Don't make waves or she might not do it, she told herself. But, for the rest of the day, the niggling thought that she was right kept invading her mind almost like a warning.

Richard raised his eyebrows when she told him the news that night.

'It's very good of her,' he said in surprise. 'Is she so helpful to all her staff or are you getting preferential treatment?'

Delia merely smiled, still convinced that her suspicions were founded, but until she could prove them to be she thought it best to stay quiet about them.

'Perhaps she's looking forward to being taken out for dinner by you afterwards,' she said.

Richard looked startled but said nothing and Delia wished she hadn't said it. It was putting ideas into his head and surely he wouldn't want to have to take Peggy out for a meal every time she came and picked George up from school. Perhaps she ought to make sure that she prepared a big casserole, so that there was enough for Peggy to be included in their evening meal at home. She decided that as she began to get things organised for the next day.

At midday Peggy made a point of letting her know that she hadn't forgotten that she was collecting George from school that afternoon.

'Perhaps you had better give me your door key now,' she said. 'You may be busy this afternoon and not able to get to your locker to find it, perhaps I ought to ask Richard to get one cut for me,' she added half-jokingly, her eyes on Delia's face to see her reaction.

Mary and Bill also reminded her of the Peggy's generosity, when she stopped for a brief word with them, after she found them sitting outside the consultant's surgery waiting to be called in.

'It's so good of her to give up her time off like this,' Mary said gratefully.

'It certainly is,' Bill agreed. 'I was for ringing the hospital and saying that because it was in the afternoon and sprung on us so suddenly there was no chance of me getting here, but Mary said I wasn't to do that if it was at all possible to arrange something.'

'I do understand,' Delia told him, patting his arm. 'Your eyes are very important and it's great that you are getting so much attention.'

'Oh, I agree,' Bill said

'They do need to see to your other eye,' Mary murmured.

'That's unfortunately so,' Bill agreed. 'And I thought one injection a month was quite enough for me, now I'll have to have one in each eye. Two per month!' He grumbled.

If it's known that his other eye has AMD, why weren't both injected at his first appointment? Delia mused. She then felt that it confirmed her suspicion that Peggy had some dealings in this error, so that she had an excuse to visit Richard. Determinedly she put it all from her mind, time enough to think about it when she got home.

When she did reach home late that afternoon, things were in a state of panic and very different from anything Delia had imagined.

'What's wrong?' she asked when she saw a police car parked on the road outside their gate, with two policemen standing inside the hall taking a statement from Richard.

'George has gone missing,' Peggy told her.

'Missing? What do you mean?'

'Just that,' Peggy snapped. 'I collected him from school and he was here when Richard came home. Then, half an hour later, when we called him to come and have a drink and some biscuits, we couldn't find him anywhere.'

'How strange!'

'We searched the house from top to bottom, the garage, the garden and the nearby streets. We asked everybody we saw if they had seen a small boy and described him, but no one had. Then Richard phoned the police,' Peggy told her.

'How on earth could he go missing?' Delia asked in a mysti-fied voice. 'There were only the three of you here, weren't there?'

'Yes, I told you, I picked him up and brought him home.'

'Was he playing outside?' Delia looked out through the window at the cold grey sky and shivered.

'No, of course he wasn't,' Peggy said indignantly. Then she added, 'not unless he had gone out without our knowing it and I suppose he must have done that, since he isn't in the house.'

'Was he wearing his outdoor clothes?' Delia asked.

'Not as far as I know,' Peggy said. 'He took them off and hung them up in the hall when we came in like he always does.'

'There aren't any children's clothes out here,' commented one of the policemen who had been listening to the exchange. 'Are you the boy's mother?' the policeman asked, looking down at the clipboard in his hand and frowning.

'No, I live here with George and his father, I'm the . . . housekeeper,' Delia explained.

'And the other lady?' he asked looking at Peggy.

'A family friend,' Peggy told him quickly.

Before he could ask any more questions Delia turned and spoke to Richard.

'Was he all right when you got home?' she asked.

Richard gave a small shrug. 'He seemed to be. He and Peggy were talking to each other when I came in. From the sound of George's voice he wanted to do something and she wasn't sure about it. Then he saw me and came and gave me a hug and that was it.'

The policeman looked at Peggy. 'Can you remember what he was asking you?'

She coloured up and shook her head.

'What did he do afterwards? Did he stay here with the two of you or go up to his room?' Delia asked.

'As far as I know, he went up to his room. Half an hour later when we called him he wasn't there,' Peggy said.

'You mean that neither of you heard him come back downstairs, collect his coat and scarf from the hallstand and go out?' She asked incredulously.

'No, we didn't,' Richard said. 'We were talking and assumed he was playing upstairs. We never gave it a thought that he would go out on his own, not even into the garden on such a cold evening. Especially since it was getting dark and George doesn't like the dark.'

The two policemen exchanged looks and one of them made more notes on his clipboard, while the other one walked out into the hall and they could hear him talking on his phone. When he came back into the sitting room, he told them that he had given the details and description of George to headquarters and that all the cars and policemen in the area would be notified.

'Now don't be worried, we'll soon track him down,' they promised. 'He can't have gone far and a small boy, all on his own at this time in the evening, is bound to be spotted and the police informed.'

'What else do you want us to do?' Richard asked as they made obvious moves towards the door.

'Stay here, Mr Wilson. We will telephone you the moment he is located or we have any news of his whereabouts. If you think of anything else that might be useful, like where friends or relations in the area live in case he has gone to visit them, then let us know.'

'We've given you his grandmother's address and that of Bill Thompson who usually picks him up from school,' Richard said.

'Yes, one of our team has been to his house but he's not at home.'

'No, I don't suppose he is,' Richard said. 'He went to the hospital this afternoon for eye treatment and my mother went with him so he is probably still at her house.'

'Yes, yes, you've already told us all that and we have verified it.'

'So, all we can do is wait?' Richard said.

'I'm afraid so, sir. I hope we will have news for you very soon but, as I said, if you think of anything that might be of help to us in our search, then get in touch right away.'

FORTY-TWO

George hated the dark. He felt scared. Being out in the dark on his own frightened him so much that he was shaking all over. He had never been out in the dark before; he'd never been out at all on his own. Bill came and collected him from school and when he went to the park it was with his dad or Delia, and when he went to the shops it was with his grandma or Delia.

He tried to imagine that one of them was with him now, but it was no good, he knew he was very much on his own.

He broke into a trot, every bush moved as if about to grab him and pull him into their darkness and every tree waved menacing arms. Shadows became grotesque and played tricks on him. One minute they were alongside him then behind him and then vanished up a wall or into a bush. There were strange sounds all around him, rustling in the branches of overhanging trees, scuffing sounds under the hedges, tiny squeals from some-where and the whistling of the wind as he went round corners. They all scared him.

Tears pricked at his eyes but he brushed them roughly away with the back of his clenched fist. Only babies cried and he didn't want a tear-stained face when he found Delia.

He wished Delia was there with him now, to hold his hand and explain all the strange shapes and noises. She wasn't afraid of anything. She was the most wonderful person in the entire world. He loved Delia and he wished she hadn't wanted to go nursing again. It had been lovely coming home every afternoon and finding her in the kitchen getting a teatime snack ready for him. It was always something special, always a surprise and always yummy.

He didn't feel very well. His head ached and his throat was hurting and he was hungry. Peggy hadn't given him a snack or a drink before his daddy came home and then, the moment she had heard his key in the lock, she had said, 'Go and say hello to your daddy and then go up to your room and eat this, and I'll call you down later.' Then she had given him a bar of chocolate. He'd done as she told him, but he knew Peggy wouldn't call him down, not until Delia arrived home and their supper was ready.

He didn't like being sent to his room. He liked his room and he was happy to play there, but only when he wanted to be there. Being sent to his room was almost like a punishment for being naughty. If he couldn't see Delia, until she came home from the hospital, he could still tell his daddy that his head was hurting and so was his throat. He might be able to do something about it because, when he had tried to tell Peggy, she'd pushed away and told him to stop whining.

He knew he was being naughty now, coming out on his own and not telling anyone but he wanted Delia to help him. He didn't want to wait for another whole hour until she got home. It was a cold night and now it was starting to rain. He couldn't stop shivering and thought about turning round and going back home. Now, he wished he had stayed in his room, where it was warm and dry and there were books and games to play with if he wanted something to do.

He trudged on. He wouldn't give up. He was on the main road now and there were plenty of lights and people about, so he didn't feel so scared. It was still a long way to go to Windsor though, he thought ruefully. Before he had left, he had taken all the money out of his moneybox and he had enough to pay his bus fare to Windsor. He knew where the bus stop was because he had gone to Windsor several times with Delia, so he joined the queue and clambered onto the next bus that came along.

'You on your own son?' the driver asked as George held out his money to him.

George nodded, took the ticket the driver held out to him and went and sat at the back of the bus, hoping no one would notice him. He wasn't too sure where he ought to get off. He knew he should have asked the driver, but he'd been afraid that if he didn't know where he was going the driver mightn't let him on. He peered out of the window hoping to recognise a shop or building. As the bus turned onto the relief road, he could see Windsor Castle and the Round Tower in the distance and he gave a big sigh of relief. He knew where he was.

He liked Windsor. Delia had taken him there to see the soldiers. He loved it when they all marched down the road and up the hill to the castle for the Changing of the Guard Ceremony. The old Guard – the soldiers who had been guarding the queen for the last twenty-four hours – went home and the new Guard took over. Delia had taken him inside the castle to watch them doing this and, for days afterwards, he had walked very tall with his shoulders back, stamping his feet every time he turned around just like they'd done. He thought he might be a soldier when he grew up, but he didn't like the big furry hats they had to wear that came right down on their face and almost over their eyes. Delia called them busbys or something like that.

The people who had got on the bus, when he had too, seemed to have all got off, but he still wasn't sure where he ought to get off and wondered if he had better ask someone. There was a middle-aged man sitting two seats away and he looked as though he might know, but George remembered that Delia had warned him that he must never speak to strangers.

Was the man a stranger? George wasn't sure when the man had got onto to the bus but he seemed to have been sitting there for a long time. Before George could make up his mind, the man rose from his seat ready to get off, so George followed him. Once they were in the street, the man walked away so quickly that George didn't have a chance to speak to him.

He stared round at the big, high, Victorian houses that seemed to be frowning down at him as if they knew he was in trouble. He walked to the corner of the road and looked both ways. He didn't recognise where he was and there seemed to be no one about, except a man in dark uniform about to turn down the next road. George raced to catch him up, then stopped just yards away from him. The man was a policeman.

'If ever you find yourself in trouble, then find a policeman to help you.' Delia's advice rang in his ears as plainly as if she was standing there at his side. Taking a deep breath, George did just that. The policeman listened to what he said.

'So you are looking for the King Edward Hospital, is that right?' the policeman asked.

'Yes, that's right,' George nodded.

'This lady called Delia, is she your mother?'

George shook his head. 'No, I wish she was.'

The policeman frowned. He studied George for a minute and then he spoke into his phone, looking at George all the time as he did so. Holding the phone away from his mouth he asked, 'Is your name George Wilson?'

George nodded. 'Yes, that's right.'

'And you live in Burnham?'

George nodded again. Suddenly he felt frightened. What was

going on? Had he done the right thing in asking the policeman for help, he wondered.

'Right!' The policeman put away his phone and held out a hand to George. 'Come on, we've a short walk to the station and then you will be taken home.'

'No! I don't want to go home, I want to find Delia,' George muttered, pulling away.

'She is already at home and telephoned us and asked us to look for you,' the policeman told him. 'She was very worried because you weren't there when she came home from work and no one knew where you were.'

'Are you sure?'

'Of course I'm sure. Come along. When we get to the station they will tell you the same thing and then they'll put you in a police car and take you home.'

Delia and Richard came running down the path to meet George, when the police car drew up at their gate and George and the policeman who had found him got out of the car. Delia held out her arms and he ran to her and hugged her fiercely.

She held him tightly, saying, 'Oh George, you gave us such a fright!' Over and over again.

Richard ruffled his hair and said, 'Let's get inside before we all catch our death of cold out here in the rain.' When they reached the shelter of the house, Richard invited the policeman in, but he refused. 'Have to report back to the station, sir.'

Richard thanked him for bringing George home then followed Delia and George into the warm sitting room.

'You were a very naughty boy running away like that,' Peggy told him crossly.

'Never mind, he's safely home again now,' Richard said quickly.

'I'm not feeling well,' George complained, clinging to Delia. 'My head hurts and my throat hurts when I swallow and I'm hungry.'

Delia put a hand on George's forehead. 'You're burning!' she said in surprise.

'That's what happens when you're naughty,' Peggy told him.

'It's rather more than that,' Delia murmured worriedly as she held his head between her two hands and studied his face. 'Look.' She opened the neck of George's shirt. He was covered with small red spots.

'Oh my god!' Peggy gasped 'he's got something contagious. Keep him away from me.'

George burst into tears. He didn't feel well and now he was really frightened.

'What's going on?' Richard demanded.

'That child is covered in horrible red spots,' Peggy said, a note of revulsion in her voice.

'Really? Let's have a look,' Richard said turning to George. George pulled open the neck of his shirt and displayed the spots for his father to examine. 'Hmm, well that's either measles or chicken pox. We'll know for certain tomorrow. It's rampant at my school.' He placed a hand on George's forehead. 'I'm pretty sure you have a temperature. Do you know where the thermometer is Delia?'

'Yes, I'll go and fetch it.'

They checked and decided George had quite a high temperature.

'Get out of those wet clothes, have something to eat and then straight off to bed,' Richard ordered. 'It's a good thing that Delia made us a casserole for tonight. It's all piping hot in the oven and there's enough for all of us,' he said looking at Peggy.

'Not for me,' she said quickly. 'I haven't had either measles or chicken pox and I certainly don't want them. I'll escape while I am still safe and hope I haven't already picked it up from any of you.'

'See you tomorrow?' Richard asked.

'No,' she shook her head vehemently. 'I've got a training session coming up so I'm afraid I won't be able see you again for ages.' As she reached the door, Peggy paused and looked back at Delia. 'This means that you shouldn't come to work tomorrow or probably not for a couple of weeks. I'm not at all sure that we can keep your job open for that long,' Peggy told her.

'I'm sorry, but George comes first and he will need nursing,' Delia said stiffly.

'I'm thinking of the safety of our patients not about him,' Peggy snapped. 'It's all very inconvenient,' she added irritably.

Delia was about to apologise but Peggy's tone riled her.

'In that case you'd better find someone else,' she said with a little smile. 'I don't think I want to come back at all, at least not for the next few years, until George is old enough to look after himself. Richard is right, I can't do two jobs at once.'

FORTY-THREE

George was not an ideal patient. He wanted Delia to be at his side every minute of the night and day. When she wasn't at his bedside, he called out for drinks or complained that he was either too hot or not warm enough, or that he had a pain somewhere. Mary and Bill were very good, they sat with him while Delia went out food shopping, but George wouldn't settle while she was out. As he gradually recovered and was well enough to sit propped up by pillows, Delia tried to persuade him to amuse himself looking at his books and comics.

'I can't stay with you all the time,' she said as she gently released his hands from around her neck. 'I have jobs to do around the house.'

'Can't you do them another day?' he pleaded.

'There are some, like getting supper ready for when your daddy comes home, that I have to do right now,' she explained.

Richard was as helpful as he could be and as soon as he came in from work he would take her place at George's bedside to give her breathing space. Yet he had other things that he needed to deal with, things concerning Megan and making their divorce official. He had no objections to it at all; in fact, he was pleased because it would mean that she was out of his life for good. He'd had some concern that, at some point, Megan could change her mind about George and want to claim him back. Although he didn't think she would have much success, seeing that she had deserted George when he had been so young, it would be good to know that there was no danger of her ever trying to do so. For George's sake, he would have hated it if it had been necessary to go to court about it.

He wanted the divorce to be as quiet and discreet as possible. His solicitor had pursed his lips when he had said this.

'People are getting divorced all the time,' he said dismissively. 'Nothing to worry about.'

Richard wondered if he should tell his mother about it, also Delia and perhaps Bill, but decided it probably wasn't necessary. They all seemed to have taken it for granted that Megan wouldn't ever be coming back. George never mentioned her name, nor did he seem to miss her, so it was probably best to say nothing, Richard decided. George was so happy with Delia and she seemed to understand his little ways.

I'm very lucky in that respect, Richard reflected. Peggy had made it quite clear that she didn't want George around all the time and George, whilst showing appreciation for the helicopter gift she bought him, most certainly hadn't liked her. Richard had noticed the look of frustration on George's little face, when Peggy sent him upstairs to his room the moment he came home, so that they could chat together without any interference. Any other child would have rebelled probably, but George had been so well brought up by Delia that he was too polite to do so, Richard thought with a smile.

Yes, in many ways he had very little to complain about, Richard thought, except that they did live a rather isolated life. He must try and take George out and about more and do some of the things, like going to a football match or a cricket match, like other fathers seemed to do with their sons. Perhaps he should try and get to know some of the other parents and encourage play dates; that might help George to have a better social life. George seemed to have very few friends, he reflected. He never seemed to be invited to other children's parties and he never brought friends home. He wondered if that was his fault, because Delia wasn't sure if he wanted other children in the house. He would have to make it clear to her that he didn't mind in the least. All he wanted was for George to be happy.

George recovered from measles in record time; keeping him happy and occupied until he was fit enough to go back to school was another matter. The brunt of doing so fell on Delia's shoulders because Richard was away all day, but Bill was a great asset. He came to see George most days and would play board games with him or read to him. Although his eyesight made reading difficult and half the time he made up the stories. George knew this but he didn't mind and he laughed about it to Delia afterwards. When they played board games, George usually won. Half the time George was making moves for Bill and telling him what card he had drawn, and Delia suspected that George might be cheating. Mary did her share of entertaining George, but she didn't like games very much.

A major problem arose, however, when the time came for Bill to visit the eye hospital again. It was not only on the same day, but at the same time as Delia had an appointment at the dentist. Delia offered to cancel her appointment but neither Bill nor Mary agreed to her doing that.

'It's Bill's fault for not telling us the date sooner,' Mary said.

'I thought I had told you,' Bill mumbled.

They waited until Richard came home to see if he had any ideas but he shook his head.

'I know that it is quite impossible for me to get time off,' he said apologetically.

'I can go on my own,' Bill insisted but Mary refused to let him do that.

'It's a pity we can't call on Peggy to come and look after George,' Richard said, 'but I don't know if she would be free at such short notice. I can try phoning her, she gave me her mobile number.' As Richard stood up to go and phone her, George, who had been playing with his train set in a far corner of the room, ran over and caught hold of his arm.

'No, Daddy, don't do that. We don't want her here again, not ever,' he pleaded.

'George! Why ever not? You can't stay here on your own and grandma doesn't want Bill going to the eye hospital on his own.'

'Why can't I go to the hospital with them?' George said sulkily.

Richard and his mother exchanged looks. 'Is there any reason?' Richard asked. 'He's not ill now; in fact he's going back to school next week.'

'I don't know,' Mary murmured. 'What do you think Bill?'

'It would certainly solve the problem for all of us,' Bill agreed.

George was delighted and said he would be on his best behaviour.

In the taxi, he was excited as they drove down the relief road and he could see Windsor Castle and the Round Tower looking resplendent in the early spring sunshine. At the hospital, he sat on a chair between Bill and Mary, fascinated by all that was going on. When Bill was called into the examination room, George sat holding his coat until he came out. When they moved from one department to the next, George helped to carry things. The only time he seemed to be uneasy was when Bill was called in for an injection.

'Will he be all right, Grandma?' he asked worriedly.

'Of course he will be. He's had it all done before. He might not be able to see very well when he comes out, that's why I wanted to be here. When he does come out we'll all go the restaurant and have a drink and you can have a cake or some biscuits,' she promised.

George's face brightened, then it clouded over again as he saw someone in a dark blue uniform coming over to them and recognised Peggy. He had quite forgotten that this was the hospital where she worked.

'What's this – a family outing? Where's Delia today?' she asked as she greeted them.

George closed his eyes and pretended not to be there and hoped she wouldn't speak to him.

'Delia had to go to the dentist,' Mary explained, 'and, as there was no one to look after George, we had to bring him with us.

'I see. You should have let me know, then I could have come and looked after him, he's not infectious now?'

'No, he's going back to school next week,' Mary said.

'Good. Tell Richard I'll pop in and see him, possibly tomorrow. After all, it is Valentine's Day,' she said and laughed.

George didn't understand what Peggy had meant. He thought about it while they walked to the restaurant and while he munched his way through the little packet of biscuits that Mary had bought for him, and drank his lemonade, but he still couldn't work it out. He was about to ask his grandmother to see if she or Bill knew, when the taxi driver appeared and there was no time to do so. Bill swallowed the last of his tea, George quickly finished his lemonade and they all went out to get in the taxi. As they started on their way home he could contain his curiosity no longer.

'What is Valentine's Day?' he asked.

'Well, it's a special day like St David's Day on the first day of March, or St Patrick's Day on the Seventeenth of March,' Mary explained.

'You mean like Christmas Day?' George said.

'Yes, that's right,' Bill agreed.

'It's a very special day; it's when you propose to the lady you love and ask her to marry you,' the taxi driver said, giving a loud guffaw. 'That's what I did and now I've got a wife, three kids and a mortgage.'

'You married her!' George exclaimed.

'Yes, that's right son, so make sure you don't get carried away and ask someone to marry you on Valentine's Day.'

George shuddered. Peggy had said that she was going to come and see his father on Valentine's Day. What did she mean? he wondered.

'Can a lady ask a man to marry her on St Valentine's Day?' he asked worriedly.

'Only if it's a leap year,' the taxi driver said.

George said no more. He wondered if it was a leap year, but he didn't know what that meant either and he was afraid to ask in case this was one. Somehow he had to try and think of a way to stop Peggy coming in case it was a leap year.

She'll probably ask him anyway even if it isn't, he thought miserably, and he couldn't think of any way of stopping her from doing so.

FORTY-FOUR

George couldn't sleep. He tossed and turned and thumped his pillow. He crept into Delia's room but hesitated about waking her. So instead, he went into his father's room and crawled into bed beside him. Richard woke with a start. George had been wandering about for such a long time that his feet were icy cold and he was shivering. Richard wrapped his arms around him and held him tight, and George burst into tears.

'I don't want her here, I want just us, like it is now, just us: you and me and Delia,' he sobbed.

'What are you talking about?' Richard said. 'Have you had a bad dream, or a nightmare? What are you crying about?'

'Peggy!' George said in a choking little voice.

'Peggy! You must have been dreaming. We haven't seen Peggy for ages and I doubt if we will ever see her again.'

'We will, she said she would.'

'You've been dreaming,' Richard told him and held him tighter, rubbing his back to try and calm him.

'No I haven't!' George struggled to sit up. 'We saw her at the hospital yesterday and she said she was coming to see you today, because it's Valentine's Day and if you didn't propose to her then she would ask you to marry her.'

'She said what!' Richard asked in disbelief.

Choking and hiccupping, George repeated what he had said. 'That's what happens on St Valentine's Day,' he added. 'The taxi driver said it was. He asked someone to marry him on Valentine's Day and he says he now has a wife, children and a mor . . . mor something.'

'Mortgage?' asked Richard, trying not to laugh.

'I think that was it,' George agreed.

'I don't think we have anything to worry about,' Richard told him. 'I won't be proposing to anyone on Valentine's Day and if they ask me to marry them I shall say: no thank you.'

George snuggled back down in bed, clinging on tight to Richard. He was so quiet that Richard thought he was asleep when George said, 'Why don't you ask someone to marry you, Daddy?'

'I don't know anyone who would want to marry me, except Peggy, of course, and you said that you don't want me to marry her.'

'I don't!' George said vehemently. 'I want you to marry Delia.'

Richard's laugh was so loud that it brought a sleepy Delia in to find out what was going on.

'What are you doing in here disturbing your daddy's sleep?' she asked George.

'He couldn't sleep,' Richard said quickly. 'He's all right now and he's going back to his own bed. Isn't that right, George?'

'Well, since I am up, I'll take him and tuck him in,' Delia offered. She walked over to the bed to pick George up. He grabbed her by the neck and pulled her towards him so hard that she lost her balance and toppled over on top of him and Richard.

'Ask her now, go on, go on,' George said, holding on tight to Delia as she struggled to stand up.

'Ask me what?' Delia said

'It's Valentine's Day and Daddy wants to ask you to marry him,' George said.

'George!' Richard protested. 'Delia doesn't want to marry me.'

'Yes she does, I want her to. I want you to marry each other,' George said stubbornly. 'You tell him Delia! You ask him to marry you.'

'Bed!' Richard said in an authoritative voice.

'Come along,' Delia took his hand very firmly. Sensing that he had in some ways upset them both, George went meekly back to his room.

After that Richard tried to go back to sleep but his mind was in turmoil. He tossed and turned until the bedclothes were all tangled. He thumped his pillow, then turned it over to find the cool side. He closed his eyes but all he could see was Delia's lovely face. So cool and calm, a delectable kissable mouth, and when he looked into her eyes, they were so bright and honest that it was as if he could see right into her very heart. He could hear her voice inside his head. Firm yet gentle when she was speaking to George. George adored her and most of the time obeyed her without question. Richard didn't know what George would do without her. What would he do if Delia decided to leave them?

He would also miss not only the care and attention she gave them both, but he would miss her as a person. She was so much a part of both of their lives that he couldn't imagine living without her. Did she feel the same way about them, he wondered. She seemed to be very much at home with them and never seemed to want time off to do anything else. He wondered about her friends and then realised that she didn't seem to have any. Like him, she was something of a loner.

His mother and Bill liked her. They all seemed to get along quite happily. There never seemed to be any altercations about the way she was bringing George up. Then, how could there be, Richard reflected, when Delia was doing such a splendid job. Soothed by the feeling of satisfaction that his life was so well ordered, Richard fell into a dreamless sleep.

Delia wasn't sure whether she was having a dream or a pleasant nightmare. Richard was there, an amorous charming Richard, who was expressing his love for her and beseeching her not to leave him, because both he and George would be devastated if she did.

It was such a wonderful dream that when morning came she didn't want to wake up to the rather hard realities of life.

George seemed none the worse for his restless night. He came down to breakfast grinning cheerfully and, as soon as they were all sat around the breakfast table, he reminded them that today was Valentine's Day and did they remember what he had told them about Valentine's Day?

'Yes, we remember,' Richard affirmed, catching Delia's eye and noticing how the colour was staining her cheeks.

'Well,' George persisted, 'are you going to do what you are supposed to do or is Delia going to be the one to ask you to marry her?' he asked.

Richard and Delia both looked startled.

'Don't you worry about it,' Richard told him.

'It's important,' George told him.

'I know,' Richard agreed. 'I'll do it as soon as I've finished my breakfast.'

'Now!' George insisted. 'I want you to do it now.'

'I think I would rather wait until we are on our own, in case she says no,' Richard told him.

'She won't say no,' George stated. 'You won't, will you Delia?'

Delia felt her colour rising. 'I think we had better wait until we are on our own, like your daddy says,' she prevaricated.

'I said, ask Delia *now*, Daddy,' George persisted, tears coming into his eyes.

'All right, all right!' Richard agreed. He took a deep breath, rose from the table and came round to where Delia was sitting. 'Will you marry me?' It was so stiff and formal that Delia was sure he didn't mean it and that it was all part of a charade to keep George happy.

'Yes,' she said, holding out her hand, 'of course I will.'

To her surprise, Richard pulled her out of her chair and kissed her. It was not a peck on the cheek or even a formal kiss on the lips, but a deep passionate kiss that left her breathless. George was so excited that he cheered and, as Richard pulled Delia into his arms and kissed her again, he hugged them both around the waist.

Finally they let him squeeze in between them and all three hugged and kissed until they were breathless. Delia wondered if it was really happening or whether she was still dreaming. This wasn't being done for George's benefit; this was a fantasy come true. Then her bubble of happiness burst and the black cloud of reality blotted out her happiness. How could she have forgotten? This was a farce! Richard couldn't marry her; he was already married to Megan.

Sensing something was worrying her, Richard whispered quietly, 'What's wrong?'

'You're already married,' she said sadly.

'No, I'm not!' he assured her. 'Megan filed for a divorce and it's all gone through. Everything is legal and above board. I'm a free man.'

'You are!' Delia couldn't believe it was true. As if to clear her mind of any doubt, Richard swept her into his arms and kissed her again.

'I think this calls for a glass of champagne, don't you,' he smiled.

'At this time in the morning!' Delia said in mock horror.

'I suppose it is rather early,' Richard admitted.

'Why don't we invite your mother and Bill round and let them celebrate the news with us,' Delia suggested.

'Great idea,' Richard agreed and kissed her once more.

Mary and Bill were delighted by the news.

'About time,' Bill said. 'I was getting tired of waiting. What took you so long?'

'Needed a bit of prompting,' Richard laughed. 'Cupid here helped,' he added, ruffling George's hair.

'I told them what the taxi man told us yesterday about Valentine's Day,' George said. 'You know about asking someone to marry you.'

'Yes, I remember,' Bill told him. 'Clever boy.'

'It worked,' George said proudly. He stopped and frowned at Bill, 'Why don't you ask grandma to marry you?'

'George!' Mary said sharply. 'You mustn't say things like that.'

'No,' Bill said quickly. 'The boy's quite right. Why don't we get married? Mary, will you marry me?'

Mary Wilson looked flustered. She looked hesitantly in Richard's direction, then as she saw the smile of encouragement on his face, said, 'Yes, why not!'

There were more hugs and kisses all round and then Richard fetched the champagne. As it was such a special occasion he even poured out a small glassful for George. They all congratulated each other again before clinking glasses and drinking their champagne.

'Perhaps we should make it a double wedding,' Bill suggested, as he put his empty glass back on the table. The two women exchanged glances, Mary gave a little shrug and Delia smiled to show she was in agreement.

'Right then, if everyone agrees, shall we set a date?'

They all suggested different dates but Bill was impatient. 'What about making it an Easter wedding,' he suggested.

'That's only a few weeks away,' Mary protested. 'We won't have time to get everything ready.'

'We've wasted enough time already,' Bill muttered.

'Right, Easter it is,' Richard affirmed. 'George will be on school holidays and so will I, so it's perfect.'

FORTY-FIVE

For the next couple of weeks all conversations centred on the coming weddings. There were so many conflicting ideas that Mary was in despair and thought they would never settle anything. Finally, it was agreed that their double wedding would be on Easter Sunday, which left them with only a few weeks to get everything ready. Since three of the people involved had been married before, they agreed that it should be a very quiet civil wedding, with a meal at a top restaurant afterwards.

'What about your honey holiday?' George asked. He was deeply interested in all the conversations and arrangements and was determined to make it a special occasion.

'Honey holiday?' Richard asked in bewilderment.

'I think he means honeymoon,' Delia smiled.

'Yes, that's right,' George agreed. 'I meant your honeymoon holiday.'

They all looked at each other with raised eyebrows.

'I don't think we are planning to have one of those,' his grandmother told him.

George's face fell. 'Why not?' he asked in surprise.

'Well . . .' Mary hesitated not knowing quite what to say.

'I think it would be a very good idea,' Bill interposed.

'No, not really,' Mary protested. 'We are too old to fly, think of the insurance.'

'We might be, but what about Richard and Delia.'

Richard and Delia looked at each other questioningly.

'I hadn't thought about it,' Richard said.

'I think we should leave it until the weather is warmer,' Delia said.

'Easter is quite late this year, so the weather should be

excellent,' Bill said. 'Anyway, I wasn't thinking of flying, I was thinking of somewhere in this country and, as I just said, the weather should be pretty good.'

'Well I suppose that's a possibility,' Mary agreed.

'We could all go together and stay at the same hotel but split up each day and go off on our own and then meet up again in the evening,' Bill suggested.

'Sounds feasible,' Richard agreed.

'Of course if you wanted to go out in the evening then we would be happy to stay with George,' Mary said quickly. She had been feeling uneasy about what they were going to do with George if they took separate holidays, but this seemed an ideal solution. Much as Mary loved George, she thought it would be asking too much of her and Bill to look after him for a whole week or perhaps even longer. If, as had been suggested, they all went away together, then they could certainly have him for the odd day so that Richard and Delia could go off on their own. Or they could keep an eye on him in the evening while Delia and Richard went out.

Although it solved one problem it brought another. Where were they to go? It had to be somewhere they all liked and once again ideas and suggestions flowed thick and fast.

After a great deal of deliberation, they settled on North Wales. There was sea and sand, there were castles to explore, the scenery was breath-taking and, for those with the energy to do it, there was Mount Snowdon to be climbed. That settled, the next thing on their agenda was making sure they had the right clothes to wear on their special day.

Mary and Delia enjoyed a shopping trip together in London. Because the weddings were to be low key, they both decided on something smart but simple. Mary chose a matching dress and short jacket in a pretty shade of lilac, while Delia went for a very smart matching skirt and jacket in deep turquoise blue. Both women agreed that their outfits could be worn again afterwards and they regarded this as a boon.

Mary chose a picture hat trimmed with artificial roses at one side. Delia didn't like hats, but Mary persuaded her to buy a fascinator. It was little more than a velvet band the same colour as her suit and was trimmed with a concoction of feathers and lace.

Both men were proposing to wear smart suits so they bought them new white shirts.

'What is George going to wear?' Mary asked as they travelled home on the train. 'I suppose we should have bought him something new as well.'

'I'm planning to ask Richard to buy him a new suit, but he needs to be with us when we do that. I thought perhaps dark grey with a little waistcoat and, of course, long trousers. A real man's suit if you know what I mean.'

'He'll love that,' Mary smiled. 'He's really taking an interest in all the preparations.'

'Indeed he is,' Mary laughed. 'We've booked the hotel for the meal afterwards and he wanted to see the menu to make sure we hadn't picked things he didn't like.'

'I think he'll be too excited to eat when the time comes,' Mary laughed.

'Not George!' Delia exclaimed. 'He's eating like a horse these days. I think he must have hollow legs.'

'He's a healthy growing boy,' Mary said with a smile. They returned home feeling exhausted but happy. Apart from kitting out George, everything was done.

'I've told them at the hospital that we are going to be away on holiday, until the beginning of May. So that Bill doesn't get an appointment and upset all our arrangements,' Mary said.

Delia looked startled. 'Did you tell them why?'

Mary shook her head. 'No, I just said that we would be away on holiday.'

'Good!'

'Why does it matter?' Mary asked in a puzzled voice.

Delia flushed. 'I'd rather Peggy didn't know, not until it is all over,' she said. 'I wouldn't like her turning up uninvited.'

'She can hardly do that at a register office. It's not like a church wedding where anyone can stand and watch the bride arrive or leave.'

'I don't know,' Delia said, pulling a face. 'You don't know Peggy like I do.'

'I don't think I want to,' Mary said with a laugh. 'From what little I've seen of her I don't like her and George certainly doesn't. Children often have an instinct about these things.'

While they had been out shopping, George had made a special calendar showing how many days there were left before the wedding day.

'I'm going to cross each one out so that we don't forget when it is,' he told them.

'I don't think we are likely to do that,' Delia told him, with a warm smile towards Richard. 'It might have been better if you'd made a list of jobs still to be done.'

'Surely everything has been done,' Richard frowned.

'Not quite: buttonholes for you men, hairdressers for Mary and me, and then haircuts for you Richard, and Bill, and for you George.' Delia told them. 'Also, there is the packing to be done. That must all be ready by the night before, so that we can put it all in the boot of the car before we set off for the register office. Then, when we've had lunch, we can get on the road right away. It's a long drive from here to North Wales.'

'I agree with you about that,' Richard told her. He looked concerned. 'After a celebratory lunch I don't think I will be in a fit state to drive. Don't forget about drink driving.'

Delia looked taken aback. 'You're right. So what are we going to do?'

'We could go by train, I suppose,' Richard suggested.

'Surely we're going to need the car to get around when we get there,' Delia pointed out.

'We could hire a car when we get there.'

'And then have to come back home on the train?'

They looked at each other and laughed. 'Not a very good idea, is it?' he agreed. 'We could stay overnight in the hotel where we are having our meal and then drive up to North Wales the next morning.'

'Or we could come home to sleep and start off the next morning.'

'We'd better see what Mary and Bill would prefer to do,' Delia said. 'We still have to make sure that we are all packed and ready.'

Richard pulled her into his arms and kissed her. 'You choose whichever suits you best. As long as we are married, I don't give a damn where we sleep as long as it is together.'

Richard's words kept going round and round in Delia's mind after she got into bed. 'I don't give a damn where we sleep as long as it is together.' Did he mean it?

She wondered and worried. Apart from kissing her very passionately since they had fixed their wedding date, he had shown no signs of desire. She had to admit there were often messages in his eyes when they met hers that left her wondering if perhaps he did have deeper feelings for her than she knew. She certainly loved him, but that didn't mean she was prepared to fall into his arms, not if he was merely playing the part that he thought was expected of him. To stop herself from thinking about it, she went through a mental list of all the things she had done in preparation for their wedding.

It hit her like a punch; she had forgotten to hire a photographer. They really ought to have their pictures taken, a permanent record of such a wonderful occasion. It was probably too late to hire anyone now, perhaps she could ask somebody to take one with her mobile phone. It would be better than nothing. She must remember to put it in her handbag. What else had she forgotten? She couldn't remember and drifted off into a restless sleep, positive that there was something.

FORTY-SIX

I t was a pale misty morning on Easter Sunday, with the promise of a fine and sunny day ahead if the weather forecasters were to be believed. Delia was up at her usual time but the house was very quiet, so she assumed that both Richard and George were still sleeping. She and Mary had decided that Mary would bring her new outfit to their place to put on. Richard could take George around to Bill's place, so that neither of the respective brides and grooms saw each other before they were all ready to leave for the register office.

'Not quite what tradition calls for but near enough,' Delia laughed when she told Richard of the arrangement.

'You want us to meet you there?' he suggested.

'Actually, that would be even better. You drive there with Bill and George and we'll get a taxi.'

The ceremony was simple and straightforward, and Delia had a feeling of unreality as Richard slipped a ring on her finger and kissed her.

'Mrs Wilson!' She savoured her new name in her mind. That too sounded unreal; Mary was Mrs Wilson. Well, she had been, that was all in the past, she was now Mrs Thompson! As they emerged into bright sunlight there was a clicking of cameras from the small gathering outside. There was a crowd of smiling schoolchildren and their parents, who had heard rumours that their teacher was getting married. There was the photographer from the estate agents handling the sale of Bill's house and various others who had come out of curiosity, when they had seen a small crowd waiting.

With smiles and waves to everyone, the happy family followed Richard to where his car was parked and climbed in for the drive to the hotel, where they'd reserved a table for a late lunch. It was a leisurely meal and afterwards they enjoyed their coffee in the big conservatory with the doors opened wide, enjoying the sun and fresh air.

'A week of weather like this would be wonderful,' Richard said as he stretched his long legs and savoured his tea.

'Certainly better than all the fuss of flying off somewhere and then finding it was too hot for us,' Bill agreed. Before they parted they arranged what time they would meet the next morning for the start of their journey to North Wales.

By now, Delia was feeling nervous, wondering what the next few hours were going to bring and almost wishing they had decided to leave for North Wales right after the ceremony.

Persuading George to go to bed at his usual time seemed to be out of the question. He was still excited and so full of questions that they played board games to try and calm him down.

Then, much later than usual, he finally capitulated and agreed that he was tired and ready to go to bed, as long as Richard promised to come up and read him a story.

Once Richard agreed, George flung his arms around Delia's neck to kiss her goodnight.

'Do I call you mummy now or Delia?' he asked innocently.

Delia felt nonplussed.

'Mummy of course,' Richard said without hesitation.

'What happens if I forget and call her Delia?' George asked.

'Why would you do that?' Richard asked. 'You have always said you wanted to be able to call her mummy.'

'I do, I do,' George protested.

'You can call me either,' Delia said quickly, hoping to settle the discussion.

'Bed!' Richard said firmly. 'Right now, or there won't be any story.'

While Richard read a story to George, Delia tidied around and then left everything ready for the morning, so that they could keep to the early start they'd arranged with Bill and Mary. It was almost nine o'clock and she could hear Richard still reading aloud, so she decided to have a bath. She lay back in the hot water trying not to think about the next few hours. The water was so soothing that she closed her eyes, and relaxed. She stifled a small scream when she felt someone soaping her body.

'Can I come in with you?' Richard said softly in her ear. She giggled and opened her eyes to find Richard standing beside the bath. She felt perfectly at ease as he divested himself of clothes and slid into the bath at her side. It was very cramped but they lay with their arms around each other and relaxed in the hot water, content to kiss and talk for the next twenty minutes.

Then, because the water was no longer hot, they got out and Richard wrapped her in a big fluffy bath towel and carried her over to the bed. They made love as if their bodies were already attuned to each other, as though they knew exactly how to please one another, as if they had had a lifetime of making love to each other. Delia experienced none of the embarrassment or awkwardness she had feared. They drifted off to sleep, still entwined in each other's arms. It was a deep dreamless sleep of utter contentment.

FORTY-SEVEN

They were all up and ready to leave the next morning at the agreed time. George was a little tetchy because he had had such a late night, but once they were on the road he snuggled down between Bill and Mary in the back of the car and dozed off again. They made three stops for refreshments and to admire the spectacular views, and give George a chance to run around and use up some of his energy.

They arrived at their hotel in time for an evening meal, bed for George, unpacking and then a short walk for Richard and Delia. Bill and Mary were feeling worn out and happy to stay and have a quiet drink, listen out for George and then have an early night.

The week that followed was a panorama of castles and filled with excitement. George never grew tired of visiting castles. Harlech Castle and Caernarvon Castle were his two favourites. Harlech was one because it had such a grey and mysterious look about it. George was fascinated by Bill's story that – when invaders tried to take it – those who had taken refuge inside it would pour boiling oil down from the battlements over them, to stop them entering. Caernarvon Castle was a favourite with them all. The picturesque view of the river, packed with small boats that ran alongside and the wonderful outlook over the Welsh mountains, made them linger there for an entire day.

At first, George wasn't too pleased at having to spend a day climbing Mount Snowdon.

'There must be some more castles that we haven't seen,' he protested. 'I love castles. I wish I could be a knight and live in one.'

When they did reach Snowdon however, he stared up at it in awe and was more eager than any of them to climb up it. Bill and Mary decided that it would be too much for them, so they would take the train that carried people right to the top.

They would sit there and enjoy a cup of coffee, until Richard, Delia and George reached the top. It was a long, hard climb and several times they had to stop and have a rest. At one point, Richard thought he was going to have to carry George who was loudly complaining that his legs were hurting.

Yet all this was forgotten when they reached the top and joined Bill and Mary in the café. George was proud of his achievement and devoured a bun and a cake, as well as an ice-cream, to give him the energy to walk back down.

'We're not going to walk down,' Delia told him. 'Oh no, we're going to take the train.'

'We could walk, Daddy, and Delia could go with Grandma,' George said looking hopefully at Richard who shook his head.

'No, we are all going on the train. I want to find out what it's like; it's quite different from the big trains we're used to.'

George was also impressed by their visit to Llandudno and the Great Orme and happy to spend an entire day there. Before they came home, they spent a day at Llangollen and found time to visit Owain Glyndwr's Mount. Bill once again told him wonderful historical story, about the man who had been the last true Welshman to be Prince of Wales, and who had fought the English King Henry IV in an attempt to keep the English out of Wales.

'He lost,' Bill told him, 'and was driven from his stronghold, but managed to avoid capture.'

'I can see when we get back home we are going to have to change out bedtime stories,' Richard laughed. 'After the tales you've been telling him since we came up here, Bill, he will want something quite different.'

'It's not a bad way to learn history,' Bill said.

All too soon the holiday was over. They broke the tedium of the long drive back by taking a detour so that they could take George to see Cardiff Castle.

'It looks a bit like Windsor Castle, but not as grand, it hasn't got a Round Tower,' he told them.

'No, but it has got the original old castle still there in the grounds,' Richard told him pointing out the Norman Keep that stood a few yards away. From Cardiff they picked up the M4 motorway and in less than three hours were home again.

Delia was glad that they had had the 'honey holiday', as George persisted in calling it. The break from home and familiar surroundings made it easier to accept the changes in their relationship when they returned home. They dropped Bill and Mary at Mary's house and arranged to see them the following week.

It no longer seemed strange, when it came to bedtime, for her and Richard to share the same room and it seemed perfectly right to be sharing the same bed.

It might be the start of a new way of life, but it was now accepted by all of them.

ACKNOWLEDGEMENTS

My thanks to Robert Harris and Carmel Bevan for their help in preparing the manuscript and also to my agent Caroline Sheldon and to Megan Middleton of the Caroline Sheldon Literary Agency.